Charlie's Hope

by
Dean Ream

PublishAmerica
Baltimore

ISBN: 1-60610-507-8
PUBLISHED BY PUBLISHAMERICA, LLLP
www.publishamerica.com
Baltimore

Printed in the United States of America

Charlie's Hope

For my wife.

And a special thanks to Ruth Elliot.

Chapter One

The storms blow hard across the western plains of Oklahoma, and the rains tumble from thunder and turn sideways on the wind, and there's no escaping when it hits a man in the face saying he was never welcome. Then comes the heat and burn, crops wilt, bend, want to die and reach for water, and the dirt says no. Farmers are married to the soil. They sit on their haunches and scrape at it, take it up in their hands and feel it and let it drift through their fingers. They watch it, kick at it, taste it, too. It's good soil but it's still just dirt, and when the rains stop and the sun laughs and burns down on the earth there's nothing can help it. And when the farmers kick the dirt in their frustration, it jumps and runs and everything dies.

Clive Stinson knew about dirt. A third generation farmer on the Oklahoma plains and it hadn't suffered any less on him than it had on his parents. From rains to drought and freezing cold to scalding heat, from blizzards in the winter to tornados in the spring, it was like walking the line between heaven and hell. And the dirt, when it wasn't mud it was dust. A man didn't need anymore problems in this country. What he needed was a sign, something letting him know it might get better, something to give him hope. He was thinking that very thing while looking through the sheets of rain slapping his face and had for years.

The road he was on was black, wet, and deep with mud, and Clive wished the day had been better for this trip. Rachael, Clive's daughter, was on the far side of the wagon seat, her coat pulled tight to her neck, a gloveless hand gripping the collar close under her chin. Her old full-brimmed hat was heavy with rain, water falling in front of her face, splashing at her knees and feet. Her left arm was draped around Charlie, holding him close, trying to keep him warm, giving up on keeping him dry.

Charlie was small for his age and his hat was packed with paper to help fit, but now the paper was wet and falling to pieces and Charlie's hat was sitting on his eyebrows, the water, like Rachael's, draining off, but Charlie's was landing in his lap and he was soaked and cold, but he wasn't complaining. Charlie rarely complained. He had good days and bad, but most things didn't carry the weight of failure like it did with everybody else. When he couldn't figure something out he sat quietly and waited for his dad or sister to finish the job. In school, other kids made fun of him, but Charlie didn't seem to understand why, and when the teacher got frustrated he'd shove his hands in his pockets and look at his feet, and they'd always shake their heads and take his hand and lead him off. Rachael hated it when they did it, but she wasn't always around when it happened. The teachers didn't like having to spend so much time with him, so they stuck him in the back of the room and did their best to avoid him, and Charlie was just as happy being by himself. He knew the kids were making fun of him, and he understood the adults were irritated with him, he could see it in their eyes, but it was beyond him how to fix it and so being alone seemed like a good answer. This was not a good day to be alone and Charlie knew it. He was wet and cold and held himself close to Rachael, her pulling him in. Rachael was cold too, and worried. This was a bad storm and they were still a long way from home.

The two mares pulling the wagon weren't any better off, and Clive was having problems keeping them in line. At times the rain came down so hard it was impossible to see, and the mares were skittish, always had been. They didn't like thunder or lightning, and there were both in this storm. Clive could only recognize the road when lightning struck, and the mares were wandering on and off the path in panic. At times it was all Clive could do to hold the slick reigns to keep the horses from bolting.

Now Clive wished he'd waited before leaving the doctor's, but he had chores to do, cattle and hogs to feed, mules in the field, and the small creek they had to cross in front of their cabin wouldn't be so little by nightfall.

The trip had been of no consequence anyway—nothing had come of it. Nobody could offer any help to Charlie. His growth wasn't keeping up, and he was slow understanding things, the schoolteacher saying there was nothing she could do with him, and he was taking too much of her time. Rachael tried to help him along, but other than Charlie loving the attention, she wasn't making much progress. The doctor said Charlie was just slow—he might come out of it—and he might not. Everything seemed fine, his eyes were bright and they followed well, his reflexes were good and his heart was strong. His lungs were good and he was hearing well, but Charlie's thoughts scattered too quickly, and when he wrote something it all came out backwards. He could hardly read, but he could talk fine, but sometimes he got lost before he was done. Charlie should have been taller and stouter for his age. He was six but looked four, and other than everybody saying how cute he was it didn't help his stature any. He was getting to the age where the other boys were picking on him and it was keeping Rachael busy protecting him, and having your big sister defending you wasn't the best way to gain approval.

Clive looked at Rachael and Charlie and knew they were miserable. They were still ten miles from home and it would take five more hours to make it in this weather, and by then the dark would make things worse. He spotted an old barn and turned the mares. One small stop wouldn't hurt and maybe the rain would quiet down. It would give the kids a chance to dry out and stretch their legs.

Six years ago Louise had died three days after Charlie arrived. The midwife had never showed and Clive tried but failed to keep her alive. It had always gnawed at him that he hadn't done better and he blamed himself for her death. Rachael was only four years older than Charlie and the burden of raising two small kids had taken a toll on him. He hadn't minded though, the kids were good and life threw some stones in the road. Over the years Rachael had taken on the chores of her mother, growing into them by hard work and harder times. Living on the plains of Oklahoma offered little, but neither child saw the obstacles, and if they did they never said.

It seemed at times that Rachael was Charlie's mother. She held him as soon as she was able—fed him and cleaned him and by the time she was five was reading him to sleep. She was a fast learner and she cared for Charlie like Clive had never seen a sibling do. Charlie had to be watched, he didn't seem to understand the things that would hurt him, and he wandered off, sometimes in the night when he should have been in bed. Rachael took to tying a string to him just in case he decided to take a stroll. He was a sweet child, and his innocence was the best part of him, but Clive believed living held little time for those in awe.

Clive drove the team to the old barn and jumped to the ground. He pulled the unhinged door as wide as he could and led the mares and wagon inside.

Rachael hopped down and Charlie stepped into her arms and she helped him to the ground.

It was dark in the barn, just the light of the opened door with a flash of lightening, and little of it. There was some straw lying around and Clive dished out a small spot in the dirt floor and started a fire. He found a few old boards and dropped them on top of the burning straw.

"Pull in close, kids," he said. "We'll wait out this rain for a bit, but we can't wait too long. Try to get as dry as you can."

"Papa, what did the man say?" Charlie asked.

Clive looked at Rachael and then squatted next to the fire and Charlie. "He said there wasn't nothing wrong. He said you were as good as gold, brighter'n brass, and better'n silver."

"He did? Then why can't I read?"

"Shh," Rachael said. "Don't talk yourself out. Get closer to the fire and get warm. We've got a long way to go."

Charlie shuffled closer to Clive and rubbed his hands together the way his dad was doing. He took off his hat and set it as close to the fire as he dared and watched as the steam floated above it.

Rachael took her coat off and held it over the fire, turning her face sideways to avoid the smoke. Clive stood and took her hat from her head, her short-cropped auburn hair hanging in strings, and slapped it against his leg to shake off as much water as he could, then he set it next to Charlie's.

The mares were restless because of the smoke and Clive backed them farther toward the door, just enough so they were inside but not hit by the rain.

"They don't like the storm," Rachael said.

"They don't like much at all today," Clive said. "I'll be glad to get home."

"So will I," Rachael said. "We should've left a fire going."

"It'd be out by now anyway," Clive said. "It'll heat up soon enough."

Charlie had walked away from the fire and was snooping around the old barn, tiptoeing back into the dark corners, when he heard a loud screech. He ran back to the fire and stood next to Rachael.

"It's just a barn owl," Rachael said. "Probably thinks you're after his mouse."

"Why does he eat mousers?" Charlie asked. "They're hard to catch."

"Not for an owl. They can see 'em in the dark, and they can fly so quiet you can't hear 'em."

"I heard him."

Rachael smiled. "Yes, you did, and so did I. Stay close to the fire and dry out, you'll be wet through soon enough."

At ten years old Rachael was mature beyond her years. Somehow it had come to her at an early age that she had to take care of certain things, Charlie being one of them. She had never had a childhood—couldn't remember playing. She had a doll stuffed with cotton, made from an old shirt with buttons for eyes. She'd never worn it out.

Rachael had known that Charlie was special all along. He didn't catch on to things the way she had, or for that matter the way the kids his age did. He was quiet a lot, but he was just a kid, and she wondered if he might always be. She had made the decision that he would be with her forever—she loved Charlie. He meant no harm, and very seldom did he cause any. His mind was just as inquisitive as anyone's, but he forgot some of what he learned. Maybe it was still in him, he just didn't know how to get it back out. It didn't bother Rachael, he did what he was told, although sometimes it came out backwards.

She knew that Charlie was only misunderstood, and that if folks would just take the time to talk a little slower, show him one more time, Charlie could get done what needed done. Most folks just said he was dense. It was unfair—Charlie was better than most—it just took him longer.

Clive went to the door and looked at the sky. It was still raining hard and the storm was set in. It wasn't going anywhere for some time. He hated the thought of getting back in it, and wondered if they might stay in the old barn until it stopped. He didn't want the kids to get sick and this was the kind of weather that could bring on such things.

Clive wasn't too interested in making the rest of the trip in the dark either, but it couldn't get much darker than it already was. The thunder was rolling and the mares were upset and they were hard to handle. He should've brought the rain slickers but the morning had been clear and warm. It was a mistake he wouldn't make again, if there were another time. He didn't think there would be.

The schoolteacher had suggested it, taking Charlie to see the doctor, but Clive hadn't put much use in it. He wanted Charlie to have a chance at a good life, though. He wanted him to learn to read and write, but he also knew Charlie wasn't the only kid that had problems.

He saw Rachael and Charlie huddled close together sitting by the fire and knew that he was lucky. After his wife had died it had been hard the first couple of years until Rachael was old enough to do her mother's chores, but they had made it through. Rachael was still just a kid herself, but she'd taken on the responsibilities of an adult without complaint. He was proud of her for that, even though he knew she was missing out on being a kid. It would make her a strong woman, but he worried that some day she might look back with sadness on her childhood. Clive wished he could do more for the both of them, but he hadn't much hope. He was a hardscrabble farmer, and the outlook was grim.

Clive needed a wife but there hadn't been much time to find one. Living so far from a town didn't help matters, and he wondered at times why a woman would even consent to live like he did. The work was hard and unrewarding for the most part, and the accommodations were less than pleasant—it had been that way his whole life. Three generations of dirt farming hadn't changed anything. He wondered if somehow it was inbred, to keep going in the same direction knowing it had started out bad and had never gotten better.

Clive walked back to the fire and knelt beside Rachael.

"What do you think, Rachael, should we keep going or stick around here?"

"I wish it would quit raining," she said. "But it doesn't seem to want to. It might rain all night and we've got the cattle to think of. Maybe we should keep going."

"What about you, Charlie?" Clive asked. "What do you think?"

"Let's stay here," Charlie said. "It's no good out there."

Rachael pulled Charlie close and smoothed his hair back. "We better keep going, Charlie. The sooner we get home the sooner you can get to bed. You'll be warmer then than you are now."

"You're probably right," Clive said, standing. "Let's get on home."

Clive backed the mares out of the barn and Rachael and Charlie stomped out the fire, put their wet hats back on and got back on the wagon. What comfort the barn and fire had been was gone as soon as they stepped through the door.

It took five hours to make it to the farm and Clive was stopped in front of the creek across from the cabin. They would have to get over its swollen banks and the mares wouldn't walk into the rushing water.

"I'll have to lead 'em across," Clive said. "They're scared."

"Be careful, Papa," Rachael said.

Clive rapped the reins around the brake handle and got down. He went to the mare and grabbed the bridle and pulled. The mares didn't want to move and tried to back up but Clive held on and tried talking to them to calm them down, then he pulled again and they fought but obeyed enough to get their front feet into the rolling water.

Rachael was holding Charlie but she was scared. The creek was the highest she'd ever seen it and the wagon was going forward a few feet and then back as the horses fought Clive's attempts to force them forward.

"Papa, let's wait," Rachael yelled.

But Clive couldn't hear over the rain and thunder and rushing water. He kept pulling on the mares. Both horses were standing in the water belly deep by then and wouldn't go any farther. Now Clive felt he'd made a mistake by leading them in that far because they were frozen in fright. He should have found a different spot to take them across, but the horses were half way into the creek now and there was no turning back. The front wheels of the wagon were in the creek bed and water was running up to the footboard. Rachael and Charlie had their feet up on the seat and were hanging on to each other. The wagon was jostling against the weight of the water and the mares were fighting against Clive every time they felt the wagon move.

Clive was standing in front of the horses, stomach deep in the water. He'd grabbed both harnesses and was trying to coax the mares backwards but they were staying their ground. He could feel their panic and knew it wouldn't be long before they made a decision one way or the other, forwards or backwards.

None of them saw the brush coming. It was a large limb pushed by the current but it was so dark there was no way to make it out, and Rachael was holding Charlie, and Clive wasn't paying attention to anything but the mares.

When the brush hit the first horse, she reared up, lost her footing and fell into the other mare. Then both of them were down, pushed and pulled by the raging water, searching for some stable footing, not finding it, fighting each other, pulling the wagon farther into the raging current. Clive was holding on to the bridles, struggling to get a foothold, straddling the doubletree, but his weight was pulling the mares heads down. The wagon was being forced down stream and starting to pull the horses, dragging them sideways and Rachael was screaming at Clive, holding Charlie and looking for a place to jump off, but they were in the middle of the creek now and it was too far to either bank.

"Papa, Papa!" She yelled, but could hear nothing except the frightened horses and the crashing of the water against the wagon.

The horses were on their sides now, struggling to keep their heads above the water; they were drowning and the wagon was twisting around and floating down stream. Rachael could see Clive fighting with the harnesses trying to climb up on the horses and get to the wagon. The wagon was turning on its side and Rachael was screaming for Clive and watched as he went under, the mares fighting, crushing him between them as they fought for a footing.

The tail of the wagon turned in the current and forced and pulled ahead of the horses, taking them with it. The wagon spun, got close to the far bank and Rachael saw her chance to jump. She made a run at the end of the wagon bed dragging Charlie with her. She lifted him up by his armpits and with all her strength threw him as far as she could. Charlie landed in the water close to the bank but not close enough to pull himself out, and the current took him with it and Charlie was kicking at the water and clawing at the mud until he finally pulled himself onto the bank. As he did the wagon flipped over taking Rachael with it. It broke in half and the rear end passed on down with the raging water and the dead mares floating behind it. There was no sign of Clive.

Charlie lay on the bank, cold, frightened, and wondering where Rachael was. Everything was past him, pushed on by the furious roll of the water. He yelled for his sister and father but there was no reply, only the sound of the rushing water, of wind and rain, and the deafening rolls of thunder.

Chapter Two

Charlie stood on the platform of the train station in Springfield, Missouri with a satchel containing his clothes. It was mid-morning in November, and he was waiting for his uncle to pick him up, and he was the only person left on the dock. He stood there watching the train roll out of sight and wanted back on it. He wasn't quite sure what he was doing here anyway and it had been his first train ride and he hadn't slept a bit the whole time. He had never seen such territory, moving from the plains across the fertile grounds of Oklahoma to the edge of Missouri, and then north into the hills of the Ozarks. It had been almost too much for his imagination to grasp and his wide eyes drank it in like the breath in his lungs.

It had been a month since he'd lost his sister and father to the flash flood. He had stayed with a neighbor until they could contact Clive's brother who lived in the Ozark's close to the Arkansas line. Beryl Stinson had not been receptive to the letter. He was a loner and lived in the hills for that reason. He had written back that the boy should be put in an orphanage, but Martha Henson, the neighbor Charlie was staying with, wouldn't hear of it. She wrote Beryl back and in the letter made no attempts at kindness. He would take the boy and he would not put him in a home, no matter how difficult the situation. Children went to orphanages because they had no kin, and Beryl was kin, and he would take the child.

Beryl Stinson was not the kind of man who took orders, especially from women. He had no use for women and he had no use for children, and if you had the one you had the other. He would pick up the boy and deliver him to an orphanage himself. He had made no commitment to his brother about anything, especially his kids. Clive shouldn't have gotten himself killed—it wasn't Beryl's problem.

The two days it took to get to the train station was as disagreeable to him as meeting the boy, and he would make no apologies about taking care of the situation to his own liking. He hadn't seen Clive in twenty years and had no knowledge of his kids and he'd be damned if he'd be straddled with his brother's offspring.

Charlie was crying. He had been crying a lot in the last month. That stormy night, sitting on the wet bank of the creek, he'd waited for daylight to come. He had called out for Rachael and his father until his voice gave out. He was scared and alone that night and he was scared and alone right now, and sitting on the deserted platform waiting for his father's brother didn't make him feel any better.

Martha Henson had told him his uncle was glad to have him, but Charlie had overheard Martha and her husband talking. He knew Beryl Stinson didn't want him and he guessed the Hensons' didn't either. Since his sister and father had drowned nothing had seemed real to him. He kept looking for clouds and rain and running from the dark, and he wouldn't get any closer to that creek than a man could throw a stone.

It hadn't been any better for the Hensons. The nights had been the worst, Charlie not sleeping, opening and closing doors and windows, searching for his sister and father, and Martha gathering him up and taking him to bed with her, listening to him cry and crying herself, holding on to Charlie, pulling him back in, forcing him to stay in bed.

Charlie couldn't get it straight about what had happened on that night. They were just crossing the creek and then he was alone, and he'd been looking for his family ever since. He was at the church when they put two boxes in the ground but he didn't know what was in them. Mrs. Henson said it was his papa and sister, but Charlie didn't know why they'd want to live in the ground. He went to the church every day and waited by the graves, hoping his dad and sister would come out of their boxes and take him home, but they never did, and then one day Martha Henson told him he had to go away. She told him his father's brother was going to take care of him from now on. Charlie didn't know what an uncle was, he'd never even heard of him, and he didn't understand why he had to leave. He wouldn't be able to go to the church and wait for his sister and papa if he had to leave. They'd be looking for him and he wouldn't be there and Rachael would worry.

Charlie did know one thing—he was alone. He had been alone on that night after Rachael had pushed him off the wagon, and now he was sitting alone on a wooden porch. When Martha Henson put him on the train she had asked a woman to sit with him, so he hadn't been alone on the train. It was his first train ride and Charlie liked it. He sat next to the window and watched as the scenery changed from flat land and sagebrush to green hills and trees. He thought he might be able to hide in those trees and no one could find him and he would make his way back to the church, but when the train stopped the woman sitting next to him wouldn't let him leave his seat. She was a kind woman and Charlie liked her, but she wasn't Rachael and he wanted Rachael.

The woman had waited with him on the platform until she said she couldn't wait any longer. She told him to stay put and his uncle would be there soon. Charlie didn't know if Beryl Stinson would be there soon or not—he knew Beryl Stinson didn't want him.

Charlie spread himself out on the boards, curled up and put his head on his arms. He wasn't so much tired as he was nervous, but he didn't know what else to do. Maybe Rachael had told the woman to tell him to stay, and if so, Rachael would be worried if he didn't.

Beryl walked up the steps of the platform on the far end. He could see a boy lying on the platform and the first thought through his mind was it took a lazy boy to lie down in the middle of train station, and it made him mad. The boy couldn't even stay on his feet long enough to wait for him. He wouldn't coddle the boy and there's no better time than now to let it be known.

Beryl's steps were heavy, he was a big man, much bigger than Clive had been, but he was thin too, and lanky, his arms swaying at his sides as he walked. His tanned weather-beaten face was lean with sunken cheeks that seemed to make straight rock ridges out of his cheekbones. With dark eyes that fixed themselves on faces like leeches, and full bushed brown eyebrows and a beard stubbled face, Beryl Stinson did not give off an impression of affability. He was eleven years older than Clive and he'd gone his own way when he was fourteen, not liking the close confines of family or the caked summer soil his father called dirt. He didn't like the plains either, the flats that brought drought in the summer, tornadoes winter and spring, and mud deep enough to swallow a bull in the fall. Beryl had headed for the hills where he heard the game was plentiful and the dirt was rich. A man could get lost there, he'd heard, and that's what suited him. Now he was blindsided with a child and the more he thought about it the madder he got.

He walked up beside Charlie and stared at him. He thought the boy was supposed to be six or seven, but this boy didn't look that old. Either that or he was a runt, and Beryl didn't like runts. He kicked Charlie's shoe with his boot.

"What's your name, boy?"

Charlie was startled by the kick and pulled himself up to a sitting position with his hands in his lap. He tilted his head back and looked up at a grizzled man looking down on him.

"Charlie Stinson."

"Get up," Beryl said.

Charlie stood and faced the man. If this was his father's brother then he didn't look much like his dad. And he didn't act like him either—Papa was a nice man.

"Get your bag and follow me, and don't drop behind. I'm not one to wait on slouchers. I thought you were older."

Charlie didn't know how old he was supposed to be. He picked up his suitcase and lugged it with both hands dragging it beside him and trying to keep up with his new uncle. The man was walking fast and Charlie was getting behind when another man stepped up beside him and grabbed the satchel.

"Hold on there, mister," he said. "This boy can hardly carry this bag. Does he belong to you?"

Beryl turned to face the man, who had stopped walking and was standing with his hand on Charlie's shoulder.

"Mind your own business," Beryl said.

"This boy ain't a pack animal," the man said. "You can't treat him like a dog."

"I've more use for a dog," Beryl said. "If you want to help him, then help him, but don't stand there like a fool."

Beryl turned and walked off the platform.

"Is that your pa, son?"

"He's my new uncle. I've come to live with him."

The man shook his head and took Charlie by the hand and followed Beryl to the wagon. When they got there Beryl was already sitting in the seat with the reins in his hands.

"Mister," the man said. "You're a hard case."

He threw the satchel in the back of the wagon and lifted Charlie up to Beryl, but Beryl didn't take him, he just kept staring forward. The man put Charlie back down and walked him around to the other side and lifted him up to the seat.

"You ought to be beat for treating this boy that way," he said. "I'll be surprised if he lives another year with the likes of you."

Beryl looked hard at the man and slapped the horses with the reins.

Charlie kept quiet on the ride south. Beryl was quiet too, but he never had much to say. Charlie kept his eyes on the constant bobbing of the horses' heads as they plodded forward on the dusty road. The wagon creaked along and when the ruts became larger it fell in and out with a twist, shouldering Charlie from side to side. When they passed other wagons most folks waved or nodded or tipped their hats, but Beryl Stinson made no attempt at returning the greeting. Once, Charlie raised his hand in reply and Beryl scolded him with a slit-eyed stare. For the most part Beryl kept his attention fixed above the teams' heads, somewhere in the dust behind the oncoming wagons.

Charlie had no idea where they were going. The farther they went, the fewer the fields and pastures became. The countryside was slowly turning into masses of trees, so thick there was no seeing between them. They had passed through more creeks than he had ever known were on land. The day was warm and at one point he'd taken his jacket off and laid it in his lap, but his thoughts were in other places and it had slid from his legs and off the side, falling from the wagon. He had looked at Beryl but had said nothing, and the wagon had kept moving.

By noon Charlie was tired and sat with slumped shoulders, head bent, and hands clamped together in his lap. He had tried to lie down on the seat but when he did Beryl grabbed him by the shirt and pulled him up, so he fought to stay awake, afraid that he might fall off the wagon like his jacket had. He was hungry, and had already eaten the only sandwich Martha Henson had given him for the trip. Once, Beryl had reached under the seat and came back with a canteen. He took a long drink, then screwed the cap back on and put it under the seat again. It made Charlie thirsty and when he bent down to grab the canteen Beryl had moved his big boot backwards and blocked his hand.

By the middle of the afternoon Beryl stopped the team at a small creek to let them drink and rest. He sat under a hickory tree in the shade with a paper sack. He reached in and pulled out a sandwich and began to eat it. Charlie was so hungry and thirsty he didn't know what to do, but he was afraid of his uncle and didn't want to ask, but now he felt he must do something.

"I'm thirsty," Charlie said.

Beryl chewed on his sandwich and stared at him. Then he said, "See any water around here?"

Charlie looked at him and the canteen, and stood in front of him with his hands at his sides.

"What do you think Rosie and Mattie are doing?" Beryl asked.

Charlie looked at the horses standing in the water, dipping their heads to drink.

"They're drinking water," Charlie said.

"You ain't as stupid as I thought," Beryl said.

"I'm not stupid," Charlie said. "Rachael said so, and so did Papa."

"They weren't very smart themselves," Beryl said. "Or they wouldn't be dead."

Charlie looked at the horses again and made a timid movement in their direction. He'd never drank water beside a horse before and the most vivid memory he had of horses in the water were on that night, and he was afraid these horses might do the same thing, but he was so thirsty he walked to the bank anyway.

He stepped as far away from the horse as he could without getting out of sight of his new uncle, afraid he might be gone if he lost sight of him. He squatted down by the edge of the water and cupped his hands together and dipped them in the muddy water. The water he was used to wasn't this murky, although it did taste bitter most of the time, and Charlie wondered if all the drinking water would be dirty where he was going. He drank what was left in his hands and dipped again until he was full.

When he walked back up to the tree where his uncle was still stretched out he saw that Beryl had an odd look on his face. His new uncle had a lot of different looks to his face but so far none of them had been pleasant.

"You are a stupid runt, aren't you? You don't drink water downstream from animals, boy. You drink upstream so the water ain't muddy and filthy."

Charlie's bottom lip trembled. He knew then that his uncle had made a fool of him. He looked at the ground and was fighting back his tears, but he couldn't hold them, and they were dropping in the dust at his feet. Charlie walked over to the end of the wagon and laid his head on his arms on the boards and cried.

Beryl Stinson stopped smiling and quit chewing. He set the last half of his sandwich down on his leg. The boy was slow, he could tell that, but he ought to know something. Clive hadn't done much in the way of teaching him and that wasn't Beryl's fault. He might have felt different if the boy was his, but he wasn't.

Beryl had never felt sorry for anyone in his life. You made your own mistakes and paid for them. No one was expected to give help. Too many folks got by on the sympathies of others and from then on they thought it was a tool.

"Come here, boy," Beryl said.

Charlie didn't move, he was still crying and sobbing. He hadn't done anything that he knew of to hurt his uncle and he couldn't understand why he was mad at him.

"Get over here," Beryl said.

Charlie wiped his eyes with his sleeve and walked over to the shade of the hickory.

Beryl handed him the other half of his sandwich and Charlie took it. He ate it as fast as he could, thinking his uncle might take it back. Charlie didn't know what to expect anymore. Then Beryl handed him the canteen.

"Don't drink downstream from the animals," Beryl said.

Beryl got up and hitched the horses back to the wagon and climbed back on the seat. Charlie walked up to him and handed him the canteen.

Beryl took the canteen and shoved it under the seat. He reached down and held his arm out. Charlie took it and Beryl hauled him up.

Charlie was feeling better—at least his uncle was talking some. He decided to ask where they were going.

"Home," was all Beryl said.

"When will we get there?"

"Tomorrow."

Charlie watched the road as the day passed. He'd never seen so many trees and some of them were turning colors and some were even losing their leaves, blowing across the road and drifting on the air. He tried to catch a few but couldn't.

Close to dusk Beryl pulled into a grove of trees and unhitched the team, tied them to a tree to let them graze and pulled a basket from the wooden box behind the seat.

Charlie watched and wondered if they were spending the night on the ground. He'd never slept on the ground before. He shared his bed with Rachael; there were only two beds in their small sod house in Oklahoma.

"You know how to build a fire?" Beryl asked.

Charlie only looked at him. Beryl picked up a stick and pitched it at Charlie's feet.

"Gather up an armload of sticks just like that and bring them to me," Beryl said. "Can you do that?"

While Charlie was gathering sticks, Beryl picked up a few rocks and made a circle in a small opening between two trees. He piled some leaves in the middle and put a match to it. As the flames rose he added some twigs and then some larger sticks. Charlie came back with all he could carry, which wasn't much, and dropped them beside the fire.

"Go get more," Beryl said. "I'll tell you when to quit."

Beryl went back to the wagon and opened the lid on the box and took out a frying pan and a pot, a coffee pot and a sack of grounds, two cans of beans, and a paper sack full of biscuits. He carried them back to the fire and went back to the box and retrieved his rifle.

Charlie was standing by the fire when Beryl got back.

"Stack some bigger limbs on that fire," he told Charlie. "I'll be back in a few minutes."

Charlie stacked limbs on the fire and watched it grow. He didn't know where his uncle was going with a gun and wondered if he should follow. He didn't like being alone in the dark even with the fire. He watched the horses grazing under the trees. It was a clear night and he could see the moon even though it wasn't dark yet. It was easier to see the moon in Oklahoma than it was here. He had to move around to catch a glimpse of it through the limbs of the trees. He didn't have that problem on the plains. Soon he heard the crack of the rifle and it scared him. Now he wondered if his uncle was coming back. He stood by the fire and heard the crackle and whistling of the limbs. Then he heard sounds he'd never heard before and didn't know what it was. Some were high sounds and some were low, and some were constant, seeming never to stop. They sounded like they were coming from the trees, but he could see nothing in the trees, and now he wondered if the trees had voices and what they were saying.

Then Beryl came out of the woods holding a rabbit in one hand, blood dripping from its nose.

"You know how to clean a rabbit, boy?"

Charlie didn't, had never seen a rabbit cleaned, and didn't see any need to clean a dead one.

Beryl could tell the boy didn't know how to cut up a rabbit, and it was another sour point to him. Clive had done a poor job of raising the boy. By the time a boy was six he should be able to shoot his own food and clean it and cook it. Clive had spoiled the child and hadn't given him the chance to stand on his own. It was a disappointment that his brother had been so lax.

"Go get me that canteen under the seat," Beryl said.

While Charlie was gone, Beryl gutted the hare and skinned it. He cut off the feet and head and threw them in the brush.

Beryl squatted down oh his haunches and held out the rabbit.

"Pour some water over him," he said.

Charlie poured water over the rabbit and Beryl washed it off. Then he walked back to the fire and tossed the hare in the frying pan and cut it into pieces. He placed the pan over the fire and filled the coffee pot with the rest of the canteen's water and poured in some grounds and put it in the fire.

"There's a creek down there to the left," he said to Charlie. "Take that canteen and go fill it up."

He handed it to Charlie who took it cautiously and held it while he stood in what Beryl thought to be a dazed state.

"What's wrong, boy?"

"I…I don't like going to the water in the dark."

"Why not? It gets dark every night. What're you gonna do, have somebody do your chores for you?"

"I…guess not," Charlie said.

"I don't like guesser's, boy. You got to know things, not guess about 'em. Now get on with it."

Charlie slowly turned and forced his feet to move. His bottom lip was trembling again. Even though he could hear no water running it didn't help. At night is when the water takes things, it's when it took Rachael and Papa. What might happen at the water in the dark had become his biggest fear. Just at the edge of the firelight Charlie stopped and twisted, looking back at his new uncle. Beryl was busy turning the rabbit in the pan so it wouldn't burn, and he was opening the cans of beans and pouring them in the pot. Charlie was still hungry, the half of a sandwich had only buffeted his hunger pangs for a short time, and the smell coming from the fire made his mouth water. He sat down and stared at the fire and food.

Beryl was stirring the beans and flipping the rabbit. He reached for the coffee pot but jerked his hand back from the heat. He reached in the back pocket of his overalls and brought out a handkerchief and used it to move the pot. Then he spied Charlie sitting on the ground in the low glow of the firelight.

"Boy, what are you doing? I told you to get the water."

Charlie was silent. He was sitting cross-legged, the canteen in his lap, his head hanging to his chest.

"What about the downstream?" Charlie asked. "Maybe there's animals in the water."

"What are you talking about? The horses are tied to the tree. You're as useless as a hole in a bucket."

Beryl pulled the rabbit and beans and coffee pot off the fire and set them in the dirt. He stomped over to Charlie and grabbed him by the arm and jerked him up, pulling him so fast behind him that Charlie's feet were dragging the ground.

When he got to the creek he took the canteen from Charlie's hands and unscrewed the cap, bent down and submerged it in the water.

Charlie watched as the air bubbles were forced from the container as it filled with water. It reminded him of the froth on the creek that night—bubbles everywhere, mingled with screams and thunder. He backed away from the edge of the water but Beryl caught him by the shirtsleeve and pulled him back. When the canteen was full Beryl capped it and shoved it at Charlie's stomach.

"Do you think you can carry it back, or do I need to do that too?"

Charlie didn't answer, but broke from his uncle's grip and ran back to the fire.

Beryl stood by the water's edge and watched the boy scramble back to the light. He thought of the man at the train station and what he'd said about Charlie not living out a year, but it wouldn't be because of Beryl, it would be because of his own weaknesses. Some folks don't make it long in this world, mostly those timid of mind and weak of body, and it seemed to him that Charlie had both.

He made his way back to the fire and found Charlie sitting on the ground, the canteen next to him. Beryl looked at him long and hard before he squatted down again and put the frying pan back on the fire, and then the beans, and then the coffee.

The evening was cooling and the fire felt good, but Charlie wasn't feeling anything right then. He knew he wanted to be with Rachael and Papa, even if they were living in a hole in the ground. He shouldn't have to go to the river in the dark—no one should make him do that. He knew the people he needed the most wouldn't be there, and that was the only reason to go.

"Scared of the dark, are you, boy?"

"No," Charlie said.

"Scared of the water then?"

"No."

"Well what is it then? You ain't gonna live very long if you're scared of either one, you know that don't you?"

Charlie looked at Beryl and for the first time Beryl saw fire in his eyes, and it wasn't the fire he was squatted by. So there was some spirit in the boy after all. Maybe he'd misjudged him a little. It better not be defiance, Beryl wouldn't take deviance.

"Don't stare at me, boy."

Charlie looked back at the fire but his expression didn't change. Then he said, "Take me back."

Beryl flipped the rabbit pieces one last time and pulled the pot of beans from the fire.

"You ain't going back," he said. "There ain't anybody there that wants you."

"You don't want me," Charlie said. "I heard 'em talking. I can't read or write, but I hear."

"Why would I want you, you can't fetch water and you're scared of the dark. That's about as useless as they come."

"I'm better'n you," Charlie said.

It took Beryl by surprise and for a moment he could only look at the boy with a bewildered expression.

"Rachael said I was better'n people that were mean, and you're mean."

"I ain't done nothing to you, boy. You're the problem here, not me."

"You ain't done nothing good either," Charlie said.

Beryl huffed. He stood up and walked over to the wagon and got out two tin plates and two forks and a tin cup. He rested his arm on the side of the wagon for a minute and looked back at the boy, still sitting cross-legged by the fire, his eyes searching through it for something Beryl didn't understand.

Beryl had never felt loss. Even though his parents were both dead and now Clive, it didn't pull at him like it did others. He liked being alone and he didn't make friends. If a man could stand, then leaning on others wasn't an option. Death came—that's all there was to it. Forget about it and move along. The boy couldn't see that though, and it made Beryl think that he might be too hard on him. The boy was slow witted and probably couldn't understand the simple truth of it. He was sorry to see it, but the boy would have to come to terms with it.

He walked back to the fire and dipped out some beans on the plate and speared two pieces of rabbit, then reached in the sack and put a biscuit on the plate, and handed it to Charlie. Charlie didn't take it and Beryl set the plate next to him on the ground. Then he filled his own plate and began to eat.

Beryl waited for a few minutes before he said anything. He thought the boy would soon get over his tantrum but it appeared it was set in.

"Better eat something," Beryl said. "We've got a long way to go tomorrow."

Charlie had lost his appetite. It had been the first time he'd ever talked back to a grown person and he didn't know how he felt. In one way he felt good about it—he'd finally said what was on his mind, but in another way he was ashamed, because Rachael had told him not to do it. Charlie felt there was some good and bad in it, but he'd gotten the attention of his new uncle and that meant something to him.

He looked at the plate beside him and thought he should say thanks, but somehow he didn't want to. The steam was rising from the beans and the aroma was drifting under his nose and he knew then he'd have to get at it. He reached to pick up the plate but he was leaning over too far and fell against his elbow, and the plate dropped out of his hands and turned over on the ground.

Charlie looked at the plate and then up at Beryl. Beryl acted like he hadn't seen anything, just chewing on his food and staring into the fire. Then he set his plate down and reached over and picked up Charlie's plate and scraped it off into the fire.

He forked out more beans and two more pieces of rabbit and took another biscuit from the sack and handed it back to Charlie.

"Sorry," Charlie said.

"Just eat, boy," Beryl said. "We've got a long day tomorrow."

Chapter Three

Beryl was up before daylight and had a cup of coffee in his hand when he nudged Charlie with his boot.

Charlie had slept all night on the ground on a blanket next to the fire. He hadn't even heard his uncle rustling around early in the morning.

Beryl handed him a biscuit and started kicking out the fire. Charlie went behind a tree to relieve himself while Beryl hitched up the team to the wagon. When he was ready, Beryl helped Charlie up onto the seat. If he was going to get anywhere he might as well help the boy. As soon as he got him home he'd figure out what orphanage to take him to. The boy needed more guidance than Beryl had the patience to extend, but he didn't want to think about it, for the most part it was trouble he hadn't looked for. Beryl had built his stake by himself and had no intentions of sharing it with anyone else.

The forty acres he owned had taken him most of his adult life to accumulate, buying parcels next to his as he could. He'd built a cabin in the middle of it to make sure he was surrounded by nothing closer than the trees, and he lived off the land, taking what food it provided and planting what else he needed. He knew his neighbors and they knew him, enough to know he didn't want anything to do with them. The closest town was Berryville, Arkansas, and he went as seldom as possible, and when he did he offered no conversation. His life was his and he needed no others in it.

Martha Henson had sent word to the sheriff in Berryville that Charlie was coming, just in case Beryl decided not to show up, and word had spread as Beryl and Charlie headed south that he was coming home with his dead brother's son. Most of the men laughed at his situation, knowing how much he must have hated it, but the women felt sorry for the boy, expecting him to be treated poorly.

Charlie saw that his uncle was at least nodding at folks as they past on the road, and he guessed they were getting closer to his new home. He also saw that many of the people were staring at him. It made him uneasy because he'd always had Rachael with him when he went somewhere and she would stay close to him. At times she would let him stand behind her so he wouldn't have to face the people staring at him. He had no protection here though, because his uncle didn't appear to care if people stared. He barely acknowledged them and looked straight ahead.

By now Charlie was getting excited. He wondered what his new home would look like and if there were animals like at his old home. He wondered if there was a Mrs. Uncle that would be there, and what she was like and if she might be like Rachael.

He missed his sister and father. People thought he didn't understand death, but he did. He knew they weren't coming out of the hole in the ground, but he didn't care. He wanted them to think he didn't know any better. If they thought he did, they might not have let him go to the church every day. He only went because he hoped they were all wrong, but as the weeks went by, he knew better.

That night on the flooded creek bank he had seen Rachael standing on the wagon bed as it flipped over, and had seen her struggling to hold onto the side and looking his way all the time. He had seen the horses strapped together by the halters, floating behind the wagon, and had seen his Papa's head and shoulders caught between the horses heads. He had followed them on the bank as far downstream as he could until he gave out. The next morning the neighbors had come to make sure they'd made it home and had found him sitting in sight of the creek, his blond hair matted against his head, his blue eyes fixed on the wagon and the mares snagged against the bank. The water had passed through by then and nothing was left but mud and brush.

Because he wouldn't talk they thought he was hurt, but he wasn't hurt, not on the outside anyway. They didn't want him to see, but he'd already been down to the wagon. He couldn't find Rachael, but he had seen his father. He looked farther down for Rachael, but he couldn't find her and went back above where the horses were wedged, and waited. He didn't know what he was waiting for, but Rachael had always told him if they got separated to stay put and she'd find him, so he had done just that, only she never did find him. That's why he wanted to go to the church everyday—so she might come to him. Now he wasn't waiting anymore, but he wasn't sure he'd been found either.

They turned off the main road onto a wagon track that led into the woods. The trees were so close to the sides of the wagon that Charlie could reach out and touch the bark at some places. The limbs hung over them like a roof as they passed under, and it was cool and quiet in the shade. Charlie had never seen such trees, so grand and tall, with limbs so long.

Soon they came to a clearing and Charlie could see fences on both sides of him, and then they rounded a bend and he could see a cabin with a front porch. It was the first house he'd seen with a front porch. All the homes in Oklahoma were sod, and they had no porches. In back of the house was a barn with a rail fence around it. Such a big barn he'd never seen. His uncle must have a lot of money. Rachael had told him once that folks with money had wood homes and big barns and they even had wood floors, not dirt floors like theirs.

Beryl guided the horses toward the barn and stopped them in front of the gate. He got down and unlatched it and swung it back, and then walked the team inside.

"Let's get these horses unhitched," he said. "You've got to take care of your animals before anything else."

Beryl felt that the biggest part of educating kids was teaching them how to stay alive first, and then let the schools teach them the rest. In his opinion it was the biggest mistake most folks made, letting their kids play till they were old enough to start school and then they were gone most of the day when all the work was being done. They had to know how to manage first, putting food on the table, taking care of the livestock, and planting the fields and harvesting. Schooling would do no good if they didn't know how to feed themselves. It was obvious to him Charlie didn't know the first thing about staying alive, and it was a disservice that Clive hadn't taken the time to teach him. He'd always thought Clive had better sense than that, but of course he'd been gone for most of Clive's life. Beryl's parents had taught him those basics and he couldn't understand how they'd slipped with his brother.

Charlie helped with the horses, mostly standing by Beryl and holding what he handed him. He'd helped with the teams before but he was still skittish around the animals. Rachael and his father had always been overprotective with him because of his size and his tendency to misjudge situations. Charlie had a lot of trust, even with the animals, and didn't seem to comprehend the dangers around him.

Beryl had already seen the timidity in the boy and his first notion was to get that out of him. Charlie may not be with him very long, but it was something that irked Beryl. A child had to learn as fast as possible what needed to be done and there was no room for hesitation. It could get you hurt, or even killed. The quicker it was taught the better.

"Take the harnesses to the barn," Beryl said. "We'll brush down these horses and give 'em some grain. They've worked hard these past few days."

Beryl led the horses into the barn and Charlie followed. Beryl put them in separate stalls and hung the harnesses on the wall. He handed Charlie a brush and told him to start brushing down one of the horses.

Charlie was scared of getting into the stall with the horse, he barely came up to the horse's belly and his father had always done the brushing and combing. He'd watched him but had never done it himself.

Beryl saw his nervousness and was quick to admonish Charlie.

"These horses aren't gonna hurt you," he said. "Right now they're tired, worse than you or me. They want some grain and they'll be more interested in that than you."

Beryl hung a bucket of grain on the front of each stall and grabbed Charlie by the arm and walked him inside one of the stalls.

"I know you can't reach their backs, so I'll do that, but you can brush down their sides and legs. Now get to it. You work on this one and I'll start on the other."

Charlie put the brush on the side of the horse and pulled down. He watched as the hair smoothed out. The horse swung his head from the bucket and looked at him. Charlie stepped away, but the horse went back to his grain. Then Charlie brushed again and this time the horse didn't look back and he kept brushing.

Charlie liked the looks of the straightened hair and remembered Rachael's and the way she used to comb it, how the brush pulled it back and left it straight and perfect. The hair on the horse was shorter and coarser but it reminded him of the same pattern as he worked the horse's side.

"Put some muscle in it," Beryl said from the other stall. "I don't want to have to do it twice."

Charlie put all of his strength into the next pull and could see the dust and dirt coming off with the brush. The horse didn't act like he noticed and Charlie worked harder.

By the time Beryl was finished with the other horse Charlie had only gotten one side done and was working on the front leg. Beryl went around to the other side and started on the horse's neck and back. When they were done Beryl put up the brushes and walked back to the wagon. He handed Charlie the frying pan and coffee pot and grabbed his rifle and the sack containing what was left of the biscuits.

Evening was closing in and Beryl knew he still had the cattle and hogs to feed. The chickens needed fed too. They'd go to the house and put their things up first, and then do the chores.

Charlie wanted to see the inside of the house and was excited about where he might sleep. He was also getting hungry and wondered what they might eat. He remembered the meals Rachael cooked at home, they were all much the same, but they were tasty, not that the rabbit and beans his new uncle had made were bad, but the meat was tough, and the biscuit was stiff and tasted like caked flour. Charlie had eaten his share of beans and pork and corn bread. He liked fried chicken and his mouth watered for some like Rachael might make, it had more taste than the rabbit.

He followed Beryl to the rear of the cabin, veering off to the side at one point so he could catch a glimpse of the porch. He could see himself on that porch, sitting, watching out the front at the cattle across the yard. He had heard stories of folks that did just that, sat on their porches in the evening after supper in the shade. He had asked his papa once why they didn't have a porch, and his papa had said there wasn't anything to hook it to. Charlie wasn't sure what he'd meant and he stretched his neck at the porch to see what it was hooked on. He thought maybe it could be moved around to the side or the back just by unhooking it and latching it again.

Charlie saw the privy off to the side and a small shed next to it. There was no door on the shed and he could see tools lying in the corners and hanging from the walls, and in the middle was a grindstone for sharpening axes and saws.

When he followed his uncle through the back door they entered the kitchen and Beryl placed the rifle in the rack on the wall. There were other guns there too, and Charlie wondered why he would want so many guns. His papa had a rifle and a shotgun, but that was all. His new uncle had as many as the fingers on Charlie's hand, and Charlie thought it was too many to carry at one time.

Beryl put the biscuits on the shelf beside the cook stove, took the coffee pot and frying pan from Charlie and set them on the counter by the wall. He lit a lantern and placed it on the table, then leaned against the counter and folded his hands across his chest. He was tired—more tired than he'd felt in years. He wasn't used to traveling such distances—hadn't traveled that far since he could remember and he hated being away from his chores for so long.

He'd had to ask his neighbor, Josh Danner, to check on the place while he was gone. If there was something he hated doing it was depending on others, and what he hated even more was asking favors. He paid all of his bills with cash money and owed nothing, and intended to keep it that way. Now he owed a favor and he considered it a debt.

He looked at the boy, who was standing beside him looking into the front room around the corner of the wall, then closed his eyes and let out a breath. The boy didn't want to be here anymore than Beryl wanted him here. He couldn't hold it against him, but he sure would like to. He couldn't hold it against anyone—they were all dead and gone. He guessed he had to hold it against himself for not making it clear to his brother he wasn't caretaker to his kids.

Beryl wondered what had caused this sour turn in his life. He'd never asked for nothing from anybody, and now that he'd worked so hard to have a life to himself, he had a small child in his care. If he'd wanted a child he would've done it himself. He was too old to be raising a boy anyway. He was almost fifty and considered himself lucky to be alive. The boy would have to go to a home, that was all there was to it.

"Let's feed the chickens and check on the cattle, boy," Beryl said. "Then we'll get something to eat."

"Will I be sleeping inside?" Charlie asked.

"Where'd you think you'd be sleeping?"

"I don't know."

"I'll show you after we get back."

Beryl walked out the back door and Charlie was right behind him. He caught up to him and took his uncle's hand in his without even thinking, just like he used to do with Rachael and his father. Beryl jerked his hand away.

"You don't have to hold on to me," Beryl said. "I ain't running off."

Charlie stared at the ground while he walked. He didn't know what he'd done wrong, but it seemed to him he couldn't do anything right. Nothing had gone right since that night. Rachael and Papa always held his hand when they were going somewhere. He didn't want to lose them and they didn't want to lose him, that's what Rachael had said. He should have been holding her hand that night and maybe he wouldn't have lost her. His uncle didn't want to hold his hand, and to Charlie it meant he didn't care if he lost him or not.

He fell behind Beryl and stopped. He walked over to a tree and leaned against it and fought back the tears. He wanted his sister so bad it hurt.

He wiped at his eyes with his hands. He knew his new uncle didn't like him crying, he'd seen it on his face. He didn't want to make him mad. Then he felt a hand on his shoulder.

Beryl kneeled down beside him and turned Charlie to face him.

"I know you didn't mean any harm. Why don't you go back to the house and wait for me."

"But I want to go with you," Charlie said. "I don't like being alone. I don't know nobody."

"Well, there ain't nobody here but me and you anyway," Beryl said. "You ain't alone, I'm right here."

"I want to go with you," Charlie said.

"Are you tired, boy, is that what it is?"

Charlie wiped his eyes again and nodded.

Beryl stood with his hands on his hips and his eyes to the sky. "Come on," he said. "Let's go to the house. We'll feed these chickens and then get something to eat. I'll check on the cattle later."

They walked to the chicken house and Beryl gave Charlie a tin can of feed and they both spread it. Then they walked to the house.

Once inside Charlie sat in one of the chairs and watched as Beryl rustled around for a while and then stood against the counter again.

"I don't eat much," Beryl said. "I can't remember the last time there was more than me here for dinner."

Charlie sat silently at the table, looking at Beryl with a turn of his head.

"What about the biscuits?" Charlie asked. "We could eat the biscuits."

"They're harder than that chair you're sittin' in," Beryl said.

Charlie looked at him, his feet swinging in the air because the chair was too tall for him to touch the floor.

Beryl thought how meager his supply of food was. He shouldn't have felt that way, it had never crossed his mind before. Eating was something that was more nuisance than anything. He ate a good breakfast, some bacon and eggs, maybe some biscuits when he had them. He'd made the biscuits for the trip, thinking it was too much trouble to hunt down something. The rabbit had been an afterthought, because he'd been hungry, the biscuits not turning out so good—they were stiffer than hardpan and almost as gritty.

Beans and meat were more than enough for Beryl, and vegetables when he had them. He wasn't much on preserving food for the winter. There was always plenty of game, and the simple things, like milk and butter, were close at hand.

"Well then, let's eat the biscuits," Beryl said. "I expect Josh took the milk home, so we'll put some butter on 'em. In the morning I'll gather the eggs."

Beryl pulled the biscuits from the sack and took the tin of butter from the cabinet and sat at the table. He placed two in front of Charlie and they ate in silence, spreading butter on the biscuits and gnawing at the hard chunks, the glow of the lantern spreading a thin light between them.

Beryl didn't know where the boy would sleep, he guessed maybe in a corner. He had another blanket he could spread out, and an extra pillow. The boy wouldn't be with him long enough to worry with, so there was no reason to go out of the way to set up something more suitable. He'd go back in to Berryville tomorrow and pick up a few supplies and get some information about orphanages. Maybe the town sheriff might know something.

He felt a little sorry for the boy but it wasn't any of his doing. The boy was too small to be of much help and Beryl wasn't that interested in having him around anyway. If he'd been a little older and some bigger he might have come in handy, but as it was the boy was of no value. Just another mouth to feed and something else to keep track of was the way Beryl saw it.

Charlie sat quietly chewing on the biscuit and butter. He was tired and was glad they were at his uncle's home. He could see into the big room from where he was sitting, but there wasn't much to look at. The fireplace was at the side and there was a chair sitting beside it, but of course there was no fire. He wondered if the winters would be as cold as they were in Oklahoma. He remembered the howling winds that were a constant on the plains and the snow blowing sideways when they opened the door to go outside. His father had said there wasn't anything to stop the wind and that was why it blew so hard. Charlie thought with so many trees there might not be any wind at all here, and if there was there would be no sideways to it.

He wondered what Rachael and Papa were eating right then. Mrs. Henson had said they were going somewhere better, but Charlie wasn't sure what that meant. Maybe the biscuits were softer and he hoped it was so. Rachael made good biscuits and if he were lucky and was there when she pulled them out of the stove, the butter would run off the top and he would lick all around it and get all of the sweetness he could before he took the first bite. Sometimes she would have smashed berries with sugar and would put some on top of the butter and he bet that's what they were eating now. He was tired of chewing and sat the half eaten biscuit on the table and looked at his uncle with tired eyes.

Beryl sat his biscuit down too—in his opinion it wasn't worth eating, and he wasn't hungry anyway.

"Let's put you to bed, boy," Beryl said. "I've still got chores."

Beryl took the lantern and walked into the big room and Charlie followed. When they entered the bedroom Charlie saw the bed in the corner with a small table beside it, and his uncle set the lantern on it. It was a small room but the bed looked much the same as the one he and Rachael used to sleep in. Charlie was so tired he wanted to jump on the bed and just lay there in its softness, but he decided to wait for his uncle to tell him it was all right to do so.

Charlie stood in the doorway as Beryl went to a small dresser opposite the bed and opened the bottom drawer. He saw him pull out a blanket and unfold it and then spread it out in the far corner at the foot of the bed. He wondered why he hadn't put it on the bed as cool as it was, but again he didn't want to ask. Charlie had slept with his Papa before, so sleeping in the same bed with his uncle didn't scare him, all he wanted to do was sleep.

Beryl took a pillow from the bed and tossed it on the blanket and turned to Charlie.

"You saw the privy out back didn't you?"

"Yes, sir," Charlie said.

"There's a thunder bucket under the bed if you can't make it, but I suggest you do the best you can to get outside."

Charlie hadn't moved from the doorway and didn't know what he was supposed to do. He wondered why his uncle was sleeping on the floor when there was a big bed to sleep in, but he wondered about a lot of things right then.

"You go on to bed, boy," Beryl said. "I'll check on the cows and the horses. I get up before daybreak and you will too, so get some sleep."

Charlie was ready to get some sleep and he had no problem with getting up early. They had always gotten up at sunrise, even though there were days when Rachael would let him sleep in, but most of the time he was awake anyway, and would stay in bed and watch Rachael make breakfast.

Charlie walked over to the bed and hopped up on it and began to take his boots off.

"You're sleeping on the floor, boy," Beryl said.

Charlie looked at him and then at the blanket at the end of the bed. He still had his hands on the heel and toe of the boot, but had stopped pulling.

"Don't look at me like I'm crazy," Beryl said. "I don't know what you thought but you ain't taking my bed. There's boards on this floor so it ain't dirt, and I know you had dirt floors. You can thank me for this. When I come back I expect you to be in the corner."

Beryl took the lantern and walked through the doorway. Charlie was still sitting on the bed when he heard the back door shut. He took his hands from his boot and let his foot fall beside his other leg. He could barely see from the moonlight shining through the small window by the bed. The bed felt so soft where he was sitting and he pushed down on the spongy mattress with his hand. He dared not let himself lie down for he knew he'd fall asleep and his uncle had been clear as to what his wishes were. He didn't understand, the bed seemed big enough for the both of them and he had always slept with Rachael, and sometimes with his dad. They only had the two beds and Papa's was the biggest, but sometimes when Rachael didn't feel well his Papa would tell Charlie to sleep with him. His uncle was family, that's what Mrs. Henson had told him, but he didn't act like family, or at least he didn't act like Charlie's father.

Charlie let himself slide from the edge of the mattress and when his feet hit the floor he stayed propped against the bed. He let himself drop to the floor and then took his boots off and tossed them against the wall. He scooted on the floor to the blanket and lay down in the corner with the pillow, pulling an edge of the blanket over him as he curled up on the hard boards.

Lying in the soft moonlight Charlie wondered if he would be going to school the next day and who might be going with him. Maybe his uncle would go with him—that would be better than going alone. He hadn't heard anything about it but he was sure there was a school. He hoped the other kids were nice. Some of the kids in Oklahoma hadn't been and they'd said things that made him feel hurt and sad. Rachael had told him not to get angry, but he had never gotten angry about the things they said and did, only sad. He liked them and wanted to have fun with them, but they wouldn't let him play. One time they had let him play and told him to go hide and they would come and find him, but they had never come, and when it was time to go back inside, the teacher had had to come and get him and everyone had laughed. He thought he had hidden so well they couldn't find him, but the teacher told him they hadn't even tried.

Charlie heard the back door open and close and the thud of footsteps coming his way. The sound of his uncle's boots seemed so loud on the boards, so different from his Papa's footsteps on the dirt floor. Charlie didn't move— he stayed as still as he could. He didn't want his uncle to think he was awake. He was tired of his uncle's loud voice that never seemed to say anything nice.

He listened as his uncle's big boots dropped to the floor and heard the tired groan as he rolled into the soft bed. He wanted to ask if he would be going to school tomorrow, but then he was sure it wasn't the right time. Maybe if he closed his eyes Rachael would be there with him. He slept so good when Rachael was with him.

Chapter Four

Charlie felt the hand shaking his shoulder but he couldn't come awake. The night hadn't been long enough and when he opened his eyes it was still dark. All he could make out was a shadow looming over him and for a moment it startled him, but then the hard floor he was lying on jolted his memory and he knew where he was.

"Come on, boy," Beryl said. "I've overslept, it's almost five. Let's feed the chickens and gather the eggs. There's water in the basin—wash up."

Charlie heard Beryl's boots stomping away and he rose up and leaned against the wall. He looked at the window but could see nothing but dark. There was a dim light coming from the outer room from the lantern and he could hear his uncle throwing wood into the cook stove.

He stepped to the washbasin and dipped into the water and splashed his face. A towel was hanging on the side of the table and he took it and wiped his hands and face. He went back to the corner and found his boots and sat on the floor and pulled them on, then stumbled out the back door to the outhouse. When he was done he walked back inside to the kitchen. The fire was going in the stove and Beryl was bent over watching it, then he pushed the door part way closed and shoved the lid over the top hole, leaving a sliver of a crescent open. Charlie could see the flames licking at the slice and he stared at it wide eyed, still drifting in the clouds of slumber.

"Wake up, boy," Beryl said. "The sun's catching us and we've got things to do."

"Am I going to school?" Charlie asked.

"School? No, you ain't going to school. Your school days may be over for all I know. We've got work to do and you'll be part of it…for now anyways."

Beryl took a basket from the shelf and walked out the back door with the lantern in his other hand and Charlie followed. When they got to the henhouse he handed the basket to Charlie and hooked the lantern on a nail and began reaching under the hens for eggs.

Beryl didn't have many laying hens and they only came up with eight eggs, but it would be enough. Charlie held the basket with both hands as carefully as he could. He remembered dropping his dinner at the campfire and even though his uncle hadn't said anything he knew he was irritated by the look on his face. He didn't want to drop the eggs—that was breakfast and he was hungry, and he was sure his uncle wouldn't be as quiet as he was the other night.

"Come on, let's go," Beryl said.

They walked toward the house, Beryl carrying the lantern and Charlie carrying the basket. He was still sleepy and was having trouble following, stumbling a little trying to keep up. Beryl wasn't paying attention, walking his normal pace, which was three steps farther than Charlie's with every stride.

"Slow down, Uncle," Charlie said.

Beryl stopped and turned around. "Can't you keep up?"

"I'm trying. It's dark back here."

"If you'd keep up you wouldn't have that trouble. Now come on, you're wasting time."

Charlie decided he'd better hurry and started to jog along faster, but when he did he tripped and fell forward, the basket landing in front of him on its side.

"Well I'll be damned," Beryl said. "Can't you do anything right?"

The worst thing had happened and Charlie knew it. He scrambled up and reached for the basket but Beryl got there at the same time and jerked it from his hand. He looked in the basket and counted the eggs.

"You don't count for nothing, boy. There's four eggs broke. I guess you like biscuits so well it's what you want for breakfast."

Beryl turned and left Charlie standing in the dark.

Charlie watched his uncle walk to the house and go inside. He wasn't sure what to do—maybe he should stay outside—he knew his uncle wouldn't want him in the house. He stood in the dark, not knowing which way to turn, thinking it would do no good to say he was sorry. He was wishing he were back home on the plains of Oklahoma.

Rachael only let him carry eggs when they were close to the house.

39

Charlie's walking was unpredictable at best. His attention seemed to be diverted by the simplest things, and Charlie was curious—anything could turn his head. No matter how often Rachael told him to be careful, Charlie still had trouble keeping his mind on the next step.

Charlie tried hard, but things seemed to jump out at him and take his mind from where it was supposed to be. One minute he'd be walking to the barn and the next he'd be on his way back to the house. If the teacher said to open his book he'd be staring at the ceiling. He just couldn't stay focused from one minute to the next.

Beryl had checked the fire and was cooking saltpork. He was so irritated he hadn't even noticed Charlie wasn't behind him. He went to the back door and could see from the faint light of the early dawn Charlie sitting on the ground where the eggs had dropped.

He was having trouble feeling sorry for him. There didn't seem to him to be that much wrong with the child. He could talk straight enough, and could use his hands and legs as well as any boy. Why he was so clumsy Beryl couldn't understand. He knew Charlie was small for his age, but that shouldn't have anything to do with finishing tasks the way they should be done. And the boy couldn't take directions well at all. And then he'd sulk and pout when he was scolded for it. A more aggravating boy he'd never met.

Beryl opened the door and walked outside. He didn't want to get too far away from the stove.

"Why are you sitting in the dirt, boy? Get in here and get something to eat."

"I don't want to eat," Charlie yelled back.

"You're gonna eat," Beryl said. "No one's gonna say I ain't feeding you."

"You don't want me here," Charlie said.

"You're not gonna live too long, son, if you keep acting the way you are. Folks stop caring after a certain point. If you can't take care of yourself nobody's gonna do it for you. Being stubborn won't help."

"I'm not stubborn. I just have trouble."

"Well it's time to stop having it. You're old enough to be trusted with chores, so do it right. Now, get in here. I'm not gonna ruin the bacon cause you're too pig-headed to come to the table."

Charlie pushed himself up and walked toward the door as Beryl went back inside.

Rachael had told Charlie not to let others give him a hard time, not to be rude or vulgar, but he should always stand up for himself. It was all so very confusing. She had also said to respect his elders, and when he'd asked her what an elder was she'd said the grownups. In this case his new uncle was a grownup, and he was fighting the temptation to yell at him, even though it had felt good the night on the road, he still felt guilty about it and didn't want to do it again. He'd never met a grownup so mean.

He did remember Rachael telling him some people were just plain ornery, and the best thing to do was stay away from them, but Charlie couldn't figure out how he was going to distance himself from his own uncle when he was supposed to be living with him. Didn't his uncle know you weren't supposed to be mean? He wished someone would tell him so he wouldn't have to, because Charlie didn't know if he could.

Beryl set a tin plate in front of Charlie with two strips of bacon on it and two fried eggs and Charlie looked at it with shock. He stared at his uncle thinking he'd made a mistake—he thought he was eating biscuits.

Beryl saw the look on Charlie's face and frowned. "Just eat it, boy," he said. "And be quick about it. We've got to milk yet and then we're going to town. I've got business to take care of."

Charlie was so hungry he had the plate cleaned before Beryl sat down, and when Beryl saw it, it caught him off guard. He leaned down at the edge of the table and peered under it, thinking the boy must have dropped his food again, but there was no sign that he had. Charlie wasn't even chewing, he must have swallowed everything whole.

Beryl could see why the boy was hungry—they'd only had the biscuits on the second day coming back, and then last night he'd been too tired to fix anything. He looked at his plate and then at Charlie and decided he wasn't hungry.

Beryl pushed his plate across the table. He wasn't going to let a child go hungry, no matter the trouble.

"Finish this up," Beryl said. "I'll go milk the cow and hook up the team."

"Aren't you hungry, Uncle?"

"I've been eating on bacon while you were out there pouting. Now eat, I want to get back as early as possible. I've been gone too long as it is."

Beryl went back to the stove and closed the vents to let the fire die and reached into the sack on the shelf and pulled out two biscuits and put them in his pocket. When he turned around he saw that Charlie was almost through with his second plate. Beryl shook his head as he walked to the door. The boy doesn't have any problems eating—if he could just think of his chores like food he might live longer than a fortnight after all.

"Pick up that blanket and pillow and put it on the bed," Beryl said as he walked out the door. "I'll be back in a few minutes."

Charlie finished his breakfast and while he was chewing he was looking out the back door. The yard was in full sunlight now, and he had never seen such colors. It was mid November, and Charlie's first look at fall in the mountains. On the plains of Oklahoma the colors didn't change much, except for the land being bare of crops, and when the snows came, and he liked the snow because it was white. He got tired of the browns and grays. His favorite time was early morning and dusk, when the sky offered its different colors. Only the sky changed on the plains.

Charlie pushed his plate away and rested his head on the table, his eyes focused on the yard. Leaves were falling in the breeze and he watched as they floated down and tumbled across the yard. Red, brown, green, and yellow. It seemed to him that they must have floated through a rainbow to have turned so many different colors. He'd seen many rainbows in Oklahoma, and when they would appear he'd stand as still as possible to watch, thinking that if he didn't move it would stay with him and not go away, but it always did. But here he could look in any direction and the rainbow of leaves stretched through the hills and through every tree. He wished Rachael could see it.

Charlie didn't know how long he'd been asleep, but when he heard the door slam shut and his uncle's heavy boots, he came awake with a start.

"Did you get that blanket put up?"

"No, sir," Charlie said. He was wiping his eyes trying to get awake and he knew at the same time he'd made another mistake. "I'll do it now," he said.

"Just stay put," Beryl said. "I'll get it myself. It's like you're not even here except for the eatin' and the trouble."

Charlie hung his head and his lip trembled. He hated it when his lip quivered, but it did it every time he tried not to cry. He bit his lip and closed his eyes as tight as he could, hoping he could stop the water, but he felt the tears roll down his cheeks and swiped at them with his arms and he pushed himself off the chair and ran outside. He didn't want his uncle to see him because he knew it would make him madder and he hated to see the mean look in his eyes.

He ran to the front of the wagon and leaned against the horse's front leg.

The horse's head turned to him for a brief moment and then forward again, as if the small pressure against its leg was meaningless.

Charlie liked being around the animals even though the big ones scared him a little, but they never had mean faces. They didn't care if he did something wrong or even if he cried. It was people that hurt him, and he had turned it over in his mind so many times it made him dizzy—people were supposed to understand, but if they did, they didn't show it.

The next thing Charlie knew he was being lifted by his arms and more thrown than put in the seat of the wagon. Then Beryl climbed up and sat down, unhooked the reins and slapped the horses. They made a half circle in the yard and started down the path leading to the main road.

While they traveled toward the town of Berryville they passed many other wagons. Most of the people stared and Charlie looked back, but very few made an attempt at smiling or waving, and he was afraid to wave because his uncle wasn't, and the day had not started out well anyway.

When they reached the town Beryl steered the team to the sheriff's office and stopped in front. He got down and tied the reins to the brake. He told Charlie to stay put.

Charlie sat on the wagon and watched the people as they strolled on the wooden walkways. He saw that many of them were looking at him as they walked by, talking to each other, nodding his way, some grinning and some, mostly women, shaking their heads and frowning. He turned his eyes away but then he couldn't seem to find any place where no one was looking at him and so stared at the footboard of the wagon.

It was much the same when he was at school—the kids staring at him and laughing, some pointing and whispering to each other, only because he'd made some small mistake or the teacher had scolded him for something. The only time he liked school was when Rachael was there, and on the days when she might be sick, he hadn't wanted to go, but Papa had made him and those were the worst days, when Rachael had not been there. The other kids wouldn't laugh as loud when she was there—they would do it behind her back, but they didn't care if Charlie saw.

Charlie had never felt so alone, sitting in the bright sunlight on a busy street with so many people around.

"And what's your name?"

Charlie was startled by the woman's voice. He'd been daydreaming and lost in his own thoughts. He looked at the woman and his eyes brightened. She was pleasant looking, with pretty eyes and dark hair. She was smiling at him and it had been, or it seemed to him, a long time since he had seen a smile.

"You do have a name don't you?"

"Charlie Stinson."

"My name's Beatrice, but folks call me Betty. This looks like Beryl Stinson's wagon. You must be his nephew."

Charlie didn't speak, but stared at the pretty face with the pleasant smile.

"You don't talk much, do you?" she asked.

"I don't guess so, ma'am."

"I've heard a little about you, young man. I've heard you lost your father and sister, is that right?"

Charlie didn't know if that was right or not. They weren't lost—he knew where they were.

"They're in Oklahoma," Charlie said.

Betty nodded and smiled and patted his knee. Then she said, "Yes, I guess they are. How are you getting along with Beryl?"

Charlie's small smile went away and he looked at the floorboards again, his hands clasped together between his legs.

"Beryl's not the easiest man to get on with, is he?" Betty said.

Charlie looked at the door where his uncle had gone in and saw it was still shut.

"We had bacon and eggs this morning," Charlie said.

"Did you now," Betty said. "Did you have some of those hard biscuits that Beryl's famous for?"

This brought another small smile to Charlie's face. Someone else had eaten his uncle's biscuits and thought the same thing he did.

"We ate some last night with butter."

"How were they?"

"Hard," Charlie said with a grin.

Betty laughed and Charlie saw her white, straight teeth and her eyes shining with happiness.

"You know," Betty said, "I've seen Beryl throw 'em to the chickens and they wouldn't eat 'em either."

Charlie thought that was funny and wanted to say something funny himself, so he said, "Their peckers must be worn out."

Betty's eyes widened and Charlie thought he'd said something wrong, but it wasn't just a moment before Betty started laughing, and folks on the sidewalk stopped and stared.

"Well, Charlie Stinson, if you don't beat all. If you're not the opposite of Beryl I don't know water from fire. You'll be good for that old man."

Charlie didn't know what she meant, but he was sure his uncle wouldn't think the same thing.

"How would you like to come over to my place sometime and have a good dinner?"

"I'd like that, ma'am," Charlie said. "When?"

"Just as soon as we can get Beryl to bring you over, and I'll tell you something else, if he won't bring you, I'll come and get you. Maybe, if we play our cards right, he'll let you stay the night, and we'll have a dandy breakfast to go along with that supper."

Beatrice Hagen owned the only clothing store in Berryville. She sold women's and men's clothes and she was forty years old. Her husband had gone to Chicago ten years earlier to buy more stock and had never come back. But Beatrice wasn't the kind of woman to let it bother her. She'd married the man more for convenience than love anyway, and it was her opinion that she might just be better off for it. She had the shop and it made her a decent income and she liked where she was living. Love was hard to locate, and it seemed to her there was more giving than getting, and she could do well enough on her own if that was how it had to be. She had thought before about Beryl Stinson living out there by himself, not that she was interested in the old coot, but simply wondered if he had the same thoughts on companionship as her own. She could see him through the window of the sheriff's office, and knew instinctively whatever they were talking about wouldn't be pleasant. Things were never pleasant with Beryl Stinson.

When Beryl stepped through the door Sheriff Stuart Burgess was sitting behind his desk looking at paperwork. He peered over his reading glasses long enough to see who was coming in, and then kept right on reading his papers. He didn't have much to say to Beryl Stinson, not that he had anything against the man, he caused no problems, but he wasn't the most likable person in the county either. A man expected a 'Good morning', or a 'Good to see ya', from time to time, but it was hard to get anything out of Beryl except a slant-eyed stare or a huff.

"I've got questions," Beryl said, standing in front of Stuart's desk.

"Have you now," Stuart said. He rocked on the back legs of his chair and placed his spectacles on the desk.

"You're the sheriff, you're supposed to know things."

"It's good to see you, Beryl," Stuart said. "I understand you've added to your family."

"That's what I've come about," Beryl said. "I need to know where the closest orphanage is."

Stuart stopped rocking. The statement took him by surprise. He knew Beryl was a loner, someone that wanted to be left alone, a man that didn't care whether his neighbors needed help or not, and preferred they didn't offer him any. But to send his brother's son to an orphanage was about the hardest thing he'd ever heard.

"Beryl, you haven't been back with that boy but one day, how can you stand there and tell me you want to cart him off to an orphanage? For the Lord's sake, he's your brother's son."

"I'm not asking for opinions," Beryl said. "Just tell me where it is."

Stuart thought for a moment before he said anything. If he had his way he wouldn't tell him, but the man would find out anyway. It was a sorry thing to do, abandoning the boy, but it wasn't something he'd put past Beryl Stinson. The boy might be better off. Living with Beryl would be no easy task, for man or child. Stuart still couldn't believe Beryl was doing it, every man had a responsibility to care for his own blood, no matter the troubles that came with it. Stinson was a hard man; he should have been living up north where there were fewer people, maybe the Dakota's, or even farther, where no one would have to put up with him.

It was something Stuart couldn't tolerate, someone as disagreeable as Beryl. He felt Beryl was more of a coward than anything, staying to himself like he did, but wanting the town close enough so he could get the things he needed. If he wanted to be a hermit then he should act like one and stay the hell out of town, let the folks that want to have a good community have it without the likes of him coming around and ruining everyone's day. As far as he knew Beryl had never offered any help with anything: no charity, no time, and no effort. It was true Beryl never caused any problems, but that didn't make him a value to the community. In his opinion it was only a matter of time before trouble caught up to him. It had a way of doing it with men like him. It wasn't just being difficult to get along with, it was how mean spirited he was, and sometimes that alone had a way of attracting trouble.

"There's one over by Harrison," Stuart said. "About three miles this side of it. You should think it over, Beryl. I've not heard good things about it. Why don't you wait until spring, see how it goes, and then make a decision. Give the boy a chance."

"It's none of your business," Beryl said.

Beryl walked out of the door without closing it behind him. It was none of the sheriff's concern how he managed his life and he needed no instructions on doing so. It was Clive's responsibility to give the boy a chance, not his. He should've remarried a long time ago if he had two kids, then the boy would've had someone that wanted to take care of him. Clive was a damn fool for not thinking of it.

Beryl saw Beatrice Hagen standing at the wagon talking to Charlie. He made no attempt to say hello. He walked around the horses and climbed up on the seat.

"This is a fine young boy you've got here, Beryl," Betty said. "It's going to start getting cold, why don't you bring him by the shop and we'll fit him into a warm coat for the winter."

Beryl turned his eyes to Charlie.

"I told you to sit here, not yak at everybody that came by."

Beryl took the reins and slapped the horses and left Betty standing on the sidewalk. Stuart came out of his office and watched as the wagon rolled away.

"I feel sorry for that boy," Stuart said.

"Maybe Beryl will soften now that he's got someone living with him," Betty said.

"Not likely," Stuart said. "He won't be staying long."

"Why not?"

"Beryl's taking the boy to the orphanage over at Harrison."

Betty's eyes locked on him—she couldn't find her voice. She couldn't understand how anyone could abandon a child. The orphanage was for children that had no family, and Beryl was family.

"You know that for a fact."

"That's what he said. If it wasn't such sorry circumstances I'd say the boy might be better off."

Stuart and Betty stood on the walkway and watched the dust cloud up behind the wagon. Both of them felt that little Charlie had few chances, with or without Beryl Stinson.

Chapter Five

Harrison, Arkansas was thirty miles to the east and Beryl knew his team could manage fifteen miles a day without wearing down. He hated asking Josh Danner to look in on the place again, but he saw no other way. It was the second time he'd had to ask for help and it irked him. Now he owed more favors, and he knew when someone had a debt the obligation would be called upon. He wouldn't call in a favor himself, but then he couldn't remember the last time anyone asked him for one, and that suited him fine. He loaned money to no man and he didn't borrow any. Over the years he'd accumulated quite a bit of money from selling his cattle and hogs, but he had no intention of letting loose of it.

There wasn't much between Berryville and Harrison and the roads were rough, some of them not what he considered roads at all, just wagon ruts for miles until they met a few homes gathered together. Then the road was better but only because of its constant use, and sometimes that could be a detriment, especially when the rains came, and they were coming. November was a bad time to be making a trip. The weather wouldn't cooperate and he knew it. They'd already had mornings that left a skin of frost on the water troughs and it would only get colder.

Beryl had made up his mind—the boy was going. He should have stayed in Oklahoma with Mrs. Henson. Beryl knew what folks were saying, that he was cruel for putting the boy in an orphanage, but he wasn't any worse than them. If they thought it was a slight, then they should step up and take the boy themselves. It was woman's work taking care of kids. In his mind Martha Henson was just as guilty as he was and so were the others. Folks might say how unkind it was, but he didn't remember seeing anyone offering to take him in either.

Without a word between them, Beryl and Charlie traveled home. They unhooked the team and let them out to pasture. Beryl headed toward the pens to feed the cattle and hogs.

"You think you can feed the chickens?" He asked Charlie.

"I think so," Charlie said.

"Well, do it then. I'll be back later."

Charlie watched as Beryl made his way down the path away from the house to the pastures. He would have rather stayed with his uncle—he wanted to see the cattle, and he didn't want to be alone. He stood in the yard and listened to the breeze rustling through the trees. It was a sound he wasn't used to, but he liked it. He heard the birds chirping and that too was a sound that he enjoyed. Since there were few trees on the plains Charlie wasn't too familiar with the many different voices of birds. He knew what vultures sounded like though, there were lots of vultures in Oklahoma. Then he heard a sound like chatter, a different noise, and it was coming from the trees behind the chicken shed.

Charlie walked in that direction and as soon as he got to the corner of the shed the sound stopped. He peered around the corner but could see or hear nothing, not even birds chirping. He listened, his head turning, spanning the forest from side to side. He stood for the longest time and then the birds started singing again and he heard a rustling in the brush. Something was running through the underbrush, something small, and then he saw the movement.

The squirrel hopped a few feet and stopped and waited. He knew Charlie was watching him. Charlie stayed quiet. He'd seen squirrels before, but this one was larger than the ones he knew, and it was reddish in color, not gray. He saw that the squirrel had something in its front paws, something round and green and he could see that he was knawing on it. Charlie made a step in its direction and the squirrel ran and jumped on a tree and hid on the opposite side.

Charlie stepped backwards to the shed and leaned against it. Then he heard the chattering again and it was coming from the same tree. Off to his left in the distance he heard the same noise, and it was coming from another tree. Then Charlie knew, there were two squirrels, and they were talking. Charlie smiled. The smile reminded him once again about his morning in town.

He wished he had someone to talk to. The woman in town had been nice and the talk had been fun. His uncle said very little and when he did there was no fun in it and very little information that Charlie could tell. Just orders mostly, things Charlie should be doing, or even worse, it was loud and gruff, telling him how useless he was.

He wondered when he might see the woman again. She reminded him of Mrs. Henson, only smaller and prettier, but just as kind. Rachael had always talked to him explaining things to him, and so had his dad and he missed it. He'd said more words to Betty in those few minutes than he'd said to his uncle since he'd met him. Maybe his uncle didn't know many words, but Charlie understood that the ones he did know didn't sound nice.

Charlie heard the chickens behind him and remembered he was supposed to be feeding them. He went to the other side of the chicken house where the gunnysack of feed was sitting on a shelf under a small tin roof. It was outside the shed so the chickens couldn't get to it, but it was higher than he could reach, so he stood on his tiptoes and stretched as far as he could but it did no good. He looked around for something to stand on and saw a wooden bucket by the barn. He brought the bucket back and set it in front of the shelf. He stepped up on it and could finally reach the bag and scoop that lay beside it, but still couldn't reach the top of the bag to fill the can. He looked around again to find something to put on the bucket.

Charlie couldn't see anything that would work, but then he noticed a large rock and he thought it might get him high enough. He set the rock on the bucket, and grabbed the shelf and pulled himself up. The rock was unstable and he was hanging on trying to keep his balance, moving his feet to get a good hold. Finally he stopped wiggling. He wasn't as high as he wanted to be but thought it was good enough. He took the scoop with one hand while holding on to the shelf with the other, and then he grabbed the sack and pulled down on the loose top. He stretched his neck to see and reached into the sack with the scoop.

The black snake was as surprised as Charlie. He slid out of the sack right in front of Charlie's face and Charlie screamed, his feet stumbling on the rock. He grabbed the sack to stop from falling but it was too late and his feet went out from under him and he fell backwards, the gunnysack and snake coming with him, landing on top of him as he hit the ground. Charlie was yelling and kicking and scrambling to get away. He kicked himself backwards and the snake slithered away.

He lay on his back a few feet from the sack. The sack had turned upside down and the feed was dumped on the ground, scattered because of his kicking. Charlie was trying to catch his breath, watching the snake as it disappeared behind the shed.

Once he stopped huffing Charlie knew he was in trouble. The chicken feed was everywhere and his uncle wouldn't be happy. He looked in the sack to be sure there were no more snakes in it and then started scooping up handfuls and shoving it in the sack. He was on his knees working as fast as could, the tears rolling down his cheeks, not because he was still scared but because his uncle would be mad at him for making the mess. He worked furiously, scraping the ground to pile the feed up so he could get as much as possible with each handful. He had feed dust all over his clothes and in his mouth and eyes and nose. The dust was caking on his face from the tears and in between scoops he'd swipe at his eyes with his hands and arms but it didn't help. Then something grabbed the back of his jacket and pulled him up on his feet and held him in the air, his toes barely touching the ground.

Beryl looked Charlie up and down. Charlie was hanging in his uncle's grip, his head dropped to his chest, his arms dangling at his sides. Beryl jerked him backwards hard enough so that when he let go Charlie fell on his back in the dirt.

"Can't even feed chickens. Get in the house and get your clothes off and wash up. You better know how to wash clothes 'cause I ain't washing 'em for you."

Charlie picked himself up and ran to the house. When he got to the door his eyes were so full of tears and dirt he couldn't find the pull and so he tried to wipe his eyes with his dirty hands but it only made things worse. His eyes stung from the dust and feed and mud and he fell to his knees, still reaching for the door with one hand. Then he felt someone pull at him, but it wasn't his uncle, he could tell by the touch, and he went limp.

"Stand up, Charlie," Betty Hagen said.

Charlie stood and Betty pulled him to her and wrapped her arms around his back and held him close and tight. She held his head against her stomach and rocked from side to side. Charlie's sobs were great gasps and he couldn't catch his breath.

"Calm down now, it'll be all right," Betty said. "You're going to be okay."

Charlie finally found his voice and said, "The snake—he—the sack—he—"

"It's okay, Charlie."

"Let the boy be," Beryl said.

Betty turned her head to face him with the coldest eyes Beryl had ever witnessed, so cold he stopped in mid-step.

"Beryl Stinson, if you ever touch this child again—"

"This ain't your—"

"I'm making it my business," Betty said. She picked up Charlie and carried him to her buggy and set him in the seat. "He's going with me tonight."

"He's not going anywhere," Beryl said, starting toward her.

Betty reached under the buggy seat and pulled out an axe handle she kept for just such problems.

"You try and stop me."

Beryl stopped again.

"Don't you come to town looking for him," Betty said.

She got in the buggy and turned the horse and headed past Beryl. She pulled Charlie's head to her lap and held him as they rode down the path.

By the time Betty pulled into her yard Charlie had cried himself to sleep. She lifted him out of the buggy and carried him inside and put him on her own bed. She went back outside and unhooked the horse and put him in the small corral and went back to the house.

In her life she had never seen a child treated so badly. She knew it happened, as disgusting as it was, but she'd never been a witness to it.

She had pulled into Beryl's place as he was tossing the boy back behind him, but it was easy to tell what had happened. Somehow Charlie had spilled the feed and Beryl was upset about it. There was no reason for him to treat Charlie in such fashion. She was almost brought to tears herself.

She'd given her own boys a swat when they needed it, but Charlie didn't need disciplined for what had happened to him, it was an accident, pure and simple. If anyone deserved to be punished, it was Beryl.

Betty stood by the doorway of her bedroom and looked at the small boy lying on her bed. She had very little knowledge of him, just the talk of the town, and gossip was useless. She knew he'd lost his mother and then his father and sister, and then his home, and to her that was enough to scare any adult, much less a child. It was Charlie's misfortune to have Beryl Stinson as his uncle, but there was nothing that could be done about that. She knew Charlie would have to go back, she had no right to take him, but there was no way she could leave him there with Beryl Stinson either.

Charlie was curled up on the bed and Betty folded a blanket over him. She thought how handsome he was, how fine his facial features were. She knew he was small for his age, but it made no difference. She smoothed back his blond hair from his forehead and listened to his easy breathing.

It brought back memories of her sons, both grown and gone now, and the many good and hard times it took to raise them. Beryl Stinson had no idea what it took to care for others, and her thoughts earlier in the day that he might soften as time went by, now deserted her. He was not a man that would soften.

Her boys were not the sons of her latest husband. Her first husband had died of pneumonia when the boys were only ten and twelve. It had been difficult raising two boys by herself but Betty had come from a family of seven children and she had been the oldest. Taking care of her brothers and sisters had been part of her life and by the time she was sixteen she was ready to leave, and so she married and had her own kids. She had never expected to have her husband die so early, but when he did it seemed to her it wasn't that much different than when she lived with her own parents, taking care of her siblings.

She married for a second time after her boys were grown, but it was mostly out of loneliness. One son moved to Oklahoma City and the other went to Houston, Texas. Boys seemed to move away, much more than girls, and Betty had spent many years fending for herself until Bernard Hagen became a suitor. He owned the clothing store in Berryville and since it was the only clothing store it was no coincidence they would meet. She had never considered him as a husband, but his unrelenting advances had finally broken her down. She hadn't loved him, but he was likable and he treated her well, that is until he disappeared. She had never heard from him after the trip to Chicago, so had no idea what had happened, but she supposed he'd met someone else or she would have been notified of his death.

His leaving had not consumed her. He'd left the store, which she'd never understood, but it made no mind to her. It was a good living and she had learned how to run it, and felt if the man was fool enough to leave his source of income behind him, he probably wasn't worth worrying about anyway.

She saw enough people during the day that having someone to talk to was not a problem, but there were times in the late evenings she did wish someone was there to share the night and pass the time. Her days were busy and she was tired when she went home, but she liked cooking and hated eating alone, and it was hard to cook for one, and the food didn't seem as tasty as it did when there was someone to share it with.

That's what she was doing at Beryl's place. She'd let her helper at the store finish the day and lock up while she went home and fixed some food for Beryl and Charlie. She thought they might appreciate some good home cooking, especially Charlie. She knew Beryl wouldn't care and would probably think it was an intrusion, but after talking with Charlie she was sure he needed something good.

It was then she remembered the basket in the back of the buggy with the food in it. She'd been so caught up with Charlie and his problems she'd forgotten all about it. Betty left the bedroom and walked outside. When she stepped off the porch she saw Stuart walking toward her.

"Evening, Betty," he said.

"Hello, Stuart. I guess I know what you're doing here."

"I heard you've got Beryl's nephew."

"I took some supper out to them and when I got there Beryl was mistreating the boy. Has Beryl been to see you?"

"No, not yet. I expect to see him soon. Josh Danner stopped by Beryl's on his way to town and he told me. Beryl don't like folks mixing in his business, and you know it as well as anyone."

"Charlie was crying, Stuart, and after what I saw there was no way I was going to leave him."

"I understand and I admire what you did, but you still can't keep the boy."

"I know it," Betty said. She crossed her arms and looked away from Stuart.

"Look," Stuart said. "I hate it as much as you do that Charlie has to stay with the likes of Beryl Stinson, and I hate it even more that Beryl's taking him to the orphanage, but the law says it's none of our business. He can do whatever he wants with him."

Betty was still staring at nothing. She was mad, not at Stuart, but at life, the life that had thrown a small, defenseless boy into the arms of a man like Stinson. She was mad at herself too. On the way home she had been so upset she'd told herself she would just adopt Charlie and it would solve the problem. But as the ride grew longer, so did her memory. She wasn't so sure she wanted to take on another child. She loved her boys, but after they were old enough to take care of themselves she had never been so thankful, and now she wondered if she still had the patience to raise another child. She might still have the patience, and she knew she had the wherewithal, but she didn't know if she had the need.

"I won't let him treat Charlie like an animal," she said. "And I don't mean just hitting and throwing him around. I mean talking hateful to him. He's got to be miserable every minute he's with that man."

54

Stuart knew there was nothing he could do. Charlie was just unlucky.

"If Beryl wants him back, I'll have to come and get him."

Stuart turned and walked away, and Betty drew a finger across her eye to catch the tear. She had never hated like she hated now.

She walked to the wagon and lifted out the basket and carried it inside. She was taking the food out when she noticed Charlie standing in the doorway of the kitchen, watching.

She smiled at him. "Did you have a good nap?"

Charlie nodded.

"Are you hungry?"

Charlie shook a nod this time.

"I'll tell you what, how about I heat up some water and you take a nice, warm bath, and then we'll sit down and have a hot meal."

"I'm hungry now," Charlie said.

"What did Beryl feed you for lunch?"

"We didn't eat."

Betty clinched her teeth and turned her head to the wall. She took out a chicken leg and handed it to Charlie.

"You snack on this then," she said, "while I heat some water. You'll feel better after a bath and the dinner will taste better too. Is that a deal?"

"Yes, ma'am," Charlie said, reaching for the chicken leg.

Betty started a fire in the cook stove and set a large pot of water on top. She covered the plates of chicken and potatoes and corn and set them on the opposite side to warm. She told Charlie to take his clothes off and gave him a denim shirt of hers she used to work in the garden. She wanted to wash his clothes while he was bathing, and she'd hang them near the fire to dry.

It didn't take Charlie long to finish his chicken leg. He was having a difficult time trying to take his clothes off with one hand and keeping the chicken close enough to his mouth to eat it. He was so intent on eating and doing what Betty told him at the same time that he'd forgotten to take his boots off first. In the end he had his pants down to his ankles with the chicken bone in his mouth, struggling to get his boots untangled from his pants.

Betty couldn't help but laugh, so she helped him with his boots and pulled his pants off one leg at a time. Charlie ended up sitting on the floor with his back against the wall, the chicken leg in his mouth, his arms lying at his sides, and his underwear the only thing covering him.

"You must have liked the chicken," Betty said.

Charlie looked up at her with a wide grin and big eyes.

"Well, there's plenty more, and there's potatoes and corn to go with it. And I've got fresh bread too, and I guarantee it's not hard. The water's warm enough to sit in. I'll pour it in the tub and you get cleaned up, and when you're done I'll come in and wash your hair for you. I've got some special soap that smells real good for your hair."

Betty reached for his hand and helped him to his feet and Charlie followed her to the tub.

"Hand me your underpants and I'll wash them too. Hop in the tub and I'll bring the water."

After Betty filled the tub she put Charlie's clothes in a large pot of hot water and washed them. She started a fire in the fireplace and hung the clothes on a chair in front of it, and then set the table. She hadn't heard anything from Charlie and thought she better check on him. She found him sitting in the tub, but the soap was still lying beside it and she could tell by the water he hadn't used it.

"You haven't washed yet," Betty said.

Charlie turned his head to her but didn't say anything.

Betty took the soap, knelt beside the tub, and washed him.

"Do you think you'll like living in the mountains rather than the plains?" Betty asked.

"I like Oklahoma," Charlie said. "Rachael's there, and Papa too."

"You know, Charlie, Rachael and your dad are in heaven. You can talk to them in your prayers, but you're not going to see them again."

"I know. Mrs. Henson told me."

"I just didn't want you to think you'd left them behind. They're with you wherever you go."

"What about the hole in the ground?" Charlie asked. "That's where they went."

"Have you ever watched the logs in a fire burning, Charlie?"

"Sure, we had lots of fires. I liked sitting in front of them with Rachael and Papa."

"Well, those logs are like people, Charlie, when they leave us. They light up the room with their flames so you can see, and they spread the warmth to keep you safe. When people leave this earth they leave their love behind, and that's the warmth you feel when you think about them."

"They're not in the hole anymore?"

"Their bodies don't work anymore, so they've left them behind, but the best parts of them rose to heaven. Now, let's wash your hair and you wrap up in this towel and sit in front of the fire while I get dinner ready, and then we'll eat a good meal and you can get some sleep."

Charlie ate like he'd never eaten before. He couldn't remember being this hungry. He was so full he could hardly move and his eyes were getting heavy and he was slouched in the chair and thought he might go to sleep right there.

Betty cleaned the table and stepped over to Charlie and poked his full stomach with her finger. "You're starting to look like a grown man instead of a boy," she said. "Are you ready for bed?"

"Can I sleep in front of the fire?"

Betty smiled and brushed his hair back. "Sure."

She went into the bedroom and came back out with a comforter, a pillow, and a nightshirt, then pulled the small couch from the wall and placed it in front of the fire. Betty held out the nightshirt and sized it up to Charlie. "It's a little tall but it'll do. This belonged to one of my boys when he was about your age. I think it might fit you fine."

Chapter Six

Beryl sat at the table and picked at his food. He'd boiled a few potatoes and beans, but the beans weren't done, so he'd mashed them, but they still had no taste and they felt like he was chewing on a tree root.

She had no right taking the boy; Charlie was his responsibility. Beryl had never shirked a task. She had no business concerning herself with him. The boy needed to learn and coddling him would do no good.

Beryl made no exceptions where work was concerned—you did it and you did it right and you stayed with it until the job was done. Having to do it twice made no sense, and that's what the boy needed to learn. Clive apparently hadn't taught him much, and the boy would not be able to make his way in the world without that lesson.

There was nothing easy in this life and being easy on a child was doing no favors. A man had to be hard and the sooner the boy learned it the better off he'd be.

Beryl got up and scraped his plate in a bucket for the hogs. He poured a cup of coffee and sat in the chair in front of the cook stove, opened the door a little so he could see the flames and rested his arms on his knees. The night was cool but he hadn't built a fire in the fireplace. No sense in having two fires going, he'd be going to bed soon.

He hadn't been that rough on the boy. The crying was just a way for kids to get folks to feel sorry for 'em, and Beryl wasn't falling for it. Hell, he hadn't punished him—all he did was get him out of the way. He might have thrown him a little hard, but he hadn't meant to. Well, Beatrice Hagen could just have him if she wanted him. No, by God, she couldn't. He didn't want the boy around at all. He didn't care what folks thought but he had no intentions of seeing his brother's son every time he went to town. It would just be a reminder of Clive's failings. Tomorrow morning he'd go get him and he'd let Beatrice Hagen know to stay out of his business. What was she doing out here anyway? She'd never come to his place before, she'd shown no interest in him, and Beryl certainly didn't have any interest in her. Women always had to stick their noses in other peoples concerns. Tomorrow he'd make it plain that she wasn't welcome and if she had trouble understanding, he'd make it even plainer.

She sure looked like she was ready to use that axe handle though. He'd never seen such fire in a woman's eyes before. It had been rare he'd seen that much fire in a man's eyes. Beryl had thought about taking it away from her but the look on her face made him think again. He wasn't afraid of her, at least he didn't think he was, but she sure did seem firm in her conviction. He had to admire her for that—she stood her ground. The boy didn't need protecting, he wasn't going to do anything to him. Beryl had never mistreated his animals and he wasn't going to abuse the boy. Animals didn't know anything—they had to be trained, and Charlie was the same way, he had to be taught. He'd taken a board to a mule once for being stubborn, but he wouldn't hit the boy, not unless he fought back.

Thinking back about it, he treated his animals darn good. They did their work and he took care of them for it. The boy couldn't seem to get anything done. Was he supposed to be treated better than the horses that did their jobs? They got things done and did what they were trained, but Charlie, he couldn't finish anything.

Beryl didn't know why he was even worrying about it. In a few days the boy would be gone and things could get back to normal. Charlie didn't want to be here anyway, so it didn't matter where he was. He'd adjust, like everyone had to. He'd be better off at the orphanage, there'd be other kids around. They could waste their days like kids do. They wouldn't learn how to get by, and that was a disgrace, but it wasn't Beryl's problem. The only problem he had right then was getting to Harrison and unloading one.

He couldn't shake the woman out of his mind though. She had been ready to fight, and for a child she didn't even know. It made no sense to Beryl, but most folks didn't make sense to him anyway, especially women. He didn't know much about her, only that her husband had disappeared some years back and she hadn't remarried. From what he gathered earlier in the day he could understand why the husband left. She was a good-looking woman though, Beryl had to give her that. He'd never put much stock in women. There wasn't any kind of work they could do that he couldn't do. They had kids and they took care of 'em, and from what he could tell that was their biggest purpose. If there were no children, it was just another mouth to feed and another dollar lost.

But Beatrice Hagen seemed different. He'd never paid much attention to her, but since their confrontation he had more respect for her. He didn't like what she'd done—she had no right getting involved, but she had brass, and she didn't back down, and that deserved a nod.

Why she would want to get involved in another man's problems he had no idea. The boy was aggravating, there was no way around it, and Beryl felt sure Beatrice would soon find it out, and if he chose to he could just bide his time and she'd be hustling him back, but there was no time to wait. The faster he got Charlie to Harrison the better for all concerned.

Beryl had thought about not picking Charlie up at all at the train depot. It would have been best if he hadn't, but Martha Henson's last telegram said she was putting him on the train, and one way or another she'd see to it he made it to Berryville, if she had to contact the sheriff and tell him Beryl Stinson's nephew was waiting at the station. He didn't have any problems with the sheriff and he wasn't about to start now, and besides, it would have looked like he was dodging his obligations, and if there was one thing Beryl wouldn't put up with, it was having folks believing he wasn't taking care of his own troubles.

Clive should've had more sense than to try and cross a flooded creek anyway. In his opinion it was no wonder the boy was dense, if he had the same inclinations as his father. Clive had never showed much promise in his estimation, marrying as young as he did and staying on the plains where there wasn't anything but dust and cracked soil in the summer and mud and freezing wind in the winter. It was a sorry place to make a living, scratching like chickens in wind-blown dirt. He'd never understood why his folks had stuck like they did. It didn't take much thinking to see it was poor place to make a stand.

Beryl had left as soon as he was able. All he'd had to do was look at the old sod house and the endless miles of wavering heat, and he knew there was no way he was staying. They'd tried to convince him to stay put, but he knew his own mind. It made him sick remembering his mother sweeping the dirt floor when there wasn't anything underneath but more dirt.

It was a poor way to live and somebody had to make the change. He'd never regretted it either. He hadn't looked back and he hadn't gone back. It was a hard life anyway and there was no need choosing to make it any worse.

Beryl didn't like thinking about those times, he needed to concentrate on the problem at hand. Getting Charlie to the orphanage was going to be trouble enough. The weather wouldn't cooperate, it seemed like it never did, and he would have to stay a few nights with those that would allow strangers in their homes, or most likely in their barns. He hated having to ask, but there was no other way; there were no towns with hotels along the way.

Beryl pitched his remaining coffee on the fire and closed the stove's door. It was time for bed. He had an early morning coming and he wasn't looking forward to it.

Chapter Seven

Betty had laid out Charlie's clothes early, before dawn. Charlie was still sleeping at daybreak. It was a sound sleep and Betty believed it was the best he'd gotten since his journey started. She hated waking him, but knew that if Beryl didn't show up at the house he would certainly be at the shop, and she wasn't interested in having a confrontation at the store with the customers looking on.

She'd made breakfast: eggs, sausage, hot biscuits with apple butter, and fried potatoes. She helped Charlie get dressed and watched as he ate. He seemed to be just as hungry as the night before and it warmed her heart knowing he was getting something good. It might be his last decent meal for a long while.

She heard the knock on the front door and so did Charlie. He stopped eating and turned his head to the noise and then back to Betty. She smiled at him and told him to keep eating.

She opened the front door and Beryl was standing on the porch with his hat in his hands.

"I've come for the boy," Beryl said.

"He's got a name," Betty said.

"I know that." Beryl said.

"Well, use it then. You name your animals don't you, and you use them?"

Beryl fiddled with his hat, staring at it while he did.

"I've come for Charlie."

"He's eating his breakfast," Betty said. "I thought I'd better feed him, seeing as how you don't think it's necessary."

Beryl looked off to his right and then back at his hat. "I need to be going."

"Are you still taking him to Harrison?"

"It's best for him."

"You'd be the one to know that, I'd suppose."

"I didn't come here to argue," Beryl said.

"No, you don't like to argue, do you, Beryl? You just want things your way and don't like anything that disrupts you're sorry life. Why don't you leave Charlie with me until you're ready to go?"

"I can't do that. I take care of my own problems."

"That's right, Beryl, you take care of *your* problems. What about Charlie's?"

"I'm taking care of 'em. Charlie!" Beryl yelled, looking into the house. "Get out here, we're leaving."

"I'll go get him," Betty said. "If he's finished eating, if not you'll be waiting."

"I don't have time to be waiting," Beryl said.

"Then leave. You haven't heard anybody asking you to stay." Betty saw Sheriff Burgess round the corner of the house.

"Morning, Betty," Stuart said. He touched his hat and nodded to Beryl.

"Sheriff," Beryl said. "I've come for the boy."

"I see that," Stuart said. "I figured you'd be here bright and early."

"The boy shouldn't be here in the first place," Beryl said.

"I'm not so sure he should be with you either," Stuart said.

"You know the law. I'm within my rights to take him back."

"Yes, you are, Beryl. But don't mistreat him. If you do I'll take him from you."

"And put him where?" Beryl asked. "The same place I'm taking him? You see, I'm right about this."

"You're only right 'cause you're wrong," Betty said.

Beryl cocked his head slightly sideways to look at her and then shook his head a little and looked at Stuart. "We're leaving in a few days. This'll be over soon enough."

Betty turned and stepped back into the house and came back with Charlie holding her hand. She knelt down in front of him and buttoned his coat. Charlie didn't take his eyes from her face—he didn't want to leave and he didn't want to see his uncle.

"Now, I'll be out to see you later in the day," Betty said.

"That won't be necessary," Beryl said. He stepped forward and reached for Charlie but Betty stood and blocked his way.

"I said I'd be out there looking in on him and I will be. I'm bringing him some clothes and a new coat, and I'll be taking *Charlie* some dinner."

Beryl looked at Stuart. "I don't need her out at my place. We're doing just fine by ourselves."

"If she wants to bring Charlie some clothes and some dinner I don't see the harm in it," Stuart said. "You don't have a problem with Charlie getting a few nice things and a good meal, do you Beryl?"

Beryl looked at Stuart and then at Betty, and then reached around her and grabbed Charlie by the arm and pulled him along, Charlie holding his hat on his head.

Beryl lifted Charlie in the wagon and got in himself, then slapped the horses and rode off.

"I asked him to let Charlie stay with me until he was ready to leave," Betty said. "I guess he wants to inflict as much misery as he can."

"I'm sorry, Betty. You want me to ride out there with you?"

"There's no need. Beryl's not going to do anything to me. He knows we're right, and he's wrong. He just wants to get Charlie as far away as he can as fast as he can. This is bringing too much attention to him and folks are starting to see what kind of a man Beryl Stinson really is. When this is over there won't be anyone within fifty miles that'll have anything to do with him."

"People have short memories, Betty."

Betty looked at Stuart and shook her head. "Not me."

"You think you're something don't you?" Beryl said. "People fretting over you like a little prince. Well, don't let it go to your head—there's lots of little prince's in Harrison."

Charlie didn't know what his uncle was talking about, all he knew was he wanted to go back to Betty's house. He was riding to his uncle's place and he couldn't remember anything nice about it, except the porch, and he hadn't been able to explore its possibilities yet. He didn't want to sleep in the corner again, not with just a blanket and a pillow. It was cold and dark in the corner, and if he had to sleep on the floor then he wanted to sleep by the fire. But there had been no fires at his uncle's house, just the one in the cook stove and his uncle put it out when it was time for bed. He had slept on the floor in front of the fire at Betty's, but he didn't wake up there. Sometime during the night she had carried him to a bed and it was soft and he had been so warmed by the fire that he thought he was back in Oklahoma in his own bed.

But now he was headed back to his uncle's, and there would be little warmth. Betty was nice—she reminded him of Mrs. Henson. Charlie didn't understand how so many people could be so nice and why his uncle wasn't. He had a good place to live—Charlie liked the house with its wooden floor and clear windows and the big porch. Maybe today he could sit on the porch. His papa had always said that he wanted a house with a porch so he could sit on it in the evenings and watch the sun go down. In Oklahoma they had sat in front of their sod house, and the yard seemed to go on forever, as far as you could see, but here it only went to the trees and brush where it stopped. Charlie liked that. It made the house seem a part of everything, not like in Oklahoma where the house was a bump on the land, out of place with the rest of the scenery.

Betty had said she was coming over later and Charlie was anxious to see her. She was bringing new clothes and a coat, and Charlie had had very few new things. Most of his clothes were handed down. And Betty said she was bringing supper too, and Charlie was looking forward to that. He bet his uncle was looking forward to it too—Betty made good food. Maybe he didn't know how to make things taste good. Charlie's dad didn't make things taste as good as Rachael did either, and Charlie had never figured out why the beans and johnnycake tasted better when Rachael made it than when his father did. He had watched them both make it before and nothing seemed different to him, but it sure tasted different.

They pulled into the yard and Beryl got down off the wagon. He lifted Charlie out and pointed to the chicken shed.

"Do you think you can feed them chickens today without making a mess?"

"The sack's too high," Charlie said. "I can't reach it. And there's a snake in it."

"A snake?"

"That's why I fell," Charlie said.

"What kind of snake?"

"Black."

Beryl had seen no snake the day before and was sure Charlie was lying. He watched carefully for snakes around the chickens. He didn't mind a few black snakes in the barn and around the house, but he didn't want any in the chicken shed—they ate the eggs.

"I won't abide a liar," Beryl said. "I was beat for lying when I was a boy and I see no reason to change the lesson now."

"I'm not lying," Charlie said, crossing his arms on his chest.

Beryl walked over to the shelf and pulled the edge of the sack down and looked inside. As he did the snake stuck its head out over his hand and started down his arm. Beryl jerked and stepped backwards, stumbling on the rock Charlie had used to reach the sack. He tripped on it and couldn't catch his balance. Beryl fell hard on his back, still holding onto the sack, it coming down with him and falling on top of him. The snake was making its way to the back of the shed while Beryl was picking himself off the ground.

Charlie was standing behind him watching.

Beryl brushed the feed and dust from his clothes and gave Charlie an ugly stare.

"You think this is funny?"

"No, sir," Charlie said. "It ain't funny at all."

"I've got things to do," Beryl said. "Put the feed back in the sack and throw some to the chickens. Leave the sack where it is and I'll put it up when I get back."

"Where you going?" Charlie asked.

"I'm gonna check on the cattle."

"Can I come?"

"No, you're too much trouble. Stay around here and don't tear anything up. I'll be back in an hour or so."

Charlie's shoulders slumped. He didn't like being alone, but his uncle was walking away and he knew he was alone. He dropped to his knees and started scooping the feed back into the sack. When he was done he threw some to the chickens and watched as they scrambled for it.

He looked around and wasn't sure what to do. He didn't want to go to the barn; the last barn he'd been in had an owl in it, and he hadn't liked the way it sounded. Then he remembered the porch. Now would be the time to investigate and find out why his papa had wanted one so bad.

When he got to the front of the cabin he walked up on the porch from the steps. It was shady and cool and the yard in front was small, the trees were close by, their limbs reaching over the roof. Charlie ran from one end to the other and then back again. He could hear the pounding of his steps as he ran and it sounded so much different than the hard dirt in front of his other home. He wished his papa could have had a porch before he left—maybe he was sitting on a porch right then, him and Rachael, watching the sun going down, wherever they were.

Charlie put his elbows on the railing and set his chin in his hands. The sun was streaming through the limbs of the trees and spotting the ground with bright circles and squares and Charlie was trying to count them. Then he saw something moving from behind one of the trees. He stayed as quiet as he could and concentrated. Whatever it was had a good size to it and he thought it might be a deer. He liked to watch deer, but on the plains there was no getting close to them because there was no way to sneak up on them. Then he saw it again, but it wasn't a deer, it was a boy. He was running from tree to tree, and he was peering around them looking at Charlie. Then the boy walked out and stood silently looking at him.

Charlie and the boy stared at each other, and then the boy walked toward him.

"You're Charlie Stinson, aren't you?"

Charlie didn't say anything.

"Don't you know how to talk? They said you were slow—are you?"

When the boy got closer Charlie saw he was barefooted.

"How come you don't have no shoes?" Charlie asked.

"I don't wear shoes when I'm tracking."

"What are you tracking?"

"Why, you, of course. You and old man Stinson."

"You don't track too good," Charlie said. "My uncle's not here."

"I know that," the boy said. "My name's Harley Eaglefeather. I'm part Injun."

"You don't look like an Injun."

"That's because I was captured and brought up by 'em. I just escaped. So, are you?"

"What?"

"Slow."

"No."

"They said you lost you pa and sister in a flood and had to come and live with old man Stinson."

"Why are you tracking him?" Charlie asked.

"I do it just to pester him. My dad told me not to, but I like doing it. Beryl don't like nobody on his place but he can't catch me. How old are you?"

"Six."

"Well, I'm nine. You sure are little for six. I've heard old man Stinson does witchcraft. Have you seen it?"

"He can turn biscuits to stone, that's all I've seen," Charlie said.

"I've seen 'em before," Harley said. "The hogs won't hardly eat 'em. You want to learn how to track?"

"Sure. Don't you go to school?"

"I skipped today. They don't teach tracking and that's all I want to know. My pa says if you want to learn how to do something then you just have to jump in and do it. Have you been to the pond?"

"No."

"It's over that hill," Harley said, pointing to the west. "But we've got to be careful. If Beryl sees us he'll skin us."

Charlie was anxious about going to the pond. He wanted to go bad, but he was afraid his uncle might not like him being gone, and he'd told Charlie to stay at the house.

"Maybe I'd better not go," Charlie said. "My uncle told me to stay put."

"You're not afraid of him, are you? He's been chasing me since I was five. I'm not scared of him."

"Why were you hiding behind the trees?"

"That's part of tracking. Let's go to the pond, there's lots of turtles there. We can track them."

"I can't be gone long."

"We won't be," Harley said. "It's just through them trees."

Charlie followed Harley into the brush and waited for him to grab his shoes hidden behind a tree. Harley put them on and led the way. Just over the rise was the pond and Harley grabbed Charlie by the arm and held him back.

"Now be quiet," Harley said, whispering. "We'll have to sneak up on them turtles. They'll be sunning on their logs and soon as they see us they'll drop in the water. Watch how I do it and then you can try."

Charlie stood back as quiet as he could and watched Harley as he took his shoes off again and tossed them next to a tree.

"Take your boots off," Harley said. "They'll make too much racket."

Charlie pulled his boots and socks off and threw them next to Harley's and watched as Harley tiptoed through the brush to the edge of the pond. Charlie could see the turtle sunning on a half-submerged limb not far from the bank, and Harley was coming in behind him. Just as he reached out to grab the turtle, it slid off the limb into the water.

Harley came back to where Charlie was sitting. "You must have made a noise."

"No I didn't," Charlie said.

"It's the first time I've ever missed, so you must have done something. You give it a try, there's one sitting right over there."

Charlie saw where Harley was pointing and the turtle was perched on a log three feet away from the bank.

"Now, when you get close to him, reach out and grab him real quick like."

Charlie had caught turtles before and didn't feel he needed any instructions. So far he wasn't that impressed with Harley's tracking skills. Charlie had seen him hiding behind the trees, so he wasn't any better at hiding than he was at catching turtles. And as far as he could see there wasn't much tracking going on. Anybody could see a turtle sitting on a log.

Charlie snuck up close to the log and the turtle hadn't moved. He looked back at Harley and he was pointing at the turtle. Charlie placed his foot on the log and it didn't move. Then he stood on the log and it seemed sturdy enough. He stepped heal to toe, watching the turtle and trying to keep his balance. When he got close enough he squatted down on the log and reached his hand out slowly toward the turtle, and just as he was about to grab him a big bullfrog, the biggest Charlie had ever seen, leapt from one side of the log in front of Charlie's face and plopped in the water. The turtle followed the frog and Charlie lost his balance and followed both of them.

He was splashing in the water, swirling up the mud, trying to get his footing, but when his feet felt the soft muck below, it scared him and he started yelling for help. Harley ran up to the edge of the bank and waded in and caught Charlie's hand and pulled him through the muddy water to the bank.

Charlie was thinking about crying, but when he saw the smile on Harley's face he thought it might be funny, and so started laughing, and then Harley started laughing too.

"You sure don't know how to track," Harley said.

"I got closer than you did," Charlie said.

"That ain't the point. You've scared the turtles off now and the frogs too. Now we'll have to come back another time."

Charlie was standing with his feet in the water and now the soft goo that had scared him before felt good. He squeezed his toes and felt the mud squish between them and for the first time in a long time Charlie was having fun.

"You sure are a mess," Harley said.

Charlie looked at his clothes all wet and covered with mud and a big smile came to his face. He reached in the water and came up with a handful of mud and let it drop down the front of his shirt and laughed. He laughed so hard it surprised Harley, but then he started laughing too, and then he grabbed a handful of mud and slapped it on the front of his chest, and then they started throwing mud at each other and jumping in and out of the pond. Soon they were worn out and were sitting on the edge of the water skipping rocks across the pond.

"When are you leaving?" Harley asked.

The question caught Charlie by surprise—he didn't know he was leaving.

"I'm not leaving," Charlie said.

"That's not what I heard. They say you're going to an orphanage."

"What's that?" Charlie asked.

"It's a place where kids go that ain't got no parents. Didn't you know?"

Charlie was confused. He thought he'd been sent to stay with his uncle because he didn't have any parents. Why would he be going to an orphanage? His uncle was supposed to take care of him.

Charlie's lip started trembling and he fought it back because he didn't want Harley to see him cry.

Harley turned his head and could see Charlie was fighting the tears. He was sorry he'd said anything, but he'd been sure that Charlie would have known.

Charlie fought the tears as best he could. He wasn't sobbing or gasping, but the tears were streaking through the dirt on his face.

"I don't think you're slow," Harley said.

Charlie wiped his face with his hands. "You don't?"

"You almost caught the turtle. Truth is, I've never got that close myself."

"Will you be at the orphanage?" Charlie asked.

"No. My parents are at home."

"What do they do at the orphanage?"

"I don't know for sure," Harley said.

"Would you want to come with me?" Charlie asked. "I don't know nobody else."

Harley didn't know what to say. He wished he'd never said anything. From what he gathered from his mother and father talking, the orphanage wasn't the best place to be. There wasn't no ma's and pa's there, and there wasn't nobody to hold you when you were sick, and you had to sleep with all the other kids and eat with them too, and if you didn't mind you got the strap and there wasn't nobody to run to when it was over.

"Maybe we ought to be getting back," Harley said.

Harley stood up and helped Charlie up and they went back to the tree and put their shoes on. Harley wanted to talk some more but he was afraid to say anything, and Charlie didn't seem to be in a talking mood anyway.

When they got close to the house Harley caught up short and Charlie stopped with him. Beryl was on the front porch looking through the woods.

"He's looking for you," Harley said. "I gotta go. Old man Stinson don't like anybody on his property. You'll be okay, won't you?"

Charlie was looking at his uncle pacing on the porch and then he looked at Harley and said, "I guess so."

"I'll try to sneak back tomorrow," Harley said. "You keep an eye out for me and we'll do some more tracking."

Charlie watched Harley disappear into the woods and then turned his attention back to the house and his uncle. He didn't want to go back to the house. He knew that Beryl was all he had—Martha Henson had told him so. He was going to live with his father's brother, the only family he had left, but now Harley had said that he wasn't going to live with him at all, he was going to an orphanage, someplace where there was no family.

Charlie hadn't known what to expect of his uncle. On the train ride he hadn't thought about it much. He assumed he would be like his dad, after all, they were brothers. But his uncle wasn't like his dad at all—he was different, he didn't seem to like anything very much. He growled when he talked, which he did very little of, and his talk was mean most of the time and he said things that hurt Charlie's feelings. Papa had said that things don't always turn out the way you want them to, and a person had to make the best of it. Well, that was what Charlie was doing, trying to make the best of it. He didn't like the mean talk and he didn't like sleeping in the corner on the floor and the biscuits were hard and didn't have any taste, but the house had a porch and he liked Betty and he'd just met a new friend.

His uncle didn't act like he liked him, and Charlie wondered what he'd done wrong. He tried to do everything he was told to do, and he knew it didn't always turn out right, but he was trying and Rachael had told him it was the better half—the trying part. Charlie thought the things he'd done wrong must have made his uncle mad and it must be why he was sending him away. Charlie didn't want to go away. What he really wanted was to go back to Oklahoma and stay with Mrs. Henson and be close to his sister and father. He wanted to talk to them and tell them he didn't want to go to the orphanage, even though he didn't know what an orphanage was, but the word sounded lonely. If he couldn't stay with Mrs. Henson, then he would rather stay with his uncle and maybe he would quit the mean talk and then he would get a real bed someday.

Then Charlie heard his uncle calling him. He was out behind the house and the sound was getting farther away. He must be trying to find him, but Charlie didn't want him to. What if he was getting ready to take him to the orphanage? No. Charlie would stay right where he was. He sat down and waited, but then it occurred to him that he didn't know what he was waiting for, except not to be found by his uncle. It would get dark soon and it was already cooling down and his clothes were wet and he was starting to get cold.

His uncle's calls were in the distance now and Charlie thought he might run to the house, but he didn't know what he'd do when he got there. Maybe he would try and feed the chickens and that might make his uncle happy and he wouldn't yell at him.

Charlie had never felt so lonely in his life. He remembered how hurt he felt after the teacher had said the kids weren't even looking for him and how they laughed at him when he went back to the school, but this was worse. There was no Rachael and there was no Papa, and his uncle didn't like him. He wondered if there was a way to be with his sister and dad. They had drowned in the water but he didn't know how to drown. Mrs. Henson had said they were in a better place and that was where Charlie wanted to be, but he didn't know how to get there. Mrs. Henson said his sister and father had died, and Charlie wanted to die too, then he would be in the better place, but he didn't know how to die either.

Then Charlie heard the wagon coming up the path and he stood to get a better look, and it was Betty. He'd forgotten Betty had said she was coming to see him and was bringing new clothes and a new coat. He ran as fast he could to the road and was trailing the wagon yelling at Betty.

Betty heard Charlie calling and stopped the horse. He came up beside her out of breath.

"Why, Charlie Stinson," she said. "You look like you fell in a pond."

"I did. We were tracking turtles and I fell in."

"Who was?"

"Me and Harley."

"You mean Harley Eaglefeather?"

"Yeah."

Betty laughed and got down from the wagon. She helped Charlie up to the seat and got back in herself and they rode to the house.

"Where's Beryl?" Betty asked.

"He's looking for me," Charlie said. "I heard him calling but I didn't want to go to the orphanage, and Harley said that's where he was taking me."

Betty kept quiet, she didn't want to have to explain it to him—not right then.

"Do you know how to die, Betty?"

The question shocked her, and again she couldn't form an answer.

"If I knew how to die I could be in the better place with Rachael and Papa."

Betty spun her head away from Charlie. Her eyes were watering and she felt confusing emotions, but the worst was hopelessness. She closed her eyes to clear her thoughts. She wiped her eyes and turned back to Charlie.

"Dying's not an answer, Charlie," she said. "Sometimes people die by mistake, and that's what happened to your sister and father. Most of the time folks die because they're worn out, but it's the good Lord's choice and not ours. You just concentrate on living, that's what your sister and pa would want you to do. Now, let's get you inside and get those wet clothes off."

Betty helped him down from the wagon and held his hand as they walked inside the house.

"Where's your bed at?" she asked.

Charlie led the way to the bedroom.

"Take your clothes off and wash up in the basin."

She saw his satchel on the floor against the wall and she dug through it for another set of clothes. She laid them out on the bed while Charlie washed his face and hands.

"Does the bed sleep good?" she asked.

"That's not my bed."

"Where's your bed?"

Charlie pointed to the corner.

"I don't understand," Betty said.

"I sleep on the floor in the corner. My uncle gives me a blanket and a pillow."

Betty stared at him. She was so mad she thought her eyes had crossed. She turned around and walked through the doorway and ran into Beryl.

"What are you doing here?" He said.

Betty didn't even think about what she did next. She slapped Beryl across the face as hard as she could. Beryl was so shocked all he could do was stare at her.

"You've got this child sleeping on the floor?"

Beryl came to his senses enough to say, "I've only got the one bed. I've slept on the floor many times in my life and worse places than that."

"That's because you were too stupid to make a bed," Betty said. "You ought to be shot, Beryl Stinson. You're no more human than those hogs you own. Get out of my way, I'm going to get Stuart."

"Now hold on," Beryl said. "This ain't your affair."

"When you put a child on a board floor with nothing but a blanket, it's everybody's affair. What'd you feed him for lunch?"

Beryl looked away.

"Charlie," she said. "Did you eat lunch?"

Charlie didn't want to answer. He looked at his uncle's unforgiving face and then at the floor. He was standing in his underwear, shivering, more scared than cold. He'd never seen two grown people argue like this before.

Betty wanted to slap Beryl again but thought better of it. He was a hard man and she might have gotten away with it the first time, only because she'd caught him off guard, but she had no idea what his reaction might be a second time.

"Did you have a bed to sleep in when you were a boy?" Betty asked.

Beryl looked away.

"That's what I thought," she said. "And you're still alive, so you must have been fed, so somebody must have fixed you something to eat, and I'll assume it was your parents. A man that doesn't have enough brains to find a bed won't be able to feed himself. Why God has chosen to let you live so long I'll never understand."

Betty walked around him and shoved him aside with her arm. She walked out the back door to her wagon.

"Why are your clothes all muddy?" Beryl asked.

"I fell in the pond."

"I told you to stay at the house. I ought to take a strap to you for not minding."

Betty was coming back through the door when she heard what Beryl said.

"You touch that boy and I'll take a strap to you," she said. "Charlie, put your clothes on."

She laid a sack on the floor and turned and faced Beryl. She stood with her arms crossed while Charlie got dressed.

Beryl was confused. He didn't know why she wasn't talking and didn't know why she was still there. He thought she was leaving, after all, it was none of her concern, and the law was on his side. She had no business butting in. He'd almost hit her, but thought better of it. He'd never hit a woman, but had never been hit by one either, but it wasn't his way to strike a female. She should have enough sense to leave.

Charlie finished dressing and stepped over beside Betty. She took his hand and walked around Beryl to the kitchen.

Beryl was still questioning what was going on. The woman had no right being there—he knew that and she knew that. But he wasn't about to manhandle her—the sheriff would get involved then, and Stuart wouldn't be on his side in this matter. He walked into the kitchen to see what she was doing.

Charlie was sitting at the table and Betty was building a fire in the cook stove.

"I don't know what you think you're doing—

"I'm cooking Charlie something to eat," Betty said. "And I'm staying here tonight with him, and we're sleeping in that bed."

"No you're not," Beryl said.

"Oh, yes I am. If you think you're stopping me then start stopping. I'd rather die than see this child treated this way."

"This is my property," Beryl said. "I don't have to let you stay here."

"No, you don't, but I'm staying. Why don't you go get Stuart and bring him out here? When I tell him you haven't fed Charlie all day and you're making him sleep in a corner on the floor, we'll see who stays."

Beryl didn't know how to fight her. He had no experience arguing with women. It crossed his mind that physically throwing her out the door would cause him more problems than he already had. He had no defense if the sheriff got involved, even though he wasn't mistreating the boy Stuart wouldn't see it his way. He was going to fix dinner, she'd just beat him to it. And there wasn't anything wrong in his opinion with the boy sleeping on the floor. Lots of folks slept on the floor when there wasn't any other place to sleep. At least he had a roof over his head and he wasn't sleeping in the dirt. Beryl had never come up against anybody as stubborn as this woman.

"You can fix supper," Beryl said. "But you're not sleeping in my bed."

"Do you plan on getting in bed with us?" Betty asked.

Charlie was turning his head from Beryl to Betty as fast as the conversation was being exchanged. He had a wide-eyed look on his face; he wasn't scared anymore, he was curious as to how the arguing was going. It looked to him like Betty was getting her way. Beryl had told her she wasn't staying, but there she was, still here. His uncle had said she wasn't sleeping in his bed, but she said she was, and Beryl had a look on his face that surprised Charlie. Most of the time his face looked rigid and mean, but now it had a look to it like Charlie *had* seen before, like when people didn't understand something and their face was asking a question.

"We'll see how you like sleeping on the floor," Betty said. "Build a fire in the fireplace—I'll not be cold tonight."

Beryl didn't like taking orders from anyone. "This is my place and I'll decide when fires get built."

Betty turned her head from the cook stove to Beryl. She was tired of arguing. She didn't want to stay out here tonight, but there was no other way. Stuart wouldn't allow her to take Charlie back home, she knew that. This was the only way to make sure Charlie was being treated well. Betty didn't know what she'd do tomorrow, but tonight she would do what was best for Charlie.

Beryl could see she was tired of arguing and so was he, but she still had that unrelenting look on her face saying she wasn't giving up. Somebody had to give a little, but it wasn't going to be him—it was his place.

To Charlie it looked like they'd come to a draw. He wondered how this last question of the fire was going to end up. So far Betty had gotten what she wanted, but the conversation was dwindling and both of them looked tired. He was twitching his head back and forth between them but all they were doing was staring at each other. He would like to have a fire. It was getting cooler as the sun was going down, and now knowing that the warmth was coming from Rachael and his father, a fire meant even more.

"I'll get the wood," Charlie said, looking from Beryl to Betty.

Betty and Beryl turned their eyes to Charlie, then back at each other.

"I'm fixing ham and fried potatoes," Betty said. "And I've got fresh bread and an apple cobbler. There's enough for all of us."

"Get the wood," Beryl said.

Chapter Eight

Beryl built a fire and sat in his chair while Betty cooked the dinner. Charlie wanted to sit by the fire but he also liked being near Betty so he stayed in the kitchen. Beryl ate his plate of food in the other room and Charlie and Betty sat at the table.

After dinner Betty opened the sack she'd brought in earlier and showed Charlie the clothes she had for him: Two pairs of pants, two long sleeved shirts, a new hat, and a warm winter coat and hat. They were the best clothes Charlie had—he'd never had brand new clothes before and he was so proud of them he said he didn't want to wear them, but he would wear the hat.

Betty washed the clothes he had on that day and hung them on a chair in front of the cook stove. Beryl had gone outside after dinner and Betty could see the light from the lantern in the barn.

By nine o'clock Charlie had fallen asleep in front of the fire and Betty carried him to the bed and tucked him in. Then she sat in front of the fire and wondered why she'd gotten so involved with this child. Something had just struck her that he needed some extra attention. She knew it had to be hard on him, losing his family and being forced to leave his home, and having to live with the likes of Beryl Stinson would be difficult on anyone, but a young child was the worst.

The man didn't seem to have any compassion. He was the most insensitive and selfish person she believed she'd ever met. It amazed and confounded her that a grown man could treat anyone as harshly as he did, especially when it was his own flesh and blood.

Then Beryl came through the back door and went into the bedroom and came out with a blanket and a pillow.

"Sleeping in the barn are you?" Betty asked.

"Just for one night," Beryl said.

"You can get another bed, you know," Betty said.

"I won't be needing one."

"Why don't you see if anyone around here might want to keep Charlie?"

"He don't need to be around here," Beryl said.

"You just don't want to see him. He'd be a reminder that you couldn't stand up to your responsibilities wouldn't he?"

"He'll be better off," Beryl said.

"You'll be better off, you mean. He knows where you're taking him—Harley told him. You didn't even have the backbone to tell him yourself."

"I'll handle this my own way. I've got no need for children."

"No, but you've got a need for cattle and hogs don't you, something you can sell and make a little money with. There's no emotion involved there, you don't have to feel one way or the other about them, do you? You probably care more about one of your hogs dying than you do Charlie. That'd be a big loss—it'd come out of your pocket. You might even shed a tear if a hog died, but you won't shed one for your brother's son who's got no one to care for him and no one that loves him."

"They'll take good enough care of him. It's what they do."

"I've never seen a walking dead man, but I'm looking at one now," Betty said. "You've got nothing inside except hate and bitterness. How does it feel Beryl, knowing you pull the worst out of people, knowing the hate is coming back at you?"

"The sooner you leave in the morning the better," Beryl said, walking past her and through the door.

Betty went to the bedroom to check on Charlie. He was spread out on the bed and had kicked his covers off. She pulled the blanket back over him and returned to the fire. She had no intention of sleeping in the bed. She only wanted to make sure Charlie had a good place to rest.

It was difficult for her to know whether Charlie would be better off with Beryl or at the orphanage. In some ways she thought it might be that he would have a better chance in Harrison. Maybe, with luck, a good family would adopt him, but in her heart she knew the chances were slim. Charlie didn't seem to have much luck.

Now her thoughts turned to Beryl and she wished she could stop thinking about him. It only made her angry. She hardly knew him; nobody did. He kept to himself and only came to town when he had to, and that was very seldom. He'd only been in her shop once or twice and the last time he was there he complained about the prices. From the way he dressed she doubted he cared what he wore anyway. The man didn't seem to care much about anything.

She looked around the cabin and could tell he had few amenities. She was sitting in the only chair in the room, and there were just two chairs around the table. There was a cloth coat hanging from a nail by the back door with gloves stuffed in its pockets, but she saw no other clothes. There were no pictures on the walls and no tables in the room she was in. She could see by the light of the fire the floors were dirty and needed swept. She'd had to wash the frying pan before she cooked with it and from the looks of the stove it hadn't been cleaned in years and neither had the table. She'd been in single men's homes before and most of them were unkempt, but they at least had some furniture, but this place looked like no one lived in it at all.

Betty wondered what a man like Beryl Stinson was thinking. Why would anyone want to live this way? Surely someone came over to visit him, but then she couldn't think of anyone ever mentioning his name, not in a friendly manner anyway. He had to be an unhappy man, but what had made him that way? No one knew much about him, and no one she knew seemed to care. She couldn't feel sorry for him, not the way he treated others, and especially not the way he treated Charlie. She wondered if God would make amends to Charlie for his luckless life, but more than that she prayed the Lord to deal with Beryl Stinson's transgressions.

Betty's eyes were getting heavy and she had to get up early. She had to go home and get ready for work the next day. She had no idea what she would do about Charlie, but maybe something would come to her. She hated the thought of him having to stay here, but some things were just out of her hands. He would be in her prayers, it was all she could promise.

Betty woke at four, her back stiff and her legs cramping. She started a fire in the cook stove and prepared biscuits and made coffee. By five-thirty she was cooking slices of ham. She went outside to the chicken house and brought back eggs. Beryl saw her in the henhouse as he walked past. When she got back to the house he was sitting at the table drinking hot coffee.

"There's no need to make breakfast," he said.

"I'm making sure Charlie has something to eat besides those white rocks you pass off as biscuits."

"They've kept me alive," Beryl said.

"I don't want to argue with you," Betty said. "Charlie needs a good breakfast to start his day, there's no telling what you're going to put him through."

She went to the bedroom and woke Charlie.

"It's time to get up, Charlie. Wash the sleep off and get dressed and come to the table."

Charlie sat up in bed and rubbed his eyes. "Am I going with you today?"

"No, you can't come with me, I'll be going to work. Just try to do what Beryl tells you."

"Will you be back tonight?"

"I'm not sure, Charlie. I'll try. Now, come on, get ready for breakfast."

Betty went back to the kitchen and finished the ham and pulled the biscuits from the stove and set them on the table. Then she started frying eggs. She sipped a cup of coffee as she did, making sure she didn't have to confront Beryl so early in the morning.

Charlie came back in from the outhouse and set at the table across from Beryl. He could smell the biscuits and reached for one, but Beryl pulled them away.

"We're not ready to eat yet," Beryl said.

Betty went to the table and took a biscuit from the pan and opened it and smoothed some butter in the middle and handed it to Charlie.

"You mean you're not ready to eat," she said, glaring at Beryl. "Not everyone's on your schedule." Betty went back to the stove.

She fixed two plates with ham and over easy eggs and set one in front of Charlie and the other in front of Beryl.

"I'm not ready to eat just yet," Beryl said.

Betty stood by the table with one hand on her hip and a spatula in the other, staring at him. "You've got to make life hard on everyone around you, don't you Beryl? You can't stand it when things are decent—everybody's got to be just as miserable as you."

She picked up his plate and went to the slop bucket and scraped it off.

"I'm sure you're hogs are hungry, they can just have your breakfast."

Beryl hadn't expected her to do that. As a matter of fact he was hungry. The dinner she'd made the night before was good. It'd been a long time since he'd eaten such a good meal, but he wasn't about to let her have the run of the place. It was his house and he'd make the decisions, but now he was disappointed, and her words about making everybody miserable had stung him. There had been no cause for saying what he did, she'd done nothing wrong. For the first time in so many years he couldn't count, someone had fixed his meals, and it struck a cord somewhere in him.

His mother had been a good cook, but that was so many years ago he'd forgotten what tasty victuals had been like. Beatrice was a good cook too, even though he hated to admit it, and he didn't know why he didn't want to admit it, it had nothing to do with the boy. He was a lousy cook himself, he knew it, but eating wasn't a priority with him, but he had to confess he hadn't tasted such fine food in a great while.

Charlie was eating slow, still waking up. Beryl watched for a moment and then stepped over to the stove and filled his coffee cup. He walked to the back door, but before he opened it he paused, his back to the kitchen.

"I didn't mean the food wasn't good," he said. "I'm just not used to eating much in the morning. I tried making breakfast for the boy—

"Charlie," Betty broke in. "His name's Charlie."

Beryl let out a breath. "It didn't turn out so good. I thank you for the meals."

He took the slop bucket from the counter and walked through the door.

Betty stared after him and then looked at Charlie. He'd quit chewing and was staring out the door, and then he turned to look at her. They were both so surprised to hear Beryl say something nice that neither one could speak. She turned back to the stove and put another slice of ham in the pan and cooked two more eggs.

It was breaking daylight and she knew she had to go. She knelt in front of Charlie and said, "Give me a hug, Charlie. I've got to be going."

Charlie stood and wrapped his arms around her neck.

"Will you be coming back?"

"I'll see you soon," Betty said. "I'm not sure if it'll be today, but I will see you again."

"Thanks for the clothes."

"You're welcome, and I'll let you in on a little secret if you promise not to tell."

"Okay," Charlie said. He liked secrets, he didn't know why, but there was something special about them.

"You remember your friend, Harley Eaglefeather? His real name's

Horace Danner. Everybody calls him Harley, but he just likes to think he's an Indian."

Charlie smiled and hugged her again.

"You be good now," Betty said. "And I'll see you soon."

She grabbed her things and walked to the wagon. Beryl had hitched her horse, but was nowhere to be seen. She turned the wagon around and headed down the lane.

Within a hundred yards she saw Beryl standing beside the road, coffee cup still in his hand. She stopped the wagon beside him.

"He seems to like you," Beryl said. "You can come back and see him if you want."

"You don't have to take him, Beryl."

Beryl looked away and pitched the remaining coffee from his cup on the ground.

"Yes, I do." Then he started back to the house.

"I cooked you another plate," Betty said to his back.

Betty dropped her head. What would it take to bring out the good in that man? At least he'd said thanks for the food. She smiled just a little. They say the way to a man's heart is through his stomach—maybe there was something to it. She slapped the reins and started home.

Chapter Nine

Beryl took a moment from fixing the busted gate and looked at the sky. It was a clear day, but it wasn't as bright as a few weeks ago. The leaves were thick on the ground and there was a hint of cold in the air. Fall was hurrying to its end and soon winter would be here. He had a few more things to fix before he started to Harrison. He would be gone at least four, maybe five days, and he didn't want to leave Josh Danner with any problems. Taking care of another man's stock was enough to ask.

He hadn't paid much attention to Charlie since breakfast. He'd told him to stay close to the house. The boy wasn't any use for working anyway.

Beryl hated leaving the place. It wasn't just that he didn't want to ask for the help, of course that irked him, but he'd worked hard to get what he had and he didn't like leaving it in the hands of others. In all the years he'd only left the place for a night at a time, selling or buying stock, but never more than that. Now it seemed he was gone all the time, and getting ready to leave again. It amounted to a lot of favors, but that wasn't the worst of it. He'd make sure Josh Danner was paid for his efforts so there'd be no outstanding debts. The worst was having to ignore his own duties to take care of someone else's problems—in this case, his brother's.

Clive should have had the sense to think things through. He should have had things in place in case he died, something that would have taken care of his kids. He didn't have a wife and that should have been enough for him to realize his children would be at risk. But Clive had done nothing, leaving everything in the hands of others. It was pure ignorance on his part.

The two brothers were so far apart in age that Beryl hadn't known his brother very well. Beryl was working the fields by the time Clive was born. He was just a howling baby when they got in from the days work, more nuisance than anything. Beryl had grown up fast. They'd lived far enough from the neighbors that he'd had few friends when he was young. Not that it mattered much, there wasn't any time for kids to play anyway. They worked from dark to dark, and it hadn't been worth it. If the droughts didn't burn up everything the rains washed it away. The wind and dust came next, like sandpaper to wood, picking up the topsoil and dropping it in Missouri. Beryl had seen the end coming, but no one else seemed to. There had been no time for schooling, which meant no time to make friends. By the time Beryl knew he was through with it, the few folks he did know only reminded him of the same stubbornness his own family had. They liked to call it determination, but he called it pigheaded.

By the time he was ready to leave the hostility had set in. He'd argued with his parents long enough about leaving the plains, but there was no convincing them. Beryl had heard of places where the grasses were green and the water was sweet, where the dirt was rich and the trees offered protection from wind and heat and erosion. There were better places to live and he was headed that way. They'd called him foolish—a quitter, worse yet, a traitor to the family. The resentment he'd held for their lack of judgment had stuck with him. They'd called him a fool, but he knew better, and it was the one thing that remained with him—he would depend on himself from then on, and would take no help or advice from anyone, and would offer none.

He looked around for the boy but didn't see him. It was for the best the boy stayed away from him, all that came of it was aggravation.

Charlie was on the front porch. He was hoping Harley would come around so they could do more tracking. He thought it funny that Harley wanted to be an Indian, all he'd ever heard about them was the trouble they caused. People talked about how glad they were there weren't any around, about how they scalped folks and killed people and tortured them. He didn't think Harley was that good of a tracker anyway. The turtles had just been lying on the logs waiting for them. He thought Harley should have been tracking the frog, he was the one that caused most of the trouble.

He wondered when his uncle was taking him to the orphanage, how long it would take to get there, and what it would be like when he got there. Harley had said there were lots of kids there, and that worried him. Most of the kids he knew made fun of him. He couldn't seem to get along with any of them even though he tried. It was something he didn't understand—he didn't steal from them or kick them or trick them, but they were always doing something to him that hurt his feelings. The only friends he had now were Harley and Betty. He didn't consider his uncle a friend—his uncle didn't like him.

Charlie heard a whistle coming from the trees. He jumped off the porch and ran to the sound and Harley stepped out from behind an oak.

"How'd you find me?" Harley asked.

"I heard the whistle."

"That was a bird call," Harley said.

"What kind of bird?"

"It was sparrow."

"I guess I don't know what a sparrow sounds like," Charlie said.

"I'll have to teach you then. Look what I've got."

Harley pulled a bow and arrow from behind his back. The bow was made from the limb of a willow tree with a string tied to each end. The arrow was whittled to a point and had chicken feathers tucked into grooves on one end.

"Where'd you get it?" Charlie asked.

"I made it," Harley said. "Well, my dad helped, but I did most of it. Let's go tracking and hunting."

"Hunting for what?"

"It don't matter, maybe bear or mountain lions. Injuns hunt everything. They even hunt elephants."

"Elephants?"

"Yeah, I seen one in a picture book at school. They're bigger'n a barn and they've got a long nose that reaches clear to the ground and they can pick up rocks and shoot 'em at you. Their ears are big as wagons, and they're tails are skinny like a possum's. Their feet are big as rain barrels and they've got swords coming out of their mouths and they can cut you in half with 'em."

"Have you ever seen one?" Charlie asked.

"I haven't, but my dad has, in a circus one time in Kansas City. They shouldn't be hard to track—Dad says they leave piles taller'n I am."

Charlie stared at Harley open-mouthed. They'd picked up cow chips on the plains before to use for the fire because there wasn't enough wood, but he'd never seen piles that big before. One pile would last most of the winter if that were the case.

"Where will we find 'em?" Charlie asked.

"They live in caves and I know where one's at. You're not afraid of caves are you?"

Charlie didn't know if he was or not—he'd never been in one. All he knew about caves were they were big holes in the ground, and they were dark and wet.

"I don't guess so."

"Come on then," Harley said.

They started off through the woods, Harley in front, bow and arrow ready, and Charlie following him. He looked back once to see if his uncle was in sight, but he wasn't, and Charlie didn't care. He was going hunting for elephants and it was the biggest adventure he'd ever been on. No one he knew had ever seen an elephant, heck, he'd never even heard of them before. He just wanted to see one, but he had his doubts if Harley's bow and arrow would kill one if they were as big as barns, and he wondered why he'd never seen one before. If they were that big you'd think they'd be hard to miss.

"How come more folks don't see 'em?" Charlie asked.

"'Cause they only come out of their caves at night," Harley said. "They don't like the daylight 'cause they ain't got no hair on 'em and the sun burns 'em. You've heard 'em before."

"I have?"

"Sure, have you ever been lying in bed and heard the thunder?"

"Yeah."

"Well, it ain't thunder, it's elephants out looking for things to kill and eat. They stay inside and sleep during the day, and that's how we'll get one of 'em. We'll sneak down inside the cave and shoot one while he's sleeping. You've got to shoot 'em in the eye—it's the only place you can kill 'em."

Charlie was just a little scared. He didn't know if he was that interested in going down in holes in the ground, and what if the elephant woke up before Harley could shoot him? And how would they see? All the caves he heard about were dark inside.

"How are we going to see 'em?"

Harley stopped walking and was thinking. Charlie was standing behind him waiting for an answer. He liked being in the woods, hearing the wind blowing through the trees and the soft feel of his steps on the leaf covered ground. He liked the rustling noise his walking made and the zigzagging through the brush trying to find a path. He saw the squirrels jumping from tree to tree and heard the sharp cries of birds as they warned their friends. It was different on the plains; what few trees were still standing were far between, and the smell was the scent of dust. There weren't many flowers either, and the forest was full

86

of different colors and smells. Charlie looked through the trees at the sky and saw a hawk high above, drifting on the wind, his wings spread wide, floating like a cloud.

"Their eyes shine like sunbeams," Harley said, waking Charlie from his daydream. "We'll have to wake him up first. That'll be your job."

"My job?" Charlie asked. "How will I do that?"

"I'd pull his tail," Harley said. "You won't want to get too close to his head, he might shoot a rock at you and kill you, or he might cut you in half with his swords."

Charlie didn't like the idea. "Are you a good shot?" He asked.

"Of course I am. I'm an Injun. See that tree over there?"

Harley raised his bow and set the arrow on the string. He pulled it back and took aim, and then let loose. The arrow missed the tree and flew through the brush, sticking in the ground.

Charlie looked at Harley and he looked back.

"Wind must have caught it," he said. "There ain't no wind in a cave, besides, elephants got eyes big as a new moon."

Charlie was getting less interested in the adventure as things progressed. Harley didn't appear to be a very good shot, and Charlie was even less interested in pulling on the tail of something that left piles taller than he was. But, it was still an adventure, and it was better than standing around his uncle's cabin waiting to get yelled at.

He followed as Harley found his arrow and pulled it free. They walked over a small hill and started down a ravine.

"The cave's right down there," Harley pointed. "We'll have to crawl on our bellies for a ways, but then it gets bigger."

When they reached the opening of the cave Charlie looked at it with a questioning stare. He wondered how something the size of a barn could fit through an opening so small they had to crawl on their stomachs to get in.

Harley saw the look on his face and offered an answer. "They shrink themselves so they can fit. They've got all sorts of magical powers, that's why nobody sees 'em and nobody's killed one before. We'll be the first."

"Have you been inside?" Charlie asked.

"No, I only found this cave the other day. See that pile over there? There's one in here."

Charlie looked where Harley had pointed, but could see nothing but a big rock.

"That's a rock," Charlie said.

"That's what folks think that don't know how to track. Their piles turn to stone so nobody can find 'em. All the big rocks are elephant piles."

Both boys were standing in front of the opening, neither one too anxious to be the first in.

"Well," Harley said. "Go on."

"You go first," Charlie said.

"It'd be best if you went," Harley said. "You're smaller, and besides, one of 'em might sneak up behind us wanting to go home and I'd have to shoot it."

"You said they only come out at night."

"Well…one of 'em might've got lost and couldn't make it back. You ain't scared are you?"

"I guess not," Charlie said.

Charlie knelt in front of the cave and peered inside. It was dark and he could only see a few feet, but it did look like it went for a ways and Harley had said it got bigger. He took his hat off and set it on the ground and poked his head in the hole. The smell was clammy and when he touched the ground his hand came back damp and muddy. He looked back at Harley.

"Go on," Harley said. "I'll be right behind you."

Charlie inched his head forward and stretched out on his stomach. He pulled his way forward with his hands and pushed with his feet. By the time the full length of his body was inside the hole he could see nothing, but his outstretched hands told him the hole was dropping in front of him.

"I can't see," Charlie yelled.

"That's 'cause you're blocking the light," Harley called back. "Once you're inside you'll see better."

Charlie was ready to back out, but he didn't want Harley to think he was scared. He was the only friend he had and he hadn't had very many. Harley might not want to do things with him if he thought he was afraid.

He pulled himself a little farther in, but the hole didn't seem to be getting much bigger. He could feel the sides of the cave on his shoulders and hips and the hole was slanting downhill much faster than he liked, and it was getting slicker too.

Charlie thought he would go just a little farther and then back out. That should be enough to prove he wasn't scared. At least he'd gotten his whole body inside and that should be enough to prove himself. He made one more pull with his hands and pushed again with his feet.

The next thing he knew he was sliding downhill so fast he couldn't stop. He screamed and his face hit the ground and his mouth filled with the thick mud and slime and then he stopped. He felt the top of the hole against his head and his sides were wedged so tight he couldn't move. He tried to push himself backwards, but it did no good.

"Help—help!" Charlie yelled.

"I'm coming," Harley said.

Harley dropped his bow and arrow and stuck his head in the hole. He could see the soles of Charlie's boots. He stretched out and pulled and pushed himself inside, but the hole was too small for him to reach Charlie. He pushed harder and when he felt himself getting wedged in he stopped. He reached as far he could and touched Charlie's foot, but he couldn't grab it.

Charlie was yelling for help. Harley could tell by his screams he was scared and it was scaring him. He wiggled back out of the hole and yelled at Charlie.

"Push yourself back out!"

"I can't," Charlie said. "I'm stuck."

"I can't reach you, the hole's too small. I'm going for help."

"No! Don't leave me!" Charlie yelled.

"I'll be back," Harley said. "I'll go get Beryl."

"No, don't. He'll be mad."

Charlie was sobbing. He was terrified. He felt cool air but it was so dark he couldn't see his hands and the smell of the damp earth was making him sick.

"I'll be back as fast as I can," Harley said.

Charlie could tell Harley was leaving because his voice was getting farther away. Then there was no noise at all, only silence, and he knew he was alone, stuck in an elephant's hole.

"Charlie?"

Harley was back at the entrance.

"What?"

"There ain't no elephants in that cave—I was making it up. So don't be afraid, okay?"

Charlie was somewhat relieved by the admission, but he was still scared.

"Okay," he said. "But hurry up."

Then the silence was back.

Harley ran as fast as he could. His first instinct was to head to his own house, but as he ran he thought better of it. It was twice as far and even though he didn't like Beryl and Beryl didn't like him, it was still quicker. He liked Charlie and he was scared for him. He might get in trouble himself if he went home. His dad had told him to stay out of the caves, but there were so many and they were so inviting and so full of mystery he'd always wanted to try one. He'd been a little frightened himself when they were deciding who would go in first, and now he felt guilty because he'd talked Charlie into being first. He never should have asked him if he was scared; he knew it was a dare and had been wrong, and he vowed he'd never do it again.

Harley's chest was burning but he didn't care. He was worried about telling Beryl what had happened. Beryl was a mean old man and he was sure there would be consequences for what they'd done, but Harley felt he had no choice—the quicker he found somebody to help the better.

He ran into the yard and up on the porch and flung open the door and ran through the cabin, looked in all the rooms, and then ran out back. He stopped at the chicken shed and caught his breath and looked around. Beryl was nowhere to be seen. Now Harley was really getting scared. Maybe he should've gone to his own house—he could've been halfway there by now. If he couldn't find Beryl he'd have to run again, and his legs were the weakest he'd ever felt them.

"Beryl!" he yelled. "Beryl Stinson." He could hardly catch his breath to yell.

He fell to his knees and started crying. He didn't want Charlie to die and he thought he might run out of air and he thought of all the things that might happen to him, like snakes crawling into the hole, or maybe a bear might reach in and grab him, and it was all his fault because he was the one that wanted to go to the cave.

"What's wrong with you, boy?"

Harley looked up and saw Beryl walking toward him from the barn.

"Charlie's stuck in a cave. It's my fault—I talked him into it. I tried to reach him but couldn't."

"Where's he at?"

Harley pointed past the house. "Over that first ridge and down the hill."

"In the draw?" Beryl asked.

Harley shook his head.

"Go get your dad and meet me there," Beryl said.

Harley was on his knees in the dirt, his hands on his thighs. He was looking down shaking his head. Beryl picked him up by his arms and shook him.

"Go get your pa. It'll be dark in another hour. Tell him to bring a lantern."

Harley started running home. Beryl went to the tool shed and grabbed a pick, a shovel, a coil of rope, and a rock bar. He walked through the house and picked up his lantern on the way out the front.

Beryl knew running would do no good; he was in no shape to be running. It would be better if he walked fast. It wasn't far to the cave, he knew right where it was. It was on his land and he'd seen it many times. Caves were scattered all over the Ozark hills, some big and some small. He'd never ventured in any, but he knew some that did. They drew no interest for him, but he could see where kids would have a hard time staying away.

He struggled carrying the tools through the thick brush. There was no path leading to the narrow gully; that side of his land was steep and the rains had cut deep troughs through the hills and going down was just as tiring as getting back up. He thought about how to dig the boy out as he walked. Most of the caves were surrounded by limestone and if he was in very deep inside at all it would be tough getting him out. Kids—trouble, just trouble.

Charlie had cried himself out. As he stared into the darkness it came to him that crying was doing no good. He wondered if his uncle would even come to help. He was trying to spit out the dirt he had in his mouth and wished he could get his hands to his face so he could scrape it out, but he couldn't bend his elbows enough to draw them back in. He rested his cheek to the ground and waited. The thought crossed his mind he might run out of air; he didn't know much about caves. The musty smell bothered him as much as anything, and he remembered the smell of the fried chicken Betty had made and all of sudden he was hungry. He tried collecting saliva in his mouth and spitting, but he was so dry it wasn't working.

Now he listened to the silence, and somehow it was comforting. Rachael and Papa were in the silence, they were in a hole in the ground, too. He closed his eyes and thought of the sunlight behind him, bright and warm, and how only a few minutes ago he was having an adventure, and how now he was stuck and it wasn't fun anymore. If he were back on the plains he wouldn't be stuck in a hole. The only holes he'd seen there were wells and they all had covers on them and he knew not to try and look down them because he'd been told him he might fall in. He had looked in the well once, but the daylight had only gone down so far and then it was dark. He knew there was water down there and he'd dropped a rock in and listened for the splash and when he finally heard it, it seemed miles away. He thought he was far away, too.

Now, somehow being stuck in the cave wasn't bothering him all that much.

He liked the silence, it was better than being yelled at. It was probably better than going to the orphanage. He wouldn't know anyone there and he was sure the kids would make fun of him, and there would be no one like Rachael smiling at him, and he would never get to leave and go home. It's what he wanted more than anything—just to go home. He wanted his father to meet him after school and lift him up on his shoulders. He wanted to run through the tall prairie grasses and sneak up on Rachael, and most of all he wanted to hold her hand and lay his head in her lap and go to sleep.

Maybe he could go to sleep now—he was tired. He was tired of not knowing where he was going to live; he was tired of his uncle's meanness, and he was tired of being afraid. He'd thought he would get to stay with Mrs. Henson, but she'd sent him away. Then he thought he was going to get to stay with his uncle, but now he guessed not. Why didn't anybody want him? Maybe God didn't like him either, after all, He'd taken his family away. He tried to do the right things and he didn't like hurting others, and he wanted to have fun, but nothing seemed to please anyone. He didn't think there was anything wrong with having a good time, but his uncle didn't like it. Then he remembered a song he and Rachael used to sing and he started whispering the words: '*Jesus loves me, this I know, for the Bible tells me so…*'

"Charlie."

Charlie thought he heard something, but he was so sleepy he wasn't sure.

"Charlie, say something, boy."

It was his uncle—he *had* come to get him.

"Uncle Beryl," Charlie yelled.

"I'm gonna get you out, boy. You just stay quiet and I'll get you out."

Charlie was so happy his uncle had come to help him he started sobbing again. Maybe his uncle did like him, maybe he wouldn't send him away. He started struggling, trying to get free. He wanted to get out and run to his uncle's arms and hold on to him. He had a home after all, he had a place to stay.

"Quit kicking, boy," Beryl yelled. "Just stay quiet. I can't reach you. I've got to figure out what to do."

Charlie stopped struggling and calmed down. Yes, his uncle would get him out, and Charlie would feed the chickens everyday, and he wouldn't drop any of the feed and he'd make his uncle proud. When he got out his uncle would hold him and they'd go home and Charlie would help on the farm and he wouldn't have to go to the orphanage. Charlie couldn't remember when he'd felt so good—his uncle liked him, and there wouldn't be anymore yelling and he'd be safe.

Outside the opening Beryl was thinking things through. The hole was so small all he could do was fit his head in to his shoulders. He tried to reach him with his arm but couldn't get a grip on a foot, and he had nothing long enough to grab him with. He would have to start digging and making the hole bigger. He looked at the sky—it would be dark soon.

Beryl started digging and picking at the rocks. He hoped the Danner boy was coming back. He might be able to crawl in and slip the rope around one of Charlie's feet and they could pull him out. It might scratch him up some, but he could think of no other way. Charlie had been in the hole for at least an hour and Beryl knew he was probably scared and cold. He was concerned about what might be on the other end—it was a good place for snakes, and one bite of a copperhead would be enough to kill him. He dug faster. No matter how much he disliked the boy, he didn't want him to die, it wasn't his way.

While he dug Beryl thought about the way he'd been treating the boy. He had been hard on him, and maybe he should've paid more attention to what he was doing and where he was going. Folks would say it was his carelessness that caused it all, and that he wasn't taking care of his responsibilities. Damn the boy anyway, he should've had more sense than to crawl into a cave. The Danner boy had said it was his fault, and Beryl would give Josh Danner a good talking to when he saw him. He'd told Harley many times to stay off his land. It seemed he came around just to irritate him, hiding behind the trees, stepping out enough so Beryl could see him and then running off. Josh wasn't any better with his kids than Clive had been. Neither one of them had taken the time to teach their kids how to behave.

He knew kids would get into some trouble, but this was uncalled for. Anybody could see the hole wasn't big enough to mess with, and they didn't even have a lantern with them so they could see. The boy needed a good whipping, both of 'em did, and Beryl would see to it something was done about it. The sooner he got to Harrison the sooner he'd be rid of the trouble.

"What's it look like, Beryl?" Josh Danner said. Josh and Harley had ridden a horse as far as they could and then hurried on foot the rest of the way.

"It looks like he's stuck in a hole," Beryl said. "These kids ought to have more brains than this."

"I've told mine to stay out of the caves before," Josh said, giving Harley a cold stare. "Maybe this'll teach 'em."

"It's a lesson that should've been taught before," Beryl said. "They ought to be whipped."

"You can't whip 'em for being boys, Beryl. Let's just hope he's not hurt. Let me have a go at it and you catch your breath."

Beryl stood back and let Josh dig. He was winded and needed the rest. He looked at Harley and Harley stared at the ground.

"I've told you to stay off my property," Beryl said. "We wouldn't be here now if it weren't for you."

Tears were forming in Harley's eyes. He knew it was his fault and he'd done what he thought was right, going for Beryl first instead of his own dad. But now he wished he'd just gone home, and maybe Beryl wouldn't even have had to know.

"Leave him be, Beryl," Josh said. "I'll take care of him myself."

"You haven't done such a good job yet," Beryl said. "He don't do what he's told."

"I said leave him alone," Josh said. "He knows he did wrong. Charlie's the one in trouble here, let's just get him out. Harley, see if you can crawl inside and reach him."

Harley slid through the opening and clawed his way toward Charlie, but he could barely touch his feet. He came back out and shook his head.

"I can touch his boot, that's all."

"We'll have to make it wider farther in," Beryl said. "Let me at it again. Light one of those lanterns, Josh."

Beryl took the pry bar and pushed himself as far inside the hole as he could and started chopping at the dirt on the sides. Josh handed him a lantern and he set it inside the hole. He could see Charlie's feet then and he thought of something.

"Josh, cut me a six foot limb—a straight one. We'll hook the rope with it and maybe Harley can loop it around one of Charlie's feet. Charlie, can you hear me?"

"Yes."

"Can you lift your feet off the ground?"

Charlie could lift them a few inches before they hit the ceiling.

"That should be enough," Beryl said. "When we holler at you lift your feet.

We're gonna try and hook a rope around one of them and pull you out. It might hurt some."

"Okay," Charlie said.

Charlie was cold. He hadn't thought about it before, but now he could feel the dampness on his body and he was shivering. He could hear them talking outside and he knew his uncle was mad, and the thoughts he'd had before about Beryl liking him had disappeared. His spirits had dropped and the hopes he'd had only moments before no longer existed. Right then he didn't care if he got out or not. What difference would it make if he stayed in the hole or went to the orphanage, neither place offered what he wanted.

"Okay, Charlie," Beryl yelled. "Harley's coming in and when he yells at you, raise your feet."

Charlie didn't say anything.

"Charlie, did you hear me?"

"You think he passed out?" Josh asked.

"I don't know," Beryl said. "He sounded fine before. Let's get Harley in there."

Harley squiggled his way in the hole with the stick, the rope twisted around it, and tried to loop it over Charlie's boot. He tried several times without luck and Charlie wasn't helping.

"Raise your foot, Charlie," Harley said.

Charlie heard him, but stayed quiet. He was determined not to cry and was afraid if he talked he would. Instead he tried to pull himself even farther into the hole.

Harley could see his feet pushing and yelled at him. "What are you doing, Charlie? You're going the wrong way."

"What's he doing?" Beryl asked.

"It looks like he's pushing himself farther in," Harley said.

"That stupid runt," Beryl said.

Josh stared at Beryl with contempt, and Beryl could see the scornful look in his eyes in the dim light of the lantern.

"Maybe he don't want to come out," Josh said.

"Why?"

"He might think he's better off in that old hole than going home with the likes of you."

Josh knelt down at the front of the hole and told Harley to crawl out. Then he pulled himself inside as far as he could.

"Charlie, it's Josh Danner, Harley's dad. Don't move anymore, son, you're making things harder. Everything's gonna be okay, Charlie, just let us help you. We'll get you out of here and get you home and you'll be fine."

"I ain't got no home," Charlie yelled back.

"Sure you do, son. You can come to my house and you and Harley can wash up and get in front of the fire and the missus can fix a hot meal. How's that sound?"

"Can I stay the night?"

"Sure you can. Now listen, raise your feet and let me get this rope on you."

Charlie lifted his feet as much as he could. Josh pushed the stick toward his boots and struggled to see. On the third try he finally got the loop around Charlie's boot. He drew the stick back and pushed it out the entrance, and then he pulled the rope tight.

"Now, Charlie, can you feel me pulling?"

"Yeah."

"This might hurt a little, so grit your teeth and push as hard as you can. The harder you try the less you'll notice the hurt. When I start pulling you start pushing."

Josh began pulling on the rope and he had to pull hard. He was afraid he might pull Charlie's leg from its socket but he felt he had no choice. If he stopped it would make things tougher on the boy, having to start over again.

"You're coming, Charlie. Keep pushing."

He could feel him coming his way and could see his boots getting closer. He reached in as far as he could and grabbed Charlie's foot. He let go of the rope and grabbed his other boot and started backing his way out.

Charlie was pushing as hard as he could. His stomach and sides were scraping the walls and he was hurting but he kept pushing and gritting his teeth. Mr. Danner had been right—gritting his teeth was helping.

Then Josh felt him come loose. He wiggled out of the hole and pulled Charlie with him and turned him over on his back.

Charlie's face was black with mud mixed with blood from a few scratches. He was spitting dirt from his mouth and his cheeks were streaked from his tears. Josh pulled him up and held him against his chest.

"It's okay, Charlie, you're all right now."

Charlie was hanging loose in his arms with his head drooped over Josh's shoulder. He could see his uncle picking up tools. Beryl stepped around Charlie and Josh and picked up his lantern and started up the hill.

"I'm taking Charlie home with me," Josh yelled at him.

Beryl kept walking.

Chapter Ten

Josh had Charlie in front of him and Harley on the rump of the horse, and both boys were nodding. When they rode into the yard, Josh's wife, Imogene, came out to meet them. Josh handed Charlie to her and then swung Harley to the ground. He headed to the barn to put the horse up while Imogene took the boys inside.

There was a crib set off to the side of the fireplace with a sleeping baby in it. Charlie noticed it as soon as he walked in and went over to look. He stood by the crib for a long time and Imogene watched. He had a smile on his face and his head turned from time to time as if to get a better look.

She stepped over beside Charlie and said, "Her name's Samantha."

Charlie looked up at her with big eyes. "She's sleeping," he said.

"Yes, she is. We have to be quiet until she wakes up. Let's get you washed up and see to those scrapes. You've had a long day and I bet you're hungry."

Imogene led both boys to the back porch where she had a bucket of water. She helped them off with their clothes and washed them. Charlie had scrapes on his face and arms, his stomach and chest, and on his hips. None of them were bad enough to have to be stitched and Imogene cleaned them and put some iodine on them. Charlie gritted his teeth when she touched his scratches with the brown liquid and it seemed to help the sting.

"You're a brave boy," Imogene said. "Harley brings the rafters down when I have to doctor him."

"It's the Injun way," Harley said. "The yelling keeps the pain away."

Imogene winked at Charlie. "Those Injuns have a loud way about them don't they? You two sit at the table and I'll get you something to eat."

Charlie and Harley went to the table and Josh was just coming in the back door.

"How's he doing?" Josh asked in a low voice.

"He's fine," Imogene said. "Is he usually this quiet?"

"I don't know, it's the first time I've met him. I saw Betty yesterday and she said he was just like any other boy, just a little small for his age."

"I feel so bad for him," Imogene said. "Beryl wouldn't take him?"

"He never offered. Charlie didn't want to come out of the hole—I told him I'd bring him home with us. It's a shame, he wasn't screaming or hollering or nothing, it was like he was content to stay. After we got him out Beryl just picked up his tools and walked away—never said nothing to him at all."

"Get washed up," Imogene said. "I've got some stew."

Charlie was famished. For the second day in a row he'd had nothing for lunch. He concentrated on his bowl until it was empty. Harley watched him as he spooned the stew in his mouth and gave a look to his mom and dad. Both of them smiled and Imogene put a finger to her lips.

"You want some more, Charlie?"

"Could I? It's very good."

"Sure you can. What's Beryl been cooking over there?"

"Betty made us breakfast," Charlie said. "She stayed the night."

Imogene looked at Josh and then at Charlie. "She did, did she?"

"She's nice," Charlie said. "My uncle didn't want her to, but she did anyway. I got to sleep in the bed."

Imogene's eyes darted back to Josh.

"Where had you been sleeping?"

"On the floor. My uncle's only got the one bed."

Imogene set the filled bowl in front of Charlie. "Well, tonight you and Harley can share his bed."

"Ma," Harley yelled.

"Hush," she said. "It won't hurt you to share a bed."

"But Injuns sleep alone."

"Injuns sleep on the ground," Josh said. "Does that interest you?"

Harley lowered his head.

"I didn't think so. You'll need a good sleep tonight, we've got some talking to do tomorrow."

Harley looked at Charlie and frowned. Charlie was devouring his second bowl just as fast as the first. As he raised another spoon to his lips he said, "Mr. Danner, it wasn't Harley's fault. He didn't make me go in the cave. I did it on my own."

"My advice to the both of you is not to fool around with anymore caves."

"Yes, sir," Charlie said.

"I suppose," Harley said. "How 'bout the big caves though? Injuns go in them all the time."

"If I catch you in anymore caves I'll swat the Injun right out of you. Have you got that?"

"Yes."

"You two go on to bed now," Josh said.

Harley got up and Charlie shoved in his last spoonful of stew and followed him.

Imogene cleaned the table and began washing dishes. Her thoughts were with Charlie though and the distraction made it difficult to finish. She dried her hands and sat at the table.

"You know Betty wouldn't have stayed the night if she hadn't felt something was wrong," Imogene said.

Josh was filling a pipe with tobacco at the table. He tamped it down and lit it with a wooden match.

"I'm sure she had her reasons," Josh said. "She's a level-headed woman. I suspect she feels the same way all of us do, that Charlie's not being treated like he should, but there's not much that we can do about it."

"He seems like such a sweet boy," Imogene said. "Surely something can be done."

"Don't be getting any ideas," Josh said. "I know what you're thinking, but put it out of your mind. We've got two kids now and barely making ends meet. I feel sorry for him, but there's lots of kids have to go through what Charlie's going through and not everybody can take 'em in."

Imogene laid her towel on the table and rested her chin on her hand. She knew Josh was right. They'd lost their second child a year and a half after Harley was born, and they thought there might not be another one, but there had been. She'd carried Samantha with no problems and the birth had been easy, as far as birthing went. She felt there would be more children and it might not be fair to her own kids to have to share what good they had—they had very little good to go around.

"You're not going to swat Harley, are you?"

"No, I think he's had a good enough scare. He did the right thing today— running to get Beryl. And Charlie was brave too. It sure took me by surprise when he was trying to get farther into that hole though."

"Why do you think he did it?"

"He's more scared of Beryl than anything else, I'd say."

Imogene got up and went to the boys' bedroom. They were both asleep, sprawled out on the bed. She adjusted the quilt over them and shut the door on the way out.

It was time to feed Samantha and she took the baby and sat in the rocker next to the fire.

Josh watched as the baby nursed. He felt bad for Charlie. He'd heard his mother had died just days after he was born. It seemed he was destined for a hard life from the beginning. There wasn't anything he could do about it—life wasn't easy for them either. Taking in another child was a burden he couldn't afford right then. Josh didn't like thinking about it—he knew he was going to feel guilty as it was. Getting attached to Charlie would do neither one any good.

He'd take him back to Beryl's place in the morning. Now he had the same thoughts he figured Beryl had—the quicker he got to the orphanage the better off he might be. Once he got there maybe someone would take him. Josh knew the chances of that happening were thin, but the boy had to get some luck sometime.

Josh picked up the lantern, kissed his wife goodnight and went to bed. Imogene rocked in front of the fire and thought of what she could do for Charlie, but there were no answers. She did know one thing—Beryl Stinson would walk in fire for eternity.

Josh let the boys sleep late the next morning. By seven Imogene had Charlie's clothes washed and dried and was making breakfast. Harley and Charlie came to the table sleepy-eyed and they both had second helpings. Harley was sipping on a cup of coffee and Charlie watched as he did.

"You want to try some?" Harley asked. He shoved the cup over to Charlie. "It's hot."

Charlie lifted the steaming cup and put it to his lips. He sipped a little and grimaced. Imogene saw him and smiled.

"Here, Charlie, try a little cream in it."

It cooled the black water and turned it brown and Charlie took another sip. This time it tasted better, sweeter, and he decided he liked it.

"Don't drink too much," Imogene said. "You'll be so fidgety you'll walk right out of your boots."

Josh came through the back door then. The horse was saddled and waiting. "It's time to go, Charlie."

Charlie stood up and Josh handed him his hat. He didn't want to leave, but he guessed he had to. It seemed the places he liked best were out of his reach, he always ended up going back to his uncle's and there would be no warm bed and no hot food.

Imogene held the baby but she put one arm around Charlie and hugged him. "You can come back anytime you want," she said.

"Thanks," Charlie said. "Will you be coming over today, Harley?"

Harley looked at his dad.

"He won't be able to come over today, Charlie," Josh said. "Maybe we can work something out later so you two can have some time together."

Charlie followed Josh out the door and Josh got on the horse first and pulled Charlie up behind him.

"I'll be back after awhile," he said.

Imogene and Harley were standing outside as they were leaving.

"Bye, Charlie," Harley said.

They rode in silence for a long way. Charlie was sitting behind Josh with his head leaned against his back and his arms stretched around Josh's waist as far as he could reach. Josh knew he didn't want to go back to Beryl's and was dreading it, but he had to take him.

"Are you going to be all right, Charlie?"

Charlie didn't answer.

"You know," Josh said, "sometimes we're harder on ourselves than we have to be. It's not your fault Beryl's so difficult to get along with. You haven't done anything to make it worse."

"Why don't he like me then?"

"That's just the way Beryl is—he don't like anybody. It's not just you."

"He's taking me to another place to live. I was supposed to stay with him, but he don't want me there."

"Maybe you'll like the other place better."

"I don't think so," Charlie said. "I like the cabin and the porch. I wish I had a bed, but I can sleep on the floor."

They came to a small creek and Josh stopped the horse to let him drink. Charlie stared at the water and watched the leaves as they fell in the breeze and landed on its surface. The wind made wrinkles on top of the water and the leaves floated with the current. The sound of the water and the wind blowing through the trees was peaceful to Charlie. He wanted to stay right there, where everything was nice and all was calm, and he could spend his time watching the leaves float downstream.

"Are you thirsty, Charlie?"

"No."

A gust of wind blew by and Josh looked at the sky. The clouds were getting thicker in the northwest and they were moving fast.

"Might be a storm coming," Josh said.

Charlie was still dreaming but he heard him say storm.

"Better get out of the creek," Charlie said.

Josh turned his head to the side and asked, "Why is that?"

"The water might carry us away. The horse won't like it."

"Are you afraid of water, Charlie?"

"No, I don't like storms."

"I can't say that I do either. We'll be at Beryl's place in a few minutes, can you think of anything you need before I leave?"

"I'd like to know when I'll be going away."

"I'll see if I can find out for you." Josh nudged the horse and they rode through the creek.

Charlie looked back over his shoulder at the water. He wished he could've stayed there; he wished he could hear the sounds of the breeze all the time, and he hoped the storm would never come, and he hoped Josh Danner would get across the creek if it did.

When they rode into Beryl's yard he was cleaning out the wagon. He saw them coming but went right on working. Josh stopped the horse and swung Charlie to the ground and got down himself.

"I've brought Charlie back," Josh said.

"I can see that," Beryl said, without looking up.

Charlie stood close to Josh. Josh had his hand on Charlie's shoulder and was holding the reins in his other hand. They stood there for some time and nothing was said. Beryl kept working on the wagon.

"Charlie wants to know when he's leaving," Josh said.

"Tomorrow," Beryl said.

"Well, it looks like there's a storm coming, Beryl. Maybe you should wait."

"We're leaving tomorrow morning. The storm's a day or two away at least. I should be in Harrison before it hits."

Josh looked at Charlie and Charlie raised his eyes to his. Josh gave him a weak smile and Charlie lowered his eyes to the ground.

"You'll look in on the place?" Beryl asked.

"Yeah, I'll look after it. I still think—

"I thank you for looking after the boy last night," Beryl said. "If you need anything for the farm just put it on my account and I'll take care of it when I get back."

Josh dropped to one knee and gave Charlie a hug.

"You'll be all right, Charlie," he said. "I'll bring Harley over to see you sometime."

Charlie bit his lip. He didn't want to start crying—he was tired of crying.

"Say good-bye to Harley and Samantha."

"I will," Josh said. "You take care of yourself."

Josh mounted his horse and turned him around, then stopped and said, "Say, Charlie, have you got any gloves?"

Charlie shook his head.

"You'll need some gloves. I'll make sure you get some before you leave."

"He won't need any," Beryl said. "Where he's going they'll take care of such things."

Josh pulled the horse around and stepped him over beside the wagon.

"You may be his boss, Beryl, but you're not mine."

Josh looked at Charlie and winked and smiled. He turned the horse and rode away.

"Get in the house, boy, and stay there," Beryl said. "We'll be leaving early in the morning and I don't want any trouble."

"What about the chickens? Don't you want me to feed 'em?"

"You'll just make a mess of it. Go on, get."

Charlie walked to the back door but before he opened it he looked back at his uncle. He hoped he might change his mind and let him feed the chickens. He could show him he could do it without making a mess, and maybe he wouldn't take him away. But his uncle wasn't paying any attention, so Charlie opened the door and went inside and sat at the table and laid his head on his arm.

Chapter Eleven

Close to dusk Charlie heard the buggy pull up in the yard. He ran to the door to see who it was. It was Betty, and she was carrying a basket. Beryl was in the barn, he hadn't been inside all day, and Charlie had been sitting at the table for most of it. He'd dozed off a few times and walked out on the porch, but there wasn't much else to do. He wished there'd been a fire, even though it hadn't been cold, but he felt a chill when he stepped through the door, and a fire would have made him feel better.

He didn't want to leave, as much as his uncle didn't like him, he still wanted to stay. Maybe his uncle would get to like him and Charlie would try to make him, but he didn't know how to tell him so, and he'd studied on it all day. Somewhere close to late afternoon he'd given up on the idea and had curled up on the bed and went to sleep.

Charlie opened the door and ran out to meet Betty.

"Hello, Charlie," she said. "You look like you just woke up."

"I did. I heard you coming up the lane."

"Here, I've got something for you. Josh Danner told me to give them to you." She reached in the basket and pulled out a brand new pair of gloves.

"Thanks," Charlie said.

"Tell it to Josh the next time you see him."

"I'm leaving in the morning," Charlie said.

"That's what I hear." Betty put her arm around Charlie's shoulders and pulled him close. "Let's get inside and I'll fix dinner. I don't suppose you've had anything to eat today?"

"I ate breakfast with Harley."

"I heard. Josh said you got stuck in a cave. I bet you won't do that again."

"No, ma'am. Josh told me not to, but I figured it out for myself."

"I bet you did. It's sort of cool out here. Have you got a fire going?"

"No, Uncle Beryl hasn't been inside all day."

"You bring in some wood and I'll start us a fire, and then I'll show you how to make chicken and dumplings. Where is Beryl anyway?"

"I saw him working around the barn most of the day."

"I suppose he'll be up soon enough. Go on and get the wood."

Charlie ran to the woodpile and started gathering what he could carry. Betty held the door open for him and when she was getting ready to follow him inside she heard Beryl.

"Beatrice."

She turned and watched Beryl as he walked toward her.

"I hope you're not planning on staying. We're leaving first thing in the morning."

"That's exactly what I'm planning. Take care of my horse and buggy. I'm fixing dumplings for dinner. You're welcome to have some if you like."

"I said you could come and see the boy, I didn't say you could set up housekeeping."

"You don't have anything to keep up, Beryl. You're chicken shed's got more furniture in it than your cabin. I'm spending the night and I'm seeing Charlie off in the morning. I've brought him some more clothes, seeing as how you're too cheap to buy him any yourself, and I'm packing his things for him. I don't suppose you've done that?"

Beryl stopped and said, "Well, tomorrow's the last of it."

"It is for everybody but you, Beryl. You'll never live this down. Get those extra blankets out of my buggy—Charlie and I'll be sleeping on the floor in front of the fire. You'll need all the rest you can get, there won't be anymore after you drop him off in Harrison."

Beryl walked toward the buggy and Betty went inside. Charlie was trying to put the logs in the fireplace and she told him to stop.

"We'll have to put some kindling in first," Betty said. "You get some small sticks of wood and bring me a handful of leaves."

She took a few of the sticks of wood and started a fire in the cook stove. She put a pot of water on to boil and dropped in a cut up chicken. Charlie came back with some pieces of wood and some leaves and she met him at the fireplace.

"Have you ever built a fire, Charlie?"

"I've watched before," he said. "Rachael and Papa always made them."

"Pay attention then, you need to know this. Put the leaves on the bottom, because they catch on fire the easiest, and then put the little sticks of wood on next, the smaller the better, light the leaves and when that gets going real good start putting the bigger sticks on it."

"Can I light it?" Charlie asked.

"Sure." Betty reached for the matches on the mantel and handed one to Charlie. "Strike it on the rock and hold it to the leaves."

Charlie did and watched as the leaves first smoked and then flamed. He put the sticks on top of it and waited for them to catch.

"Keep putting the little sticks on, Charlie. You've got to have a hot fire before the logs'll catch. I'm going to make the dumplings."

Charlie stayed at the fire laying one small stick at a time on top of the leaves. He'd never built a fire before and it made him feel good to be able to help. Now that he knew how, he'd build all the fires and he'd never be cold again.

Beryl came in and sat at the table after putting the extra blankets on the other chair. He saw Charlie building the fire and thought it was foolish letting the boy do it.

"He shouldn't be doing that," Beryl said. "He'll burn the cabin down."

"He won't if he knows how," Betty said.

"Some kids never learn," Beryl said.

"Some grown-ups don't either," Betty said.

"I didn't come in here to argue."

"No, I don't suppose you didn't. You're not used to having a second opinion, are you? You think yours is the only one that matters, but I've got news for you Beryl, I haven't met anyone that cares about your opinion."

"It wouldn't hurt 'em none," Beryl said. "I've done well."

"Have you? You must have blinders on."

"I've got land and a good roof over my head. That's more than most."

"Yes, and you've got some cattle, and you've got pigs and a few chickens. You'll be leaving a fine legacy to a stranger."

"I've got horses, too."

"Don't forget about the jackass you've got living here either."

Beryl didn't like talking to women. He didn't much like talking to men either, but women had a way about them, they didn't talk straight about things. They turned things around and blindsided a man instead of getting to the point. It was like chopping roots—if you weren't careful the axe would bounce back at you.

Beryl never had much luck talking to women. He avoided them for the most part. In his opinion they were walking trouble. They wanted things that had no value, like curtains and pictures and do-dads and things that sparkled, stuff hanging on the walls and sitting in the corners. It was money wasted was what it was, and Beryl had no inclination to throw good money away on trinkets and whatnots.

He'd been inside Josh Danner's house before and the man had four lanterns and *all* of 'em lit. A man needed one less than he could carry and that was enough. He knew it couldn't have been Josh's decision to have the place lit up like a dancehall and it made no sense to have one lit at all if there was a fire going. That was a woman's doing, and it was a costly factor at best. Women didn't seem to have much sense when it came to handing out money; they spent it like chickens dropped eggs, thinking there'd be more under the feathers in the morning. He knew one thing for certain—they could ruin your day faster than a firestorm with one sentence, and it didn't bother them at all to do it.

Beryl didn't like the idea of Beatrice staying again either. It didn't make any difference if she said her goodbyes tonight or in the morning. It would just make things worse for the boy, having someone around he liked and having to leave them behind. She should have thought of that instead of thinking of herself.

Charlie's fire was going good and he was lying on his side in front of it, and Betty had her dumplings made. The pot of chicken was boiling and she poured two cups of coffee and sat one in front of Beryl. She moved the blankets from the chair and sat down.

"You sure you won't reconsider?" she asked.

"Why would I?" Beryl said. "I'm doing what's best for him. He'll understand that when he gets older."

"All he'll understand is he was kicked around from one place to another, that nobody wanted him, not even his own uncle."

"If I'd wanted kids I would've had 'em myself."

"Sometimes surprises come along in life, Beryl. They may not be what you want, or when you wanted them, but you still have to deal with them. Throwing them to the side and walking away—it's not the way to handle it."

"You'd be one to know that, I guess," Beryl said.

"I've had my share of good and bad luck, but I'll tell you this, when the bad came along I stepped up and took care of it—I didn't put it out of sight and pretend it wasn't there."

Beryl sipped on his coffee. He leaned back in his chair and stretched out his legs and crossed his arms. They could both hear the wind rising from outside and could feel the cold of the night setting in.

"Why tomorrow, Beryl, why do you have to take him tomorrow?"

"What difference does it make which day I take him?"

Betty could only look at the man with disbelief. Nothing meant anything to him, he had no notion of family or community. Living alone for so many years had destroyed any feelings he may have had. He had no compassion for anyone, there was no hope or goodness or passion for life. It was like she was sitting across from a stone, one that could walk and talk, but still a rock so hard nothing could penetrate it.

She stood from her chair and looked at Beryl with sadness.

"Tomorrow's Thanksgiving Day, Beryl. Doesn't that mean anything to you?"

Beryl stared at her as if it *didn't* mean anything. He hadn't realized what day it was—tomorrow was just another day to him. So many Thanksgiving Day's had passed and he had paid no attention. It was just one more sunrise and sunset. Besides, the only thanks he had to give were to himself. He had depended on no one to get him what he had, it was all his own doing. He'd worked hard, and he'd asked for help from no man.

"It means it's late November," he said. "I should have gotten an earlier start."

Betty could find no words. She was through talking to him. She looked at Charlie by the fire and her heart went out to him, but she knew there was nothing she could do to change Beryl Stinson's mind. She turned back to the stove and took the pot from the fire. She pulled out the chicken to let it cool before stripping the meat from the bones. She took a deep breath and let it out; she needed to think good thoughts, but she didn't want to let Charlie see the sadness she felt. He had no idea it was Thanksgiving either, she was sure of that, and it was probably best he didn't. She would try and make this last night as warm and comfortable for him as she could.

When dinner was ready Betty called Charlie to the table. Beryl took his plate and a cup of coffee to the barn, and she was glad of it. While they were eating Charlie asked where the wishbone was. Betty went to the plate of bones and found it. She made sure Charlie got a wish.

"What did you wish for?" she asked.

"I'm not supposed to tell," Charlie said.

"It's okay to tell me, I know how to keep a secret."

"I wished I could stay here."

It was confusing to Betty why this small child would want to stay. He had to know Beryl didn't want him.

"Why?" she asked.

"I like it here. I like the cabin and the porch. Harley's my friend and I could play with him, and I like you too. Why does Uncle Beryl not want me?"

Betty wished he hadn't asked that question. She had no good answer for him, because she didn't know why herself. There was something missing in the man and she couldn't understand it, so it would do no good to try and explain it to Charlie, but she knew he deserved an explanation.

"Your uncle's lived alone for most of his life, Charlie. Sometimes folks get set in their ways and they can't accept change. Beryl's never had a wife or kids and he doesn't know how to deal with it. It doesn't have anything to do with you, it could have been any little boy or girl. Beryl doesn't know anything else except being alone."

"I'd try not to bother him. Maybe I could come over to your house in the mornings and come back at night, so he could be alone."

"You might like it in Harrison, Charlie. There's going to be lots of other kids there. I'll come and visit you too."

"You will? When?"

"Maybe I'll come at Christmas. Would you like that?"

"Sure. Will Uncle Beryl come too?"

Charlie was so naive he couldn't understand his uncle didn't want anything to do with him. It upset Betty to even think about it. There was no way to make him realize the truth without hurting him, and she wouldn't do that. It might be better for him to go on believing his uncle had some good in him. The sweet innocence of children was God's most precious gift, and she would take no part in spoiling Charlie's.

"I'll talk to him when the time comes, how about that?"

"Okay. What about Harley, will he come? He's the best friend I've got."

"We'll have to ask Josh about it, but I'll make a point of it. You and I are going to sleep on the floor in front of the fire tonight. I've brought some extra blankets so it'll be nice and soft. Are you about ready to go to bed?"

"I guess so."

Betty took the blankets and layered them in front of the fire. She got the pillow from Beryl's bedroom and the spare blanket.

"Put one more log on the fire, Charlie, and get ready for bed. I'll clean up these dishes and be there in a few minutes."

It was late when Beryl finally came through the back door and went to bed. Charlie was asleep, but for Betty, it would be a long night.

Betty was up at four. She'd packed Charlie's things and started breakfast. Beryl was up by five and doing his chores and hitching Rosie and Mattie to the wagon, and had readied Betty's buggy as well.

She'd fixed pancakes and eggs and fried potatoes and Charlie had eaten well. She had only picked at her plate, and Beryl had eaten his outside.

It was cold and windy and the sky was dark. It had spit snowflakes overnight but not enough to cover the ground. It was a poor time to be starting out on a trip and she'd told Beryl so, but he was going, no matter the weather.

Beryl was seated on the wagon and Betty was on the other side with Charlie.

"You keep you're satchel with you all the time," she said. "Everything in it belongs to you, so don't let anybody else have it. Keep your hands in your pockets to keep them warm and don't lose your new gloves."

"I won't," Charlie said.

"I'll come and see you at Christmas," Betty said. "And I'll write you letters, and you write back."

"I don't write so good," Charlie said.

"There'll be somebody there to help you. I'll miss you, Charlie."

Betty hugged him tight and kissed him on the cheek, and Charlie kissed her back. She lifted him to the seat and Beryl started off without another word. Charlie was turned around looking at her and waving as they rode down the lane. Betty was waving and wiping tears at the same time.

Chapter Twelve

They passed few people on the way out of Berryville, but those they did only stared, and Charlie noticed most of them were staring at his uncle and none of them waved and he saw no smiles on their faces.

It was a dark, dreary, day and the weather had made no attempts at getting better. Charlie was hunched on the seat with his hands in his pockets and his new coat buttoned up as far as it would go with the collar pulled up around his neck. His hat was pulled down as far as he could get it and the brim tilted down to keep as much wind from his face as possible.

His uncle wasn't talking and the few attempts that Charlie had made went unanswered. Charlie kept his eyes on the road ahead, watching the horses' heads bobbing as they pulled him farther from where he wanted to be. Once again he was leaving a place where he'd thought he was supposed to stay. He hadn't been scared when Mrs. Henson had told him he was going to live with his uncle; his uncle was his dad's brother and he would take care of him. But now Charlie was frightened—he was going someplace where he didn't know anyone and none of them were uncles and no one had said there would be anyone there to take care of him.

At noon Beryl stopped the horses at a stream and let them rest and drink. He and Charlie ate biscuits and bacon that Betty had fixed for the trip. The sky was still thick with dark clouds but it had stopped spitting flakes, now just heavy with moisture carried on a cold northwest wind.

Charlie wanted to know more about where he was going and decided to give his uncle another try.

"Are we going to the orphanage?" He asked.

Beryl was still chewing his biscuit and continued to chew as he turned to look at Charlie. He stopped long enough to give his answer.

"Yep." Beryl took another bite of biscuit.

Charlie didn't say anything for a long while. The answer had been plain enough, but he'd expected more. He knew his uncle was short on words but it seemed to Charlie that if he was being left with strangers there needed to be more said about it.

"What will I do there?"

"You'll just live there," Beryl said. "Probably do what most kids do— nothing."

"Will there be chickens to feed?"

"They've got to feed you something. I expect there's a chicken."

"How many kids are there?"

"Good lord, boy, I don't know. Quit asking questions. You'll be there soon enough."

"What kind of place is it?"

"It's a place what takes kids that don't have anywhere to live. Now that's enough."

"But I've got a place to live," Charlie said. "With you."

"Your dad wanted me to take care of things and that's what I'm doing. If you're looking to blame someone for it, then put the blame on him. I'm not my brother's keeper and I'm not yours."

"I'd rather stay with you," Charlie said.

"Clive must have thought I was an orphanage, but I'm not, so I'm taking you to one, and as far as I'm concerned it's abiding by his wishes."

"If we went back I'd try to do better," Charlie said. "I wouldn't cause any trouble, I promise."

Beryl threw the rest of his biscuit to the side. He stood up and grabbed Charlie and lifted him in the wagon.

"Now shut up, boy. I've heard enough talking to last a fortnight and it's all wasted breath. You'll find out what you need to know by tomorrow, and you ain't living with me. That should be enough for you to know."

Now Charlie was mad. He wasn't mad about being pitched into the wagon and he wasn't upset about being told to shut up, although Rachael had told him never to say those words, but he was angry about being taken to the orphanage. He was thinking back about all the things that had happened since he'd met his uncle and he couldn't think of anything terrible enough for him to be punished.

If the snake hadn't of crawled out of the sack it wouldn't have scared him, and it'd happened to Uncle Beryl too, and getting stuck in the cave was an accident, and he'd felt bad about it because he wasn't supposed to be there, but accidents happened, Papa had said so, and it wasn't nothing to get punished for. The way he saw it his uncle was just being mean because Charlie had made a few mistakes.

All he wanted was a chance to set things right and he was sure his Uncle Beryl would see he would be no trouble. He just needed convincing, that was all. Charlie didn't want to give up another place to stay. His home was supposed to be with his uncle, everybody had said it, so his uncle must be wrong. He wasn't sure how to tell him so, but he had no intentions of letting his Uncle Beryl make a mistake. If he did, then he might not ever let him come back to the farm, and Charlie was coming back—he would not stay at the orphanage—he would not.

"I won't stay," Charlie said.

Beryl looked at him with a sideways stare. Charlie was looking straight ahead with his arms folded across his chest and a decent snarl on his lips. The boy wasn't just upset—he was mad. Beryl had to smile a little—he hadn't seen this side and he kind of liked it. So far from what he could tell Charlie was a timid child with little confidence and that wasn't something Beryl admired in anyone. At least he was showing some backbone. It made Beryl think he was making the right decision taking him to the poorhouse. At least it was bringing out some spirit in him.

"You'll stay," he said.

"No, I won't," Charlie said. "Mrs. Henson said I was to stay with you, it's what Papa and Rachael wanted."

"Mrs. Henson don't know what Clive wanted. She never talked to him about it."

"Betty said it too."

"It's not her concern," Beryl said.

"I won't stay!" Charlie shouted. "I'm staying with you, everybody says so."

Beryl gave Charlie a swat on the arm and Charlie grabbed it with surprise. He'd never been hit by a grown up before and it hurt, and more than that he hadn't done anything to deserve it.

"Don't talk back to me," Beryl said. "You'll do what I tell you. Now pipe down—I'm through talking. If I hear another word I'll give you a licking you won't forget."

Charlie didn't cry. He stared straight ahead with a resilience that made Beryl take notice. Something had changed in the boy, he could tell. He wasn't the same meek, scared little child that had started out with him that morning. It was the first time he'd seen courage, persistence, and determination in him, and they were traits Beryl considered well worth having. He felt he had the same qualities of character himself, and it made him think the boy might have the same kind of mettle. But it probably wasn't, it was just anger.

By late afternoon the weather turned worse. The clouds had gone from dark to black and the wind was strong enough to blow the horses manes sideways. Something was coming—Beryl knew it, and it wasn't far off. He started looking for shelter. He hated asking, but it would not be a night to sleep on the ground.

In another hour it was sleeting and Beryl and Charlie were freezing and the horses were tired and cold. Beryl spotted a light in the distance and decided it would have to be the place. They could stay in the barn and eat the rest of the biscuits and bacon, maybe even build a fire if the owners would let them.

When they reached the turnoff to the cabin Charlie was shaking. Their hats and shoulders were covered with ice and the horses backs were wet and starting to freeze over. Beryl turned the team on the lane heading toward the light and the horses picked up their pace, smelling the hay that was close to the barn. He stopped the wagon in front of the small home and told Charlie to stay put. He walked up to the door and knocked.

An old man opened the door and stared back at Beryl.

"Evening," Beryl said, holding his hat in front of him.

The old man nodded. He had a rifle in one hand, holding the door open with the other, and his wife was standing a few feet behind looking over his shoulder.

"Sorry to disturb you," Beryl said. "I'm headed to Harrison but this storm's caught up with me. I was wondering if I might stay in your barn for the night. My horses are tired and near froze."

The old man looked Beryl up and down. Then his wife stepped to the door.

"Well, let him in, Jacob, he's freezing."

"Come on in then," Jacob said. He opened the door wider and Beryl stepped through. Jacob could see the wagon in the dim light coming from the cabin.

"You got someone else with you?"

"I've got a boy with me," Beryl said.

"Well, Lord a-mighty," the woman said. "Don't let him sit out there in the cold."

"We just need some shelter," Beryl said. "We'll stay in the barn if that's all right."

"*You* might stay in the barn if you're a mind to," she said. "But that boy won't."

She stepped in between the men and hurried to the wagon. She helped Charlie down and held his hand as they walked back to the house. Before they got there Charlie broke loose and ran back to the wagon. He stepped up on the spoke and grabbed his satchel, struggling to lift it over the side of the wagon. When he got back to where the woman was she took his hand again and led him into the house.

"This boy's shivering," she said. "Come on," she said to Charlie, leading him to the fire. "Get that wet hat and coat off and stand in front of the fire. I'll heat some water for coffee. Jacob, where's your manners? Put that rifle down and show this man where to unhook his team. I'll see to this young boy while you're gone."

"That's fine ma'am," Beryl said. "But the boy can come with me. We don't intend to bother. The barn's shelter enough."

She held Charlie's coat and hat in her hands and said, "You don't intend to let this boy stay in a cold barn tonight?" Then she looked at Beryl even harder. "Who are you?"

"Beryl Stinson's my name. I've come from Berryville headed to Harrison."

"So you're the one," she said.

"Ma'am?"

"You're the man that's taking his dead brother's child to the orphanage."

Beryl was taken by surprise.

"Well, speak up," she said. "Are you the man or not?"

Beryl looked at the old man and back at the woman, and then he looked at Charlie. Charlie was huddled as close to the fire as he could get, rubbing his hands and shaking.

"Maybe we'd better go on down a ways," Beryl said. "Come on, boy."

Charlie turned his head toward Beryl and then back to the woman. His hands dropped to his sides and he stepped in her direction reaching for his coat.

"You're not taking this child anywhere tonight," she said. "You're not likely to get a door more open than ours. We've heard you were coming, everyone has. Jacob, take Mr. Stinson to the barn and show him where the hay is and give him a bucket of grain so he can feed his horses. You can sleep in the barn or you can sleep on the floor in here, it's all we've got to offer, but this boy's staying inside where it's warm tonight."

Beryl thought better of trying to leave. It wouldn't do any good going to the next place if everyone had the same opinion as these folks. It was hard for him to believe word of his coming had gotten this far so fast, and it was even harder for him to understand the way they felt. These folks had no idea of his situation and they were passing judgment.

He looked at Jacob and the old man stared back.

"You ready?" Jacob said.

"We'll be leaving early," Beryl said.

"You'll be leaving when I've fed him breakfast," the woman said. "If you plan on staying in the barn Jacob will bring you a plate of food after a bit. We've got some leftovers from dinner."

Beryl nodded and followed Jacob as he grabbed his coat and gloves from the hook by the door. Out front he took the mare by the harness and led the team after the old man to the barn. When they reached it Jacob pulled the door open and stepped inside and lit a lantern.

"Jacob Demanche's my name, and that's Ethyl in the house. There's no stalls in here but you can tie 'em to the posts. The hays in the far corner and the buckets and grain are through that latched gate. Sleep anywhere you like."

"I've got money," Beryl said. "I'd like to pay if I could."

"You're just sleeping, mister, it's nothing to take money for."

"Your wife," Beryl said. "She don't approve it seems."

"I doubt you'll find many along the route that do. Can't say as I do either. We've raised five children ourselves and I can say it wasn't easy, but we never gave one up."

"He's not my boy," Beryl said. He didn't know why he was trying to explain himself, it'd never bothered him before what people thought, but somehow he was bringing out the scorn in folks.

"He's your blood kin ain't he?" Jacob asked.

"I can't care for him."

"Is that right?" Jacob said. "Well, it's not my affair. I'll bring you a plate in a while."

"It's not necessary," Beryl said. "I've got biscuits."

"We're not that way," Jacob said. "We share what we've got. You don't have to eat it."

Jacob walked to the barn door and opened it to leave.

"How'd you know I was coming?"

Jacob turned and said, "You ought to know how, mister. You rarely hear about what good folks do, but the bad's always ahead of you." He closed the door behind him.

Beryl went outside and unhooked the horses and brought them inside. He brushed them down and scattered some hay in front of them, and then went back to the wagon and took two blankets from the box behind the seat. He bunched up some hay across from the mares and made a bed. There was no reason to sleep inside the house, not the way these folks felt.

He had not expected to meet folks that knew he was coming. He'd been glad to get going, leaving the hostile talk and stares behind him. He figured in a few weeks things would be back to normal and all would be forgotten. It occurred to him as he sat on the blanket that this was different. Folks seemed to look at him with resentment, and it was new to him. Even though he'd kept his distance most of his life, he was sure there had been a certain amount of respect for what he'd accomplished. It was hard carving out a living anyway, but doing it alone said something about a man. Folks may not like the way he was, but they had to admire what he'd done. But now he was running into people he didn't even know, but they knew him, and they weren't interested in befriending him. Not that Beryl thought he needed any friends, but he sure didn't deserve to be despised. If the tally was put on the board everyone had things that wouldn't be appreciated by all, but it didn't mean they hadn't worked it out the best way they could. Well, he'd steer clear of any more folks. They'd make it to the orphanage tomorrow and he'd make sure there'd be no more stops, coming or going. Two more days and he'd be back to the cabin and folks could think what they wanted. They'd move on to something else, some other thing they could think was wrong and talk about it until it was dead and something took its place.

Inside the house Charlie was sitting in front of the fire. Ethel was heating up leftovers from her Thanksgiving dinner: Turkey and potatoes and gravy, corn and turnips, bread and pumpkin pie.

Charlie was still cold; he'd taken off his wet pants and Ethel had given him a blanket to wrap up in. He wondered about his uncle and why he hadn't come back to the house. He had to be cold in the barn and these people were nice. The woman warmed some milk for him and put some sugar in it and it tasted sweet and was making him sleepy. The man was sitting in a rocker behind him, smoking a pipe, and Charlie liked the smell mixed with the fire and food being warmed. It all reminded him of home, in Oklahoma, when they'd sit in the sod house in the winter by the fire and Rachael would read to him and Papa would rock in his chair. Sometimes they would sing songs and Papa would sing too and his voice would never mix well with Rachael's and they would laugh. He wondered if there would be a fireplace where he was going and if they would sing songs. It didn't matter—he wasn't going to stay. He would leave the first chance he had and would go back to his uncle's cabin and his uncle would see that he belonged there.

Ethel brought him a plate and handed it to him. "You might as well eat in front of the fire," she said. "Get that chill out of you. Jacob, I've fixed a plate for Mr. Stinson, you might as well get it to him, and take that pot of coffee too."

Jacob set his pipe down on the table beside him and put his coat and gloves on. He got the plate, covered with a towel, and walked out the back door. Ethyl pulled up a chair and sat next to Charlie.

"What's your name?" Ethyl asked

"Charlie Stinson."

"Do you know where you're going, Charlie?"

"To the orphanage," he said.

"Are you glad to be going?"

"No, I want to stay with my uncle."

"He don't seem to me to be the type of man you'd want to be around."

"I'm supposed to be there," Charlie said. "Everybody says so."

"Everybody but him, I guess."

Charlie busied himself with his plate. The food was good and it warmed him and he didn't like talking about his uncle. It seemed to him that when people talked about his uncle they didn't talk nice about him. He knew that his uncle didn't talk much and when he did the things he said weren't too happy, but he was still his uncle and he wished folks would talk better of him. If they did maybe he would let him stay. That might be part of why he was taking him away, because everyone talked bad about him and argued with him, and it might be Charlie's fault they did. It might be best if folks didn't talk to him at all, and then Charlie could say nice things to him and everything would be better. Charlie didn't care how his uncle talked as long as he got to stay with him.

"How'd you know my uncle?" Charlie asked. "You said you knew we were coming."

"Some folks got business over in Berryville. It's all the talk over there, how he's taking his own nephew to the orphanage."

"Does the orphanage know we're coming?"

"I'd say so. Word travels fast."

"I'm not staying," Charlie said, looking in the fire.

Ethel looked at the small boy sitting with the blanket around him. She felt sorry for him, not pity of course, just a sorrow for what he was going through and what he was about to go through. Some of her own kids had been problems, one of them in jail in Fort Smith for stealing as they spoke, but she'd tried to do right by him. He'd always been trouble though, more than the rest. It seemed no matter how hard they'd tried to teach him to do right, he just had a bent in the wrong direction. The others had grown up decent, all of them married now with kids of their own.

They lived close enough to the orphanage to know some of the troubles there too. Once those kids were old enough to run, they did, and for the most part they ran straight to trouble. They had little at the orphanage and few people to care for the kids. When it was time for them be let out, the kids had nothing to start with, no money, no clothes except what was on their backs, no jobs to go to, and no chances to start out with. It was more like a prison than anything. She'd heard the stories, everybody had, about the whippings and the work they made them do, about the sorry food and cold rooms, and the things going on between the older ones, things that young kids shouldn't be seeing or hearing about. This boy sitting by her fire would probably fair no better than any of the rest. The shame of it was having a chance, and it being thrown away by his blood kin.

Jacob came back in and hung his coat on the hook and sat in his rocker. He re-lit his pipe and rocked.

"Is he eating?" Ethel asked.

"Not when I left, but I 'spect he will. All he had was biscuits, he said."

"He's staying out there tonight?"

"Seems so," Jacob said.

"Is that all you know?" Ethel asked.

"I didn't have a set-down with him."

"Well, you should've. Folks'll want to know something."

"You mean you do," Jacob said.

Ethel frowned and Jacob kept puffing his pipe.

"Maybe I should go out there and check on him," Ethel said.

"He's doing fine by himself," Jacob said. "You won't get nothing to gossip about from him—he don't say much."

Ethyl untied her apron and marched to the kitchen.

"You know how to play checkers?" Jacob asked Charlie.

Charlie turned his head over his shoulder. "Yes, sir. I played checkers a lot."

"I'll just get the board out," Jacob said.

"He's got more on his mind than checkers," Ethel said from the kitchen. She was hanging Charlie's pants over the cook stove.

"He's eating pumpkin pie," Jacob said. "That's what's on his mind." He winked at Charlie and Charlie smiled. Jacob leaned towards him a little and said, "She plays a poor hand. I've not had a decent game since the boys left home."

Jacob got up and went into the other room and came back with a small checkerboard. He sat down with crossed legs beside Charlie and placed the checkers on the board. Charlie set his plate to the side and twisted around to face Jacob.

"You don't cheat, do you?" Jacob asked.

Charlie shook his head.

"Good, maybe I'll have a chance. I only cheat when I'm losing. Two cheaters can make a short game."

They played for the better part of an hour and Jacob let Charlie win all of the games, acting upset when he lost. When Ethel told them to quit because she was making Charlie go to bed, Jacob shook his hand.

"They was all good matches," he said. "You sure you don't cheat?"

"No, sir," Charlie said with a smile.

"Come on, Charlie," Ethel said. "You can sleep in the back bedroom. It's cool in there but there's plenty of blankets."

Charlie followed her into the room and Jacob picked up the checkers. He saw Charlie's satchel still sitting in the floor. He thought for a moment and then opened the case and stuffed the checkerboard and checkers on the bottom and covered it with the clothes.

"She plays a poor hand anyway," he said under his breath.

After the house was quiet Charlie still lay in bed awake. He'd thrown back some of the blankets Ethel had put on the bed, the weight of them so heavy Charlie could hardly turn over. There was a window opposite his bed and he could see from what little light the moon gave that the wind was blowing the limbs of the tree beside the house. He got up and went to the window and looked out. The night was dreary and cold and he could hear the clicks of sleet hitting the pane. He could see the barn through the tree limbs. The shape was big and dark, set against a sky of drifting blackness, with streaks of moonlight in between the hard lines of clouds.

Charlie put his shirt on, grabbed his boots and a blanket, and being as quiet as he could, walked to the kitchen. By the fading light of the fireplace he could make out his pants hanging beside the cook stove. He took them down and pulled them on, grabbed his coat hanging on the back of a chair and opened the back door. Outside he slid into his boots and ran to the barn. He found the door and pulled it back a crack and stepped inside.

The lantern was still glowing, the wick on its lowest turn, and he could make out the form of his uncle lying on the hay against the far wall. Both mares turned their heads when he walked in but stayed quiet, then turned back to the wall.

Charlie stepped slowly toward his uncle and when he got up to him he spread the blanket on top of him. Then he turned and snuck his way back out, closing the door after him.

Beryl was awake. He'd heard the barn door open and had glanced that way. When he saw Charlie he wondered what the boy was doing, but decided to wait and see. He thought he might be trying to run off and he hated the thought of having to track him down, but when he'd put the blanket over him it had surprised him. What was he thinking? Why would he do such a thing? Maybe the woman had told him to do it. She should mind her own affairs. If she thought it would make him less likely to keep going, she was wrong.

Beryl pulled the blanket closer to his head. It wasn't his fault the boy had to go. Clive should have made provisions for him, it was his slight. Well, he'd turn the tables on the meddling woman; he'd just thank her in the morning for the extra blanket, which would tell her he knew what she'd done. Women try to trick you into believing things that aren't so, he knew that much. When they didn't get their way they came at a man from the sides, not lying exactly, just with half-truths, and that was a full lie in his thinking.

Beryl wondered about folks sticking their noses in other people's affairs. He'd never done it, no sir, he'd never asked questions and he'd made it clear—he didn't want to hear about other folks' dealings. Let 'em handle it their own way—good or bad they only had their selves to blame. He had no qualms about taking a drubbing if he deserved it, but he would be the one doing the kicking, not some stranger that had no business being involved.

The old man, Jacob, he knew when to keep out. The part about blood kin, that bothered Beryl a little. Twenty years it'd been since he'd seen Clive, which made blood fairly thin in his book. Hell, the boy wasn't his brother, he had half his mother in him, and that made him somebody else's kin too. Where were they when the need came up? No one came forward from that blood, but Beryl had heard no one say anything about that. Oh no, it was just him that was to blame for the boy not having a home. Here he was taking care of things the best way for the boy, and everybody acting like he was the devil incarnate. They should be thanking him for handling the problem, for taking the time to carrying things through. It wasn't like he didn't have his own farm to run. He could've refused to take the boy, just flat out said no, but he hadn't. He'd taken him in and now he was seeing to it the boy would be cared for. He ought to be thanked for what he was doing, not beat down like a cur.

And the old man saying they'd never given one of their kids up. Beryl wasn't giving the boy up—he'd never taken him for permanent. He was just making sure the boy had a place to be. At least he was doing that much. Beryl hadn't seen anybody with arms out wanting to take the boy for real. From what he'd seen everyone was passing him along. They were sure quick to judge, standing behind a fence rail pointing fingers and saying how they'd do different. They wanted nothing to do with the problem, but they could sure come up with answers.

Charlie would have to fend for himself, that was all there was to it. There was nothing wrong with that, it would build character, and a man without character was failed from the start. A boy has to learn to make his own way. He's got to find the qualities in himself he can use the best and take advantage of them. Coddling would do no good. Beryl was doing the boy a favor and someday Charlie would see it.

Beryl wondered what time it was. He figured midnight or better. It would be a long push the next day and he wanted to get some sleep. He wouldn't stay here on the return trip, he'd be sure of that. He wrapped tighter in the blankets and closed his eyes. His problem would be gone tomorrow.

Chapter Thirteen

Beryl had the horses hitched before daylight. He could see the light in the house but made no attempt to go in. He'd made sure the team had eaten some grain and had left two dollars on the shelf by the door. It was more than the grain he'd used but it was fair for the night.

The wind was still up and the clouds were dark, threatening, even mocking, as if warning those foolish enough to start out on a trek. There was no going back, and there was no staying. He was not welcome, only the boy was. The sooner it was done the better.

Jacob had come out of the house and was walking toward Beryl. He leaned on the wagon and lit his pipe.

"She's got breakfast," he said. "Charlie's eating."

"I'll pass," Beryl said. "But I'm obliged. The sooner we leave the sooner I can get him there."

"You're still a good ten hours," Jacob said. "Depends on how much this storm holds you up."

Beryl looped the reins around the brake. "Thanks for the supper and the shelter."

"You're going through with it then?" Jacob asked.

Beryl didn't say anything. He put his blankets in the box and shut it. "I guess I'd better get the boy headed this way." He walked past Jacob to the house.

Beryl knocked on the door and opened it. Charlie was sitting at the table finishing his plate of eggs, bacon, and biscuits.

"It's time," Beryl said.

Charlie looked at him and Ethyl did too.

"It's sinful taking him out in this weather," she said. "I'll take his bag."

Ethyl strutted passed him and went to the room and got the satchel. She brought it back and set it on the table and opened it.

"I've made sandwiches." She put them in the bag and closed it, then said, "It's sinful taking him—period."

Beryl stepped up and took it. "I thank you for the food and bed and blanket."

Charlie got out of his chair and Ethel helped him with his coat and hat. She put her arm around him and gave him a hug. Charlie walked past Beryl and pushed the door open, and Beryl followed him. As he walked through the doorway he heard Ethel.

"What blanket?"

Beryl turned to her. "The one you sent Charlie out with last night."

"I didn't send him out with anything," Ethel said.

Beryl turned back to Charlie who was standing beside Jacob at the wagon. He looked back at Ethel.

"You're making a mistake, Mr. Stinson. That boy's got good in him. They'll tear it out and kill it where you're taking him."

Beryl glanced at the ground and walked to the wagon and put Charlie's case in the box and closed the lid. "Let's go."

"Take care, Charlie," Jacob said. He lifted him up into the wagon bed and Charlie climbed over the seat.

"You could wait a day," Jacob said. "This storm might run out by then."

"I meant to be farther along than I am," Beryl said. He nodded and started the mares walking.

Jacob went back to the house and sat at the table. He popped his pipe against the palm of his hand and dropped the ashes in the tray on the table.

"What'd he say?" Ethel asked.

"He said he meant to be farther along than he was."

"That's it?"

"That's it."

"It's a good thing you don't own a newspaper," Ethel said.

Jacob packed the tobacco in the bowl with his finger and struck a match off his coveralls and lit the pipe He was thinking about Charlie and the orphanage and the cold ride he had ahead of him. And he was thinking about the storm.

Two hours into the trip and the temperature hadn't changed. Charlie had his gloves on and his hands were still cold. His hat was pulled down to his eyebrows with his head bent to deflect the wind. Beryl was doing much the same. At least it wasn't sleeting or raining, but the wind made it miserable.

They rode in silence, Charlie with his arms crossed over his chest, his hands stuck under his armpits. They were the only ones on the road; they'd passed no one, coming or going. Once, they had traveled by a cabin close enough to the road that Charlie had seen a woman standing in the doorway staring as they passed. Charlie waved at her but she made no effort to return the greeting. He watched the horses heads as they bounced along in the same rhythm, their tails crossing their haunches in front of him. He wondered if they were as cold as he was.

They came to a creek and Beryl let the mares drink, but didn't climb off the wagon. He wished he had some coffee; at least it might warm his hands.

By noon it was snowing, small flakes, but thick enough it was hard to see a hundred yards ahead. Beryl thought they'd be close to Harrison in another five hours. The orphanage was supposed to be this side of the town, and after he dropped off the boy he was thinking of riding on in and getting a room, but then he thought better of it. He didn't like being gone from the farm, and with a storm on top of them Jason would have his hands full with his own place. He probably should have waited to make the trip, but it had to be done. The boy needed to get settled in, and he needed to get it over with.

The road was starting to cover and in places it was hard to see where the ruts were. The wagon kept jerking in and out, bouncing around and making it difficult on the horses. Rosie and Mattie were cold and tired. Beryl wished he'd bought some grain from Jacob—the horses would need it. He kept trying to spot cabins in the hills, but had only seen a few and didn't know if he could even find them in the dark. He'd spent nights on the ground before, in just as bad a weather. He just needed to find a bluff, or a group of trees, pines would be good, to keep the wind off, and he'd be all right.

The hills were sloped on his left—had been since they'd gotten a few miles out of Berryville. Most of the cabins were on the north side, set back in the hollows on the slant. The steep grade bothered Beryl and he was trying to stamp landmarks to his memory. He didn't want to be traveling in the dark and not able to see the road. He'd changed his mind about staying at Jacob's place, and thought he'd try and make it back there tonight. Surely he'd let him sleep in the barn again, and the horses could stay inside and get some grain, and then he'd know he could get back home the next day by nightfall.

By late afternoon the flakes were thumb sized and the road was white from side to side. There were no tracks to follow and the horses were nervous. Then Beryl saw the smoke. The long bend in front of him hid the building, but he could see the trail of smoke blowing over the trees and could smell the scent of burning wood. He looked at Charlie, huddled over beside him, head down to his chest. It was almost over, for both of them.

When they rounded the bend Beryl could see the orphanage, or it figured to be. It was a two-story building with a fireplace at both ends and a long curved road leading up to the front. He turned the mares to the right and Charlie looked up as he did. He didn't like what he saw.

The building was as wide as it was long. There were no windows on the second story and only a few down below. With the snow coming down so hard it looked deserted, if it hadn't been for the smoke coming from the chimneys. There was no porch, the flat face looking hard and worn, like it had been standing there for ages, tired, and unfriendly.

Beryl stopped the wagon in front of the door and put the brake on and tied the reins. He got down and reached in the box and pulled out Charlie's satchel. He walked around the end of the wagon and lifted his hand to help Charlie down.

"I'm not going in there," Charlie said.

"Come on, boy, we're here."

"Please, Uncle Beryl, take me back. Don't leave me here."

"I told you this was where you were coming. Now don't fight me on this. You've known it all along."

"I'll be good," Charlie said. "I won't cause no problems. I'll stay gone all day and only come home at dark. I won't be a bother, I promise. I want to stay with you."

Charlie's lip was trembling again but this time he didn't care. He didn't want to go in there; if he went in he might not get out. Uncle Beryl had to take him home—all he wanted was to go home. The ride had been so long and cold and all he could think of was turning around and heading back. Now he was here and his uncle wanted him to go inside—he was going to leave him. He couldn't believe it was happening.

"Don't make me," Charlie cried.

"Come on," Beryl snapped. "This is where you're staying from now on."

He dropped the satchel and grabbed Charlie under the arms and hauled him down.

"Now quit your crying. Act like a man. I've got to get started back."

Beryl had him by the forearm and Charlie was struggling to get free. He wanted to get back on the wagon, to sit on the seat and wait for his uncle to slap the reins and start back down the hill. Charlie was crying, gulping air, fighting to get free, pulling with all he had, and kicking at the snow, stumbling, Beryl hanging on to him, and finally jerking him up and clamping him under his arm. He grabbed the satchel and stomped up the path to the door. He put the case down and opened the door, picked up the satchel and stepped inside, kicking the door shut behind him.

It was quiet inside, only the sounds of Charlie's crying. The long hallway in front of them was dark and cold, only one lantern sitting on a small table halfway down. In the middle of the hall on either side were stairs leading to the second floor. At the end of the hallway, sitting cross-legged on the floor was a young girl, her back against the wall, hands folded in her lap, and in the dim light Beryl could see a pleasant smile on her face. She stood then, and waved them forward.

"Quit crying," Beryl said to Charlie, holding him by the arm.

When Charlie saw the girl he did quit crying. He saw her wave too, but he and Beryl stood silently in front of the door, and then the girl began to walk toward them. As she got closer something about her reminded Beryl of his brother's walk, the way she carried herself, stepping, almost bouncing on the balls of her feet instead of touching her heals first, and the movement of her arms held close to her body, and the sway of her shoulders and the tilt of her head. She stopped beside the lantern.

"You're Charlie, aren't you? I knew you were coming. I've been waiting, we've all been waiting."

"Is this the orphanage?" Beryl asked.

"Yes."

"I need to see the one in charge."

"They're downstairs eating."

"I don't have much time," Beryl said.

"You've got a new coat, Charlie. Does it keep you warm?"

Charlie nodded. Her voice sounded familiar and in the dull half-light of the hall he squinted to see better. Her hair was dark and short and she was taller than he was, almost Rachael's height, and for a moment he thought it might be his sister, but he knew it couldn't be.

"Go get who's in charge," Beryl said.

The girl turned her eyes to Beryl. "She'll be along soon enough. You must be Charlie's uncle. You picked bad weather to make the trip, but Charlie knows about riding in bad weather, don't you?"

Charlie didn't nod this time, but kept staring at the girl.

"You could stay the night," she said. "It might make traveling easier in the morning."

"I'll be leaving as quick as possible," Beryl said.

Beryl noticed that the girl hadn't taken her eyes from Charlie when she'd said it, and then when she did shift them to him, the look on her face said she hadn't directed the words to him. He stared at her, and then looked over at Charlie. They were both gazing at each other, and they were wearing tight smiles on their faces.

"Who are you?" Beryl asked.

"I'm Mindy, just another orphan."

"My business is not with you."

"No, but Charlie's is. You're making a mistake leaving him."

"So I've been told," Beryl said.

"You need him more than you know, and he needs you."

Then Beryl thought he heard something but couldn't make out where it was. He walked to the stairs pulling Charlie with him, but everything looked dark in the stairwells. Then he walked to the end of the hall and saw a staircase leading down. He heard someone coming up the stairs and saw the light from a lantern. He pulled Charlie back close to him and waited. Mindy had walked behind them and was standing beside Charlie. She took his satchel and set it on the floor and held his hand.

An old woman was plodding up the steps, slow and bent, holding her arm to the wall for support. She was white headed and had her hair tied in a bun on the back. She was carrying a lantern in one hand and held it low, at times hitting the steps with it. When she reached the top she lifted the lantern and turned her head to clear the glare.

The woman's face was rutted with wrinkles and as pale as the snow they'd left outside. One eye was half closed, squinting over the light.

"Are you in charge?" Beryl asked.

The woman looked at Beryl and then lifted the lantern higher and stared at Charlie, then took her attention back to Beryl.

"I'm Miss Winston. You the man from Berryville?"

"Yes, I've brought this boy," Beryl said.

"He's your brother's boy."

"His father's dead," Beryl said. "The boy needs taken care of."

"But not by you," she said.

"Is this the orphanage or not?" Beryl said. "If it is I'm leaving him here, if it's not, tell me where I can find it."

"You're at the right place, but we don't take children that have blood kin if they can care for them."

"You're taking this one. I'm heading back tonight and he's not going with me. If you don't want him then send him to another orphanage."

Beryl pushed Charlie in front of him. The old woman leaned forward and looked him over.

"He seems healthy enough," she said. "Why don't you want him?"

"Where's all the kids?" Beryl asked.

The old woman raised her head. "They're down in the basement eating. Are you hungry?" she asked Charlie. "Go on down these stairs and get something to eat. They're having grits and cornbread."

Charlie turned to Mindy.

"Don't like 'em?" Miss Winston asked. "You'll get used to 'em. Three times a day except on Wednesday's and Sunday's, then you get beans, but no grits."

Charlie stayed put.

"Might shy, ain't he? Well, I guess we can take him. I've lost two, so there's room."

That's what Beryl wanted to hear. He figured the kids probably got adopted sooner or later, and the fear folks had about leaving the boy at the orphanage was just so much talk.

"His name's Charlie Stinson," Beryl said. "He's six years old. You need to know anything else?"

"I don't suppose so. He's small for his age, ain't he?"

Beryl looked around. He didn't like the place but he hadn't expected much either. At least the boy had a chance of a family taking him.

"How long were those two here that got taken?"

The old woman glanced at him. "I said I lost two, I didn't say they were taken."

"What happened to 'em?"

"Don't know. They got sick. Some live, some don't."

"My home's in Berryville," Beryl said. "I guess you know that. Get in tough with me if anything happens I should know about."

"You mean if he dies? You leaving your own kin here like this tells me there ain't much else you'd be interested in."

Beryl looked down the narrow hallway to the door he'd just come in. He wanted out of the place, and he had to get going before the roads got too bad. Charlie was standing between him and the woman, stiff, his hands to his sides. Beryl couldn't see his face but he figured it was troubled. He didn't think he'd have as much trouble leaving the boy, not like he was having. He didn't like the place and didn't like the old woman, but he had to finish it, it's what he came to do.

"I'm leaving," Beryl said.

Charlie jerked around and pleaded with him. "Don't leave me, Uncle. Take me with you." He lurched to Beryl and grabbed him around the legs.

"Come on, Charlie, straighten up," Beryl said. He loosened Charlie's grip around his legs and knelt in front of him. "You're gonna be all right, boy. They'll take care of you. They'll let me know if something happens."

Charlie leaned into him and threw his arms around Beryl's neck. "Don't go, Uncle Beryl, don't go without me."

Beryl gave him a nervous hug and Charlie thought maybe he wasn't leaving him and he held on tight, but then Beryl broke free and stood up. He turned Charlie around to face the woman.

"I'm going now. Take the boy, don't let him follow me."

Beryl hurried down the dim hallway. When he was almost to the door he could hear Charlie screaming at him between sobs. "No! No! Don't leave me." And then he heard the woman ask, "You want I should let you know if someone takes him?"

Beryl didn't answer. He kept walking and then he was out the door and it was shut behind him. He climbed in the wagon and took one last look at the dark, old building. The snow was heavy like clouds and the face of the building looked dim and distant. He released the brake and slapped the mares and left it behind him.

Chapter Fourteen

"You come with us now," the old woman told Charlie. "We'll get you something to eat."

"No, I'm not coming." Charlie wanted to chase after his uncle but she held him by the arm.

"It's all over now, Charlie. He's gone and you're staying. You'll fit in just fine in a few days, don't worry."

"I want to be with my uncle," Charlie yelled.

"He don't want you, that's plain. Now don't be a hard case, we've got ways of dealing with kids don't want to follow the rules, and the first rule is you do what you're told."

Mindy held out her hand to Charlie. "Come on, come with me. I'll take care of you. I know you're scared, everybody is at first."

She stepped up and took Charlie's hand and pulled him along with her. Charlie fought a little but the touch of the girl's hand was somehow comforting and he quit fighting and slowly walked along. When they got to the stairs Charlie remembered his satchel. He had to get it. Betty had told him not to let it out of his sight.

"My satchel," Charlie said.

"It'll be fine where it's at," Mindy said. "You can get it after you eat."

Charlie and Mindy were in front of the old woman and she held the lantern high so they could see the steps. The stairway was narrow and Charlie could touch either side as he walked down.

When they reached the bottom he was standing at the rear of a great room. The fireplace was at the far end, and there were two long tables leading from where he was standing to the other wall. Kids were sitting at the tables and he'd heard them talking as he was walking down, but now they were silent, watching, looking at him. There were two lanterns on each table but they seemed to be of little help in giving enough light to offset the gloom.

One woman was standing at the end of each table and they each had a stick in their hand. They were staring at him too.

"Kids, kids," the old woman said. "This is Charlie. He's come to stay with us. He's not too happy right now, but he'll get over it."

"Geraldine," she said to the closest woman. "Make room for him at your table and get him some grits and cornbread."

"The pots are empty," Geraldine said.

"Well, then divvy some out of the other bowls. We can't let him go hungry."

"Come sit by me," Mindy said, pulling Charlie along.

She led him to two empty chairs and pulled one out and moved Charlie into it. Geraldine started her way to the end of the table, looking at the kids' bowls and as she did the sounds of spoons clattering against pottery overwhelmed the silence.

"Stop it!" She yelled. She smacked the stick on the table. "Stop what you're doing." The woman at the end handed her an empty bowl and a spoon and as she made her way back to Charlie she dipped some grits and cornbread from each child's bowl as she passed. She sat it front of Charlie and he looked up at her.

"Eat it," she said.

The kids were staring at him. He sat there waiting, taking in their quiet looks. There were no smiles in the room, and some of the older kids were glaring at him.

Geraldine lifted Charlie's arm and slapped the spoon in his hand.

"Eat," she said. Then she raised her head to look out over the tables. "Finish eating, all of you. You'll be in your beds early tonight, there's been enough distractions."

Charlie wasn't hungry. He put the spoon back on the table.

"Eat it," Geraldine said. "Everybody eats."

"I don't blame you," Mindy whispered to Charlie. "It's not very good."

"I'm not staying," Charlie whispered back.

"I know you're not. I just want you to know you'll be all right. You'll have the home you're after."

"What about you? You could come with me. We could be brother and sister."

"I'd like that," Mindy said. "I miss my brother, but I can't come."

"That's the way it's going to be, is it?" Geraldine said, noticing Charlie hadn't started eating. She stood behind Charlie and dipped the spoon in the bowl and brought it to his mouth and squeezed his nostrils together with the other hand. Charlie's mouth opened and she shoved the gruel inside. The mush was cold and tasteless and Charlie grimaced. He shoved his chair back as hard as he could, hitting Geraldine in the stomach. He jumped up from the chair and turned around. Geraldine lunged for him and Charlie spit the clabber in her face and ran past her toward the staircase.

Miss Winston was blocking the way and Charlie tried to run around her but she grabbed him by the coat. Charlie spun and bit her arm and kicked her leg and she screamed and let go. He bolted up the stairs and into the hallway and started running for the door, then he heard Mindy yelling at him and he stopped and turned around.

"Your bag, Charlie, don't forget your bag." She had it in her hand as she was running to meet him.

Mindy shoved the bag at his hands and said, "Go, Charlie, your uncle needs you."

Charlie turned and bolted to the door, opened it and ran into the darkness.

Beryl was bothered. He couldn't get the orphanage out of his head. The inside was dark and gloomy and there was the smell, a musty odor of decaying earth and rotting wood. And the old woman, she had no business seeing after kids, she was too old and feeble. The girl had bothered him too. She'd seemed to know them, not just by the rumors, but by some sense she had. Beryl had a feeling of familiarity when he saw her, and the way she looked at Charlie was like she'd known him all of her life, he could see it in her eyes.

His thoughts went back to his own childhood. Even though he'd hated living on the plains he could still remember being cared for. There was always food on the table, and it was hot and had some taste—it wasn't grits all the time. Where would the boy be sleeping? Mixed in with thirty or forty others he suspected. The corner on the floor would be better than that.

He tried to shake off the thoughts. He had to get home. Charlie would get used to it. It wasn't as bad as it looked. After all, he hadn't seen everything. The old woman was only one of the people looking after the kids, there had to be more. Maybe he should have looked the place over better, if it hadn't been so late and the weather so bad he would have. Beryl stared into the darkness and shook his head. No, he wouldn't have. He was only trying to make himself feel better.

Beryl had left his home when he was fourteen, old enough to take care of himself, not just six years old, not so young he didn't know how to hold a plow horse in line, not so young he couldn't hunt game, or build a shelter, or fight for what was his. Charlie wasn't old enough yet to do those things, and he was small to boot. He'd have a hard time getting by no matter where he was.

Now all of the things people had said about him were coming back. The man at the train station saying, 'You're a hard case', and Beatrice Hagan: 'Nothing inside but hate and bitterness, and Jason: 'The bad's always ahead of you'.

Beryl never had much to say to anyone and no one said much to him, but now everything that was said was critical of him. He didn't mind being called a loner, or cantankerous, and he knew there was worse things said, but he never thought folks believed he was a bad person, just standoffish was all. He wasn't about to let what others thought make his decisions for him, but now the words stung.

Thinking about Charlie and what he'd been through and what more he was going to go through made him think he might have been harsh. Maybe he was thinking of himself, but that's all he'd ever done—there hadn't been anybody else to think about. There were the neighbors of course, but what could he do for them? He'd helped when they'd called, of course he couldn't remember the last time one of them had, and the others, the ones in town, they treated him like an outsider, like he had no business being there. He's always paid his bills, they knew that, and he'd never caused any problems, all he wanted was to be left alone.

What Beatrice had said though had some truth in it: Life hands out surprises, some good and some bad, it doesn't mean a man has a choice on taking them.

He thought about Charlie, the boy had not brought things down on himself, they'd just come down on their own, just like Charlie had come down on him. It was no more the boy's fault than it was Beryl's. He had no right holding it against him, he could see that now. The best thing he could've done was to wait things out a little more, maybe a family might have taken him in, a decent family with a good home, a place where Charlie might have gotten another start. There would be no starting points at the orphanage, it would be up to luck, and Charlie wasn't the luckiest person Beryl had run into.

Beryl had been gone from the orphanage a little more than an hour. He looked ahead of him and could barely make out the road. The tracks he'd made on the way in were gone, and the snow was still coming. It would take another four hours before he'd be back at Jacob's and he only hoped they'd let him stay in the barn.

Beryl stopped the horses and stared at the road ahead, then turned and looked behind him. He had no idea why his conscience was nagging at him right then, he'd done nothing wrong. Sure, overall the boy had some good qualities, but Beryl had no need for a child. He'd done just fine by himself and there was no reason to change things now. It might take a while but Charlie would adjust to his surroundings. The orphanage would take care of him, that's what they do. They had more resources than Beryl did. He held the reigns with both hands and dropped his head. This was all wrong and he knew it. Charlie was the one who hadn't done anything wrong. All he wanted was some family, and an orphanage wasn't a family. The boy needed a man around to show him how to get things done, how to stand on his own. So what if he was an inconvenience, life was full of inconveniences.

It was then Beryl made his decision. He'd go back and get Charlie. He'd find him a good family to live with, no matter how long it took. He'd do better by him, not because he was his brother's son, not because he was blood, but because every man deserved a chance, and Charlie hadn't had one.

Beryl got off the wagon and walked ahead of the horses. The steep bank on the south worried him and he needed a wide swath in the road to turn around. The curve ahead had a cutout on the left and maybe it was wide enough.

He got back in the wagon and walked the horses to the curve. He pulled them to the left as far as they'd go and then reined them to the right. One of the mares didn't want to go and was acting up, and Beryl had to get off the wagon and lead them around by walking them. It was a close turn and the wheels were riding the edge and the horses knew there was a drop off. He tried backing the mares up to get another twist with the wagon, but they were skittish. He got them to go backwards enough to where he thought they could make the turn.

Beryl got back in the wagon and pulled his coat tighter. They were heading into the wind again. Another hour to the orphanage and Beryl thought he might just stay there for the night. If they didn't have a bed, well, he and Charlie would have to sleep on the floor. Depending on the weather they could start out early in the morning and call on Jacob by noon. It would put him a day beyond his plan but it would be worth it. He knew the Demanche's would give them a warm welcome this time, him bringing the boy with him, and he thought he might just sleep inside if they'd offer, next to the fire, maybe even let the storm blow out before starting off the next day.

"Let's go girls," he yelled. Rosie and Mattie started pulling but Rosie was having trouble with her footing. She was too close to the edge and fighting to get over, running into the other horse. Rosie was frightened, her back feet slipping in the snow, and the more scared she got the worse Mattie got and soon they were both panicking and trying to bolt, but Beryl was trying to steer them to the right and it made things worse. As they picked up speed the tail end of the wagon slid around and the back wheel slipped off the edge. Rosie was fighting to get her rear feet back on level ground but was slipping, and then the weight of the wagon pulled her farther down the hill. Then the wagon slid off the edge pulling the mares with it, the horses fighting to regain the road and then the wagon tipped on its side and flipped over.

The horses were screaming and Beryl was riding the wagon when it flipped upside down and slid on the wet snow, the horses on their backs and the wagon on top of Beryl. The tongue broke loose and the horses tumbled down the hill. Free from the dead weight of the wagon they finally found their legs, but were so frightened all they could do was run. Still tied together by the harnesses and doubletree, they were running through the brush pulling at each other, neither one knowing which way to turn and struggling to pull apart, each trying to avoid the tree coming at them. They split to the sides, the tongue spearing the tree, slamming the horses into the sides, breaking them loose from each other but flinging them down the hill through the brush and trees. Then everything was quiet.

Beryl was pinned under the wagon up to his waist, with one leg broken that he knew of, maybe both, he couldn't move either one. He was lying on his back looking up through the trees, watching the snow falling on his face. He could hear one of the mares down below him, struggling to get up, and he thought it was Rosie. Except for the mare grunting everything seemed calm to him. He thought maybe he was dying. He felt warm, even comfortable, the pressure of the wagon on his legs seemed to absorb the pain from the broken bones. Then he couldn't hear the mare anymore, and could only hear the wind.

The thought occurred to him that no one would know he'd been going back after the boy, and he wasn't sure why, now, it meant anything to him, but it did.

The possibility he might die was close, he knew his chances of surviving the night in the cold, lying on wet snow, his legs busted, were slim. He didn't think he was bleeding but there was no way to be sure. Then he heard Rosie again, struggling to get up. She needed to be shot, put out of her misery, but there was no way to reach his rifle, even if it were still in the box, which it probably wasn't. He bent backwards as far as he could trying to see where the horse was but could see nothing and thought he was crazy for trying. He tried to twist sideways and when he did the pain shot up through his right hip and side and it hurt so bad he yelled in pain. He let himself back down slowly and caught his breath.

He shouldn't have left Charlie there, he shouldn't have even made the trip. Why he couldn't see that days earlier confused him now. It made no sense. It was his own bullheadedness that had blinded him. Beatrice Hagen had been right—he treated his animals better than he did people. Beryl tried to think of why he'd turned out this way; he hadn't hated his parents or his brother, only the life they were living, the uselessness of trying to make something out of nothing. It had been so easy for him to see. They were struggling, trying to beat the odds that nature handed them. Year after year, one crop failure after the other, they had gone back to the same fields and replowed and replanted and nothing had come of it. He thought of his tired young mother, aged beyond her years, with Clive at her breast, her face furrowed in worry, her body beat down so thin she could hardly feed herself. He wondered if she'd ever felt like leaving, but she wouldn't have said so, he knew that much. He'd never heard her complain, never heard her fight back for what common sense had to be telling her, that there was no future in a sod house, no hope in the windswept soil, and no pride in failure.

He'd hated it most of all for her, watching as she wasted away, her courage the only thread holding the family together. It wasn't courage that held his father there, he'd just stepped along behind his own father, sliding into his boots, staying because it'd been what he'd done, blind leading blind, poor getting poorer, handing down nothing but worn out work horses, broken down plows, and skinny chickens. It was the women and kids that had it the worst. The women, suffering with one nursing and one crying for food, the father outside, keeping his distance from the torment, kicking the dirt, thinking next year the earth would fold over and the rich pulp somewhere down below would come to the top and his pigheadedness would pay off. Beryl had tried to tell her, pointing to the south, it's there Mother, trees that reach to the stars, shade below to keep you cool, dirt so black corn grows ten feet tall, and running streams so clear and sweet it taste like honey. It had made no difference, she would bear the misery and bring her kids along, committed to a man with no sight left, only following the same dust choked dreams of a past generation.

Maybe that was it, maybe he'd felt cheated. It should have been an obligation, to see to it things got better, not remain the same, to not get worse. If there was failure, leave it behind, move on, and reach for something better. If a man was to take a wife then he had to give her a good life, and if there were kids, then they ought to have a chance at something decent, not the same hardscrabble he'd been handed. The failure of his grandfather and his own father had scarred Beryl, they'd provided nothing better, they'd handed down the same ache and agony they'd endured and never felt the worse for it. Beryl had done something about it, he'd left, but he'd still fallen short. He was leaving nothing better for his own name, nothing better for his mother's hopes. Charlie might have been that chance. Beryl had done more than two generations behind him but it had made no difference, he had helped no one but himself, and now he was dying, sprawled in the snow with a wagon across busted legs and his only kin in an orphanage an hour's ride away. He had made things no better.

Charlie was walking now, looking back over his shoulder from time to time, but had seen no one chasing him. He stepped off the road beside a tree to put his gloves on and rest. He could barely make out the wagon tracks his uncle had left because they were filling over with snow, but Charlie knew which direction he was headed. He wondered if his uncle would stay at Jacob's place, and if he did he would be able to catch up to him there. How far away it was he wasn't sure, it had seemed a long ride in the wagon from there to the orphanage and he knew the walk would be longer. He wasn't cold, the running had warmed him and the wisps of white breath coming from his mouth felt warm against his lips.

He got back on the road and followed the tracks, carrying his satchel as best he could, the weight of it making him switch from hand to hand, but he wasn't letting it go, he was hanging on to it like Betty had told him.

Charlie didn't know what his uncle would do when he caught up to him, but it didn't matter much. If he needed to he'd walk all the way back to the cabin, and maybe it's what he should do anyway. He didn't want Uncle Beryl to take him back to the orphanage, and if he were closer to it than home that might just be what happened. He hadn't had time to be scared, but now as he walked along the deserted road with the darkness and the wind and the snow he began to worry. He couldn't see very far ahead and when he looked in back of him the thought occurred to him that someone might come up from behind and be on top of him before he knew it. He walked in what wagon tracks he could make out thinking it might hide his footsteps, but soon it got to be too much trouble and he gave up trying. Then he stayed closer to the side of the road so that if he did hear someone coming he could hide in the brush.

But no one came. He walked along the road with the wind at his back and the snow falling so heavily that when he did look over his shoulder his own tracks were nearly covered. Then he was starting to get cold. He had no idea what time it was or what difference it made and he wondered how far it was to Jacob's house. He could see no lights in the hills and thought he might be close to the house where he'd seen the woman staring at them as they rode past, but he could make out nothing but the falling snow. The satchel was getting heavier and he thought he might drop it off to the side of the road and they could come back and get it, but then he might not be coming back and didn't want to lose his new clothes, and he remembered what Betty had told him, so he switched it to the other hand and kept walking. He dreamed he was sitting in front of the fire again and could feel its heat, and he had a blanket around his shoulders and Ethyl had brought him a hot plate of turkey, and then he was on the bed and asleep. He wondered if Uncle Beryl was in the barn or in the house or if he'd just kept going, and if he had then Charlie should keep going himself.

Charlie's feet were wet and cold and he could feel the dampness in his socks, but he couldn't feel his toes. He stopped and set the satchel down and sat on top of it. All of sudden he was tired, and sitting in the road in the darkness was starting to bother him, and then he remembered the cave. If there were a cave nearby he could get in it and sleep and wait until daylight, but then he wasn't sure about walking along the road in the daylight—the old woman from the orphanage might come along and see him and take him back. Then he began to think he shouldn't stop at all at Jacob's because they knew where he'd been going and they might take him back too. No, when daylight came he would stick to the woods beside the road and hide behind the trees so no one would see him. If he got to Jacob's he would hide and wait for his uncle to start off again, and then he'd surprise him and Uncle Beryl would lift him up in the wagon and they'd go home.

Now he was shivering and he hadn't been so cold when he was walking, so he stood back up and picked up the satchel, but it felt so heavy he sat it back down again. He took his belt off and stuck it through the satchel's handle and buckled it and dragged the bag behind him. He walked for a long time before stopping and then sat back down on the satchel again. He didn't think he could go much farther and thought he might just lie down and use his bag for a pillow and rest. His feet were starting to ache and he wanted to take his boots off and rub them, and then he remembered he had new socks and they would be warm and dry. He opened the bag and dug through it but he couldn't see in the dark and had to take things out, and then he gave up and put everything back and closed it. Then he heard a noise. He had heard nothing but the wind since leaving the orphanage—the wind and the swish of his own boots and the quiet sweep of snow blowing through trees.

Charlie stood in the road as still as he could. The sound had come from the south, off the side of the road, down the hill from the brush. He stared in that direction but he couldn't see anything. He waited, his bag at his feet, his arms at his sides with his gloved hands clinched against the cold, and now against the fear. Then it came again, faint, weak, hurting, something down in the darkness, calling for help, a noise he couldn't understand.

Charlie felt chills run through his body, not shivers of cold, but fright shaking him to panic. He looked to the sides and then in back and then up the road he'd just come from. Nothing—there was nothing. He wanted to run and he did, away from the noise, up the opposite hillside and into the brush, clawing at the vines and the scrub, the briars tearing at his clothes and gloves, the wet snow slapping at his face, and then he tripped and fell. He sprawled face down in the snow and listened for something following him, but there was no sound, only his own hot, hard breathing. And then it felt good to be lying in the snow, the cold wetness against his cheek, and the soft sound of the wind, the feeling of comfort from not walking or standing or running. He closed his eyes and thought he might fall asleep and how he *wanted* to fall asleep, and when he woke up the sun would be out and the wind would've stopped and his uncle would be sitting in the road with his satchel of new clothes in the wagon, and he'd be waving at him to come along: *'We're going home, come along, Charlie, we're going home'*.

The noise again, the same noise again from the same place, now distant, across the road and down the hill. Charlie raised his head to hear better but there was nothing. He sat up and listened but only the stillness reached him. Then it was back, a pitiful yawing, a lonely cry of agony. Something was hurt, Charlie knew it now. Something needed help, and he should try to help it. He pushed himself up and struggled back down the hill through the brush and made it to the road. He stopped by his bag and waited to hear the sound again. Then it came—farther down the road to the bend. Charlie strained to see through the falling snow and darkness. He picked up his belt and pulled the bag behind him and kicked through the mounting snow.

When he reached the curve he saw a swath of torn and bent scrub trailing over the edge of the road, and in the distance he could see something big and dark, something that shouldn't be there. Then the sound came again, down below in the darkness, beyond the black shape.

Charlie stepped off the road and picked his way through the saplings and vines. As he got closer he could see the wooden wheels of a wagon lying on its side. He walked closer until he could touch it. He stood beside it and listened, and then he heard a rustling on the opposite side. He let go of his bag and carefully placed one foot in front of the other, as quietly as he could, and walked to the end of the wagon and slowly bent his head around the edge. There was a body lying on the ground, he could see the arms and the bulk—it was almost covered with snow. He stepped around the wagon and over to the form and bent down beside it. The legs were under the wagon and the arms were lying in the snow and the face was turned away from Charlie. He reached out and touched an arm, but it didn't move. Then he scooted up to the face and bent over to see it.

Beryl had been in and out of consciousness. He was in shock and he knew it. He couldn't feel the cold anymore and he couldn't feel his legs. He heard the mare from time to time—its groans of misery, but then he'd passed out. He'd woke up once and couldn't figure out where he was and flogged his arms about and tried to get up but the pain in his legs hit him and he remembered what had happened. He laid his head back down and waited. He thought it was about midnight but couldn't be sure—it was just a fifty-year-old guess. He knew that if he had to lie there all night he'd be dead by morning. Then he woke up again and thought he'd heard something, something that wasn't the mare, something coming down the hill in front of him. Probably a coyote, he thought, or maybe even a bear, it wouldn't matter much. It might be best to get it over with, although freezing to death might be easier, but he didn't think it was that cold because the snow was soft and there was no crust. He didn't know if his legs were bleeding or if the life was draining from him, all he knew was he was tired and wasn't sure he wanted to know where he was or what sort of shape he was in.

He'd heard the noise beside him and had felt the tug on his arm but didn't want to see what kind of animal was sniffing him out. Then he felt the warm breath on his cheek—something was getting a closer look. He decided to fight it off as long as he could; he didn't want to be torn apart for some animal's dinner.

Beryl jerked his arms up and grabbed, and Charlie screamed, and then Beryl saw who it was and he held him there in front of his face.

"Charlie, my God, it's you." He loosened his grip and lowered Charlie back down.

Beryl laid his head back down. He winced with the pain he felt in his legs.

"Charlie, how'd you get here?"

"I ran away. I wanted to be with you. I didn't want to live there."

"Oh, Charlie, I'm sorry I took you there. I shouldn't have."

"Are you hurt Uncle Beryl?"

"I'm hurt. I don't know how bad and I won't know till we get this wagon off of me."

"How?" Charlie asked.

"You can't do it, Charlie. You'll have to get help."

Then they both heard the mare.

"You've got to look after the horses, Charlie. You've got to go down the hill and see what kind of shape they're in."

"But what about you?"

"You can't do anything for me right now. The first thing to be done is to get the horses out of their misery. Open the box on the wagon and see if anything's left in it. There was a lantern and a rifle. If they're not there then you need to scrounge around and find 'em."

Charlie looked beside him at the wagon and got up and stepped to the box. The lid was part way open and everything was down at the end. He dug around and found the lantern and brought it out.

"I couldn't find the rifle."

144

"That's okay, son." Beryl reached in his coat pocket and brought out some matches. "Set it up straight, Charlie." Beryl lit the lantern and turned it up high.

"All right, take it down the hill and find the horses. Be careful the kerosene don't splash."

"What do I do when I find them?"

"I know one of 'em's still alive, so see if the other one is."

"How will I know?"

"Just look at his eyes, you'll know."

Charlie started down the hill being careful with the lantern. The mares weren't hard to find, they were both in front of the tree they'd straddled, the doubletree broken in half. One mare had slid farther down the hill than the other and was lying on its side. The other one was lying with its head uphill and was still alive.

Rosie raised her head when she heard Charlie coming and tried to get up but her rear legs wouldn't work. Charlie raised the light higher and saw the other horse lying still in the snow. He crept up to her slowly—he didn't want to surprise her, thinking she might be resting. When he got close enough to see her head he held the lantern closer. Her body was covered with snow, not like Rosie, and he wondered why, and then he touched her neck and felt the cold stiff muscle. The eye was covered and Charlie wiped the snow away and could see the dark, blank bulge staring out at nothing. He rubbed the horse's neck hoping to wake her, but there was no response. Dead, yes, Mattie was dead. He'd seen dead animals before, but only from a distance, his Papa not letting him get too close. This was Mattie, the one he'd brushed down when they'd first gotten to the cabin. She'd been so calm and had looked at him and had never made a sound. Charlie's eyes filled with tears, but then he heard Rosie.

He stumbled over to her and when he got close she struggled to get up, throwing her head from side to side and up and down, her front legs flailing at the ground, screaming and huffing all at once, but then stopped as if she was worn out, and let her head drop to the ground. The snow had melted in front of her nose and Charlie could hear the great blasts of air blowing from her nostrils. He reached to pet her but when he did he saw her huge eye staring at him with panic and fright and she tried to get up again. Charlie jumped back, stumbled and fell backwards, falling on his rear, the lantern still in his hand, sitting in the snow beside him. The mare fell back again and was quiet.

"Charlie!"

He heard Beryl calling him. He got to his feet and worked his way around the horse and up the hill.

"Which one's alive?" Beryl asked. "Is it Rosie?"

"Yes," Charlie said.

"What about Mattie?" Beryl asked.

"She's not moving," Charlie said. "And her eye's not working."

"She's dead then," Beryl said. "Rosie?"

"She tried to get up but her back end won't move."

Beryl laid his head back down in the snow. "She's broke her back, then. You've got to find the rifle, Charlie. Take the light and work around the wagon and up the hill till you find it. There's no telling where it's at."

Charlie went around the front of the wagon with the light held high. He searched on the ground from one end to the other and couldn't find it.

"I don't see it, Uncle," he said.

"Make your way up the hill then. I had it under the seat, it's fallen out somewhere. Kick around in the snow."

Charlie wandered back and forth through the broken brush, kicking in the snow, feeling with his hands, thinking every broken sapling was a barrel and every busted limb a stock. He made his way up to the road and started back down again. When he got to the wagon he picked up his satchel to take, and there under it was the barrel of the gun sticking out from under the wagon.

"I found it, Uncle Beryl, I found it."

"Bring it to me."

Charlie dropped his bag and fell to his knees pulling on the barrel of the gun, but it was trapped under the wagon.

"It's stuck," he yelled. "It's under the wagon."

"You'll have to dig it out," Beryl said.

Charlie dug with his gloved hands and now they were wet with the snow and the fingers were crumpling, so he took them off and dug with his bare hands. He pulled again on the gun but it was still stuck and so he dug some more, trying to get as far under the bed of the wagon as possible. His hands were freezing and he stuck his fingers in his mouth to warm them and could feel the cold and taste the dirt on his tongue. He unbuttoned his coat and stuck his arms inside and his hands under his armpits.

"Have you got it?" Beryl shouted.

"Not yet, my hands are cold."

"Keep digging, boy!"

Beryl thought about what he'd said. It was wrong. Charlie was doing the best he could, he shouldn't expect any more. He should be thanking the good Lord right now that he'd even showed up. The boy had more guts than he'd given him credit for anyway, running from the orphanage in the middle of the night in a snowstorm. Maybe it was a sin taking him in the first place, and he was paying for it now. Beryl had never put much stock in religion, and he never put much in anyone else either, but right now his whole life was in the hands of a small boy, a boy he'd treated like a rabid dog, and right then he wasn't sure he'd blame Charlie if he just walked up the hill and left.

"Charlie," Beryl said.

"Yes, sir."

"I'm sorry, I didn't mean to yell at you. I now you're doing the best you can. Look for a good sized limb, one the wagon broke maybe, and stick it under the wagon a ways and lift on it. It might raise the bed enough to pull the rifle out."

Charlie looked around and found a stick and started poking it under the bed. Soon he was digging dirt and shoving up on the limb and pulling on the butt of the rifle and it was coming loose. He worked on the other side of the gun for a while and finally pulled it out. Then he grabbed his bag and the rifle, picked up the lantern and walked around to Beryl.

He set the lantern down along with his satchel and handed Beryl the rifle.

"Have you ever shot a gun?" Beryl asked.

"No, sir."

"Well, you're gonna have to do something no boy should have to do."

Charlie stared at him in the white light of the lantern. He had no idea what his uncle meant, and he didn't know what the rifle had to do with anything anyway. It seemed to him that getting his uncle's legs out from under the wagon was the most important thing, and he didn't know how they would do that. Maybe he should be going to get help from Jacob, he would know what to do.

"Listen to me, Charlie," Beryl said. "Rosie's down there hurting, and there's no way we can help her. She's got to be put down. She don't know what's happening to her and she's scared, but there's nothing we can do for her. We've got to put her out of her pain."

Charlie looked at his uncle and then at the rifle. "How?"

Beryl chambered a shell with the lever and made sure the safety was on.

"You're gonna have to shoot her, Charlie. It's the only way."

"But she's alive," Charlie said. "She's trying to get up. You can help her."

"I can't help her, Charlie. Her back's broken."

Charlie was quiet. He tried to see the mare from where he was sitting but couldn't. He looked back at his uncle and then at the rifle again.

"It's best not to think about it," Beryl said. "You've just got to walk up and do it and not think about it."

Beryl knew he was the one that should be doing it, but it had to be done now. The mare was suffering and no animal should suffer.

"Look here, Charlie," Beryl said, sticking the rifle toward him. "It's loaded now, so when you get down there push this button, that'll mean it's ready to shoot. Then pull back on this hammer until you hear it click. It'll take a good tug so don't be afraid. Put the stock up to your shoulder and hold on tight. When it shoots it's gonna buck you."

"But she wants to get up," Charlie said.

"I know she does but she can't, and she's never gonna be able to." Beryl knew it was hard for Charlie to understand and he was trying his best to help him.

"Have you ever had a dog that got so old he had to be put to rest?"

"You mean shot?"

"Yeah, put to sleep, so he wouldn't be hurting anymore."

"No."

"What about a cat? Did you ever have a cat that had to be shot?"

"No. We had a chicken once that got hurt by a fox and Papa killed it and we ate it."

Beryl felt lucky he couldn't feel his legs. "It's kind of the same thing, Charlie, only a horse is just bigger. If they're hurt and you can't fix 'em, then you have to put 'em out of their misery." He handed the rifle to Charlie.

Charlie took it and held it and looked at Beryl.

"Between the eyes," Beryl said. "Get in front of him and put the end of the barrel between his eyes and pull the trigger."

They heard the mare struggling again.

"It's time, Charlie. It needs to be done now."

Charlie stood up with the rifle and took the lantern in his other hand. He walked slowly down the hill toward the mare. When he got there he made his way to the front of the horse and set the lantern on the ground.

The mare's head was up, looking at Charlie. She struggled once, but was so worn down her attempt was feeble. Charlie stared at her and wanted to talk to her, but he could see she was weak, her head swaying from side to side, her eyes fixed in a stare. He pushed the button and pulled the hammer back until it clicked, then raised the rifle and stepped closer to the horse. It seemed she was looking straight at him, like she was wondering what he was doing, and Charlie let the rifle down.

"Come on," he whispered. "Get up. Just get up."

Rosie huffed tired air from her nose and bowed her head like she was waiting.

Charlie lifted the gun again and pointed the barrel between her eyes.

Beryl was waiting for the shot. He hoped the boy could go through with it. It was a hard thing to do, even for a man, and he felt somehow like he'd let the mare down. She'd been with him for many years, both horses had, and it was sorry they had to end this way. Then the shot rang through the quiet.

Chapter Fifteen

Now that it was over Beryl started shivering. It was the one thing that had to be finished before he could concentrate on his own injuries. The pain in his legs came back and the chills ran up and down him so hard and fast his whole body was shaking.

By the time Charlie made it back up the hill Beryl was shaking uncontrollably. Charlie knelt down beside him and laid the rifle on the ground and held the lantern over Beryl.

"What's wrong, Uncle Beryl?"

"Cold, I'm cold."

Charlie reached for his satchel and opened it. He threw out his clothes looking for something to cover his uncle with but there was nothing big enough. Then he remembered seeing some blankets in the box and went to get them. He covered Beryl and watched, thinking he would stop shaking any time, but he didn't. Fire, he needed a fire to keep him warm.

Charlie began picking up sticks like Betty had told him. He kicked out the snow close to Beryl's body and laid the sticks down. Leaves, he needed leaves to start the sticks, but there were none, and the ones he could find were wet. He dumped his satchel on the ground and saw the checkers and board. He moved the sticks and put his new socks on the bottom and the checkers on top of them. He reached in his uncle's coat pocket and took out some matches and found a rock and struck it against it. The match flared and Charlie stuck it to the socks and they started burning. As the flames grew higher he laid the sticks on top, one by one, until he ran out, and then he scrounged around for more. When the fire was going good he put the checkerboard on top. He went to the other side of the wagon and picked up bigger limbs that the wagon had broken and put them on the fire. He rolled up his new shirt and pants and laid them under Beryl's head.

Beryl was still shaking but he could feel the warmth of the flames and the blankets had helped. Charlie hadn't said anything when he'd gotten back after shooting the mare, he'd just started helping like he knew what to do. Beatrice had been right about teaching him about the fire, she'd been right all along. He just needed a little instruction. It wasn't like he couldn't learn, Charlie only needed more prodding.

Beryl knew it wouldn't be enough though. He had to find out how bad his legs were busted and how much blood he was losing. He had felt the warm fluid running off his shin at first, but soon he could feel it no more, nothing but cold and pressure. He would need help and would have to have it soon.

Charlie was warming his hands close to the fire, staring at the flames. He was remembering what Betty had told him, that the flames were the spirits of his sister and papa, and how they would keep him safe and warm. He thought about Mindy and how she had reminded him of his Rachael and he wanted her to be with him now. If only she had come with him maybe they could have lifted the wagon off of his uncle. Charlie stood up and turned around to the wagon and tried to lift it but couldn't. He turned back and looked at his uncle's face. It was wet with melted snow and twisted in pain, and Charlie wanted to do something to help but didn't know what.

"Charlie," Beryl said, his eyes closed. "Can you hear me, Charlie?"

Charlie stepped over to Beryl's face and squatted next to him. Beryl opened his eyes and pulled his arm out from under the blanket and squeezed Charlie's arm.

"I'm sorry I left you there, Charlie. I shouldn't have done it, I know that now."

"I didn't want to stay there," Charlie said. "I wanted to be with you. I know I shouldn't have run away, but I had to."

"It's all my fault, son, all mine. You're gonna have to go get help, Charlie. Can you do that?"

"It's dark," Charlie said.

"I know it is, but I don't think I can stay here the rest of the night. You remember how to get to Jacob's place don't you? Just keep on the road and you'll find it. You can take the lantern if you want."

"But what about the fire, Uncle Beryl? It'll go out and you'll get cold."

"Gather up some more wood and lay it over here by the rifle. I'll put it on as I need it."

"Can't I stay here with you?"

"I need you to go get Jacob, son. Tell him the wagon's on top of me and my legs are broke, tell him to bring a team."

Charlie went around the wagon and picked up more wood and brought it back and put them by the rifle and waited for Beryl to say something. Charlie didn't want to walk on the road anymore. He remembered how scared he'd gotten just before he found his uncle and he didn't want to feel that way again. Then he looked at Beryl's face and something told him he had to go. His uncle was just lying there in the snow like he was asleep, but Charlie knew he wouldn't be sleeping on the cold wet ground. He knelt down and shook Beryl's shoulder.

"Uncle Beryl?" Charlie shook him harder. "Uncle Beryl, wake up." Then Beryl's eyes fluttered. He looked around like he didn't know where he was, trying to fix on something he knew, and then he found Charlie.

"Oh, Charlie, are you back so soon? Where's Jacob?"

"I haven't gone yet."

"Oh. My back's so cold I can hardly feel it."

Charlie took his new coat off and stretched it out as far as he could. He pulled up on Beryl's shoulder and Beryl leaned up a ways until the pain in his legs took his breath. Charlie pushed his coat under Beryl's back and helped him lay back down.

Beryl let out a gasp of air as he lowered onto the jacket. He closed his eyes and breathed heavily.

"Uncle Beryl," Charlie said. "I'm going now." Beryl didn't say anything.

Charlie put more limbs on the fire and blew on it to get the flames higher. Then he moved the other wood closer to the heat and Beryl. He picked up his old coat near the satchel and put it on, finding the sandwiches that Ethyl had gave him, and he stuck one in his pocket and took one back to his uncle and laid it next to his head. He grabbed the lantern and started up the hill.

Charlie had just gotten to the road when the lantern burst into a bright glow and then slowly dimmer and dimmer until nothing was left but a tiny low flame. The lantern was out of fuel and Charlie set it on the road. He looked ahead at the darkness and the falling snow and then back down the hill where his uncle lay. He could see the glow of the fire behind the wagon. He would much rather have stayed with Uncle Beryl but he understood he was hurt and needed help and Charlie couldn't lift the wagon.

The wind had calmed from the gusts of earlier and the snow was drifting down in quiet pieces, more like slow-motioned frozen raindrops, Charlie thought. He stood in the road and gazed up to the sky and watched as the flakes came down, some landing on his face and some falling on his outstretched hands. He couldn't feel them when they landed even though he cupped his hands and could see them lying in the fold. There were no tracks on the road anymore, just a soft white sheet leading into darkness. He listened for sounds but there were none, now only the silence of night. He thought about that night he'd sat on the bank of the swollen creek and waited for his father and sister to come out of the darkness, but they had never come, and now his uncle was waiting, down below off the edge of the road, lying on the ground like Charlie had been. As that night had lingered on Charlie's hopes had diminished as the roar of the rushing water had, and as the gray light of dawn broke over the edge of the horizon he had realized that no one was coming, and that feeling of hopelessness had seized him, and now the feeling was back again, the emptiness that had filled him was gaining momentum, rising from his chest and flushing upwards to his head. He hated being in the dark alone, not that he was afraid of the night, only scared that when it ended there would be nothing promising in the light.

The last spark of light from the lantern was gone. The small radiance from the fire below seemed far away and he wanted to go there and sit by the fire and wait. Maybe this time it would be different and someone would come out of the darkness and help, but the surrounding silence whispered it wouldn't happen. If only someone would come.

"Charlie."

His name, he'd heard his name. Charlie twisted his head and turned in the road and looked in the sky and then down the hill. The voice was not his uncle's, it was sweet and soothing—it was Rachael's voice.

"Charlie, I'm coming."

From behind, the voice was coming from behind, and he turned around and stared into the darkness, and then he saw the form coming closer, not far away, the snow kicking in puffs on the road in front her feet. It was her, it was Rachael. She had found him and had come to help. Then she was there, trudging through the snow and night and Charlie could make out her body and then her face and he wanted to run to her so she could hold him and tell him it would be all right, everything would be all right.

"Charlie, it's me, Mindy."

"Mindy? Mindy!"

"Why are you standing in the road?" she asked.

"I've got to get help for Uncle Beryl. The wagon's on top of him and he's hurt."

"Where are you going?"

"To Jacob's. It's up the road somewhere. I'm not sure how far."

Mindy took Charlie's hands in hers. "Your hands are freezing, where's your gloves and coat?"

"My gloves are wet and Uncle Beryl's lying on the coat."

She rubbed his hands and blew warm breath on them. "Put them in your pockets. We should be going."

"Will you come with me?"

"Yes, that's why I'm here. I waited until Miss Winston made us go to bed and then I snuck out. You shouldn't be out here alone."

"They'll be looking for us," Charlie said.

"No, they won't, not tonight and maybe not ever," Mindy said. She put her arm around Charlie's shoulders and pulled him in close. "We'd better hurry, your uncle needs help."

They walked together up the road and Charlie hadn't felt as good since he was back in Oklahoma with Rachael. Mindy had come to find him and help him and she was just like Rachael, holding him close and staying beside him. She would be there when he needed her and she would know what to do when things got confusing, but he wasn't confused anymore—he knew what had to be done. Now his thoughts were clearer and the road wasn't threatening. They had to get help for Uncle Beryl or he would die, and he'd said he was sorry for taking him to the orphanage, and that meant he would be going home with him, and it's what Mindy had said, that Charlie would find his home.

They walked in silence, Mindy's wool glove around his neck, warm against his cheek. The snow had quit falling and the sky was clearing. Charlie and Mindy could see the first few stars as they brightened through the breaks in the clouds, and the lip of a full moon was edging into view. Charlie didn't know how long they'd been walking, but he knew he was tired. He leaned more heavily on Mindy's side as the night wore on, and his progress had become more stumble than steps. Mindy didn't seem tired at all, pulling Charlie closer to her as they walked, supporting him as he let his head drop to his chest and closed his eyes.

"It's not far now, Charlie," she said.

"How do you know? Maybe we passed it."

"I just know we're almost there. Try to wake up. You'll have to tell Jacob where your uncle's at."

"Won't you be going with us? It's so dark I might miss it."

"No you won't."

"But what about you?"

"Don't worry, I'll be with you. I'll always be there when you need me. Look, there it is."

Charlie looked to his left and saw the dark outline of the cabin set back off the road. He remembered the path they'd turned on to reach Jacob's place and there was a soft light coming from the fireplace through the front window. His spirits rose as they neared the path leading up to the cabin and he picked up his pace to nearly a run. Mindy was beside him when they reached the porch and she pounded on the door, but they heard no movement inside.

"I'll go around to the back," she said. "You stay here and keep knocking."

She pulled Charlie into her chest and held him tight and kissed his cheek.

"Everything's going to be all right, Charlie. You'll have what you want. Your uncle's going to be good to you from now on, so treat him good back."

"Maybe you can come back with us—you could come and live with us."

"Your uncle doesn't want another mouth to feed. I'll be fine."

"He will," Charlie said. "I know he will. Without you I couldn't have done it, and he'll know it and you can come back with us."

"Maybe so, Charlie, we'll see. Now you keep knocking while I go to the back."

Mindy stepped off the porch and turned back to Charlie. "Betty was right, Charlie, about the light and warmth of the fire, and the sun and moon and stars—your sister and papa are always with you, keeping you safe." She turned the corner of the cabin and was gone.

Charlie listened for a moment as she walked away and then turned and knocked on the door as hard as he could. Then he heard footsteps and the door opened and it was Jacob.

"My lord, it's Charlie," Jacob said. Ethyl was standing behind him with a shawl over her shoulders.

"Well, get him inside," she said. "Don't stand there like a tree."

Jacob pulled Charlie inside and led him to the fire.

"What are you doing, Charlie?" Jacob asked.

"Uncle Beryl's down the hill and the wagon's on top of him. He says his legs are broke and I've come to get you. We've got to hurry."

"He's freezing," Ethyl said, pushing Jacob aside. "Get another log for the fire while I get his boots and pants off."

"Where's he at?" Jacob asked.

"Toward the orphanage," Charlie said. "Mindy and I've been walking a long ways, I'm not sure how far. She went to the back to try and wake you."

"Go on, Jacob, get the wood," Ethyl said. "We'll find out what we need to know in a minute."

Ethyl helped Charlie off with his wet boots and pants. She went into the bedroom and brought a blanket and wrapped it around Charlie's shoulders.

"Now you sit here by the fire and I'll get you some warm cider to drink. Who's Mindy?"

"I met her at the orphanage. Uncle Beryl left me there but I ran away, and so did Mindy. She followed me to where the wagon was and then walked with me here. She's out back. You've got to find her."

Jacob came back in with more logs and got the fire blazing while Ethyl started the stove and put a pan of cider on the burner.

"Did you see anyone out back?" Ethyl asked.

"There's no one out there," Jacob said.

"Put your clothes on," Ethyl said. "You won't do us any good running around in your long johns. Then go outside and look around—he says a girl's with him, she'll be half frozen herself. You stay put, Charlie, while I get dressed."

While Jacob and Ethyl were gone Charlie was wondering where Mindy was. He got up and went to the back door and stepped outside, but Mindy wasn't there. He went to the front door and walked out on the porch from one side to the other and still he couldn't see her. He yelled for her but heard nothing. He kept yelling until Ethyl came out to get him.

"You've got to get back inside," she said. "Jacob'll find her if she's out here."

As they turned to go in Charlie saw something down at the main road. It was Mindy and she was standing in the road in the moonlight, waving at him.

"There she is—it's her. She's on the road."

Ethyl stopped and looked.

"There's no one there, Charlie. Your eyes are playing tricks on you. Come on now, let's get inside."

Charlie struggled to stay on the porch, but when he looked again at the road, Mindy wasn't there. Nothing was there but a white blanket of snow."

"I'll take a look," Jacob said, coming around the side of the cabin. "If she's out here I'll find her."

Ethyl took Charlie back inside and sat him by the fire, then poured him a cup of warm cider. She rubbed his feet with the blanket and got a pair of Jacob's socks for him. She was sure Charlie was talking out of his head, delirious from the long walk and the freezing cold.

Jacob came back inside after circling the cabin and barn. Ethyl looked at him as he entered the back door and he shook his head. Charlie was looking into the fire with the cup pressed to his lips. Jacob knelt down beside him.

"Better get him dressed," Jacob said. "He'll have to show me where his uncle's at."

"He can't get back out there," Ethyl said. "He'll be sick as it is."

"The fire," Charlie said.

"What's that?" Jacob said.

"I built a fire to keep Uncle Beryl warm."

"It'll be out by now," Jacob said. "How long were you walking?"

"The bend in the road," Charlie said. "I looked for the other cabin we passed on the way, there was a woman standing in the doorway looking at us and I waved, but she didn't wave back."

"That's Clifford Shaw's place," Jacob said. "The bend in the road's just this side of it. He's walked near three hours then."

"You better get going," Ethyl said.

"I'll hitch up the wagon."

"Stop by the Marsh's—Randall and his boys will help you."

"I know that, woman," Jacob said, as he walked away.

"I'll make coffee and wrap up some blankets and bandages," Ethyl said. "Don't leave without 'em."

"I know that too, woman," Jacob said, shutting the door behind him.

Charlie was still staring at the fire when Jacob came back in, but his eyes were half open and he was drifting in and out of sleep. Ethyl was just about ready to put him to bed.

"We'll be taking him on into Harrison," Jacob said. "I hope we will anyway. He'll need a doctor."

"I know that, old man," Ethyl said with a concerned look. "Carry Charlie to the bedroom before you go."

Jacob picked Charlie up and took him to the room and put him on the bed. Ethyl brought the lantern with her and turned it down low and pulled a chair up close to the bed. She squeezed Jacob's hand as he turned to leave.

"You be careful," she said.

"I will. With any luck I'll be back by nightfall tomorrow."

Chapter Sixteen

At some point during the night Charlie's sleep turned fitful. His breathing became labored and he developed a dry cough along with a high fever. Ethyl stayed by the bed with a cool rag on his forehead but it did little good. By morning he was worse. The chills started about daylight and he complained of a sore throat. He couldn't breathe through his nose and his eyes were red and burning. Ethyl boiled water and brought the pan to the room and made Charlie breathe the steam under a towel, hoping it would make breathing easier, but the discharge was thick and yellow, and she knew then he had the grippe. She made him gargle warm salt water and kept a hot towel on his chest.

Ethyl killed a chicken and made broth and fed what she could to Charlie. He ate very little and soon it came back up. She was worried about him; she knew the grippe could kill. There was little she could do, only try to keep him quiet and keep him drinking water and what little broth he would take.

By late afternoon she was not only concerned about Charlie but about Jacob, too. She'd heard nothing since he'd left and had thought that one of the Marsh's would have come to let her know something, but there had been no sign. Ethyl considered it a good sign though, thinking that if Jacob had returned any earlier there would have been no reason to go to Harrison. Beryl Stinson must still be alive, as sorry as he was, but she would wish no harm on anyone.

She made chicken and dumplings and kept it on the stove for Jacob when he did come home, and sat in the chair beside Charlie and waited.

"You see the bone sticking out," Doctor Horace Greenbaum said. "That's what we call a compound fracture.

Jacob looked at Randall Marsh and frowned. He didn't like doctors anyway and he had a particular distaste for this one. Dr. Greenbottom, was what he liked to call him, not so Ethyl could hear of course, but he didn't mind if anyone else heard. The doctor just figured Jacob had trouble saying his name and paid little attention to the slight, but everyone else knew better. He was the only doctor in Harrison, and he worked on livestock with the same determination as he did people, which in Jacob's mind was the real reason the death rate was so high on both parts.

He'd had the doctor down to his place years ago when one of his boys had the croup. As the good doctor was leaving he heard Jacob's mule coughing and decided to treat the animal with the same syrup he'd given the boy. The boy got better, but the mule died, and to Jacob's way of thinking it appeared to be a fifty-fifty chance as to who was going to live and who was going to pass. He never put much stock in Dr. Greenbottom since then.

"It's a wonder he's still alive," Dr. Greenbaum said. "I'd say if his leg hadn't of been lying in the cold snow he wouldn't be with us now, and on the other hand it might just be the death of him yet. If he doesn't come down with pneumonia I'll have missed a guess."

"He had a fire," Jacob said. "It was keeping him somewhat warm."

"He's lucky for that. Which one of you is going to help me set this fibula?"

"Set what?" Jacob said.

"His shin bone. One of you lay across his chest and the other one grab his leg right below the knee—this is probably going to wake him up."

Randall Marsh's two boys were both teenagers and neither one of them had ever seen a compound fracture and were looking on with quiet amazement, standing behind their father staring out on either side of him.

"You boys jump on in there," Jacob said, eyeing Randall. "Your pa and I have done our share of doctoring in our time. It's best you start learning yourselves. We'll just wait for you outside. How long will it take, Doc?"

"Give me thirty minutes, take or give, and I should be done with that part. You two cowards can find something to do for that long I'd guess."

Jacob and Randall stepped through the door and into the street. It was mid-morning, two days after Thanksgiving, and the town was quiet. Normally Jacob didn't come to Harrison more than once a month, but now that he was here he thought he might pick up something for Ethyl.

"It's good your boys are learning something," Jacob said.

"A man needs to know how to set a broke bone," Randall said. "I had to set my own finger once."

"How'd you break it?"

"It wasn't really broke, just jammed, but it's close to the same thing. I just pulled on it. Lot of pain though. I was lucky I knew what to do."

"I set a dog's leg one time," Jacob said. "I couldn't keep him off of it and he limped the rest of his life. Darn good rabbit dog at one time. After that he couldn't catch nothing but ticks. Let's get something to eat and then check on Stinson. I don't think we'll be taking him back with us. He'll probably be staying here for awhile. Then we ought to head for home."

"He's lucky his boy found him," Randall said. "If he hadn't of had that fire and those blankets he might've just died out there."

"It's an odd turn, isn't it?" Jacob said. "That the one thing he was trying to get rid of ended up saving his life."

They had seen the light of the fire as they came up to the bend in the road. It was still burning from the sticks of wood Charlie had piled up for Beryl. He'd been in and out of consciousness through the night, but had had enough wits about him to throw the limbs on the hot coals when he did wake up. When Jacob and Randall had found him he was delirious, shouting for Charlie, and he didn't recognize Jacob at all. They'd unhitched the team and tied them to the wagon and pulled it off of Beryl, the boys holding him as the wagon lifted. His leg was in terrible shape, twisted and busted with the bone poking through the skin. His other leg was just bruised, but both of them were blue from the cold and weight of the wagon.

The hill was so steep they'd had to take the sideboards off the wagon and lay Beryl down so the horse could pull him up to the road. Carrying him up the hill wouldn't work, the pain of his leg wouldn't allow it. The long ride to town was difficult—every bump causing Beryl to scream out and try to grab his leg, but even that effort made things worse. Finally he'd passed out and for the last hour of the ride things had been quiet.

Jacob had found the mares and saw that one had been shot. It must have been Charlie that had done it, and he wondered how the boy felt about it. He hadn't said anything at the house and it surprised Jacob. Shooting a horse wasn't an easy thing to do, especially one you know, and it never stopped amazing him how a horse always seemed to know what was going on, and how they ended up looking at you with those big dark, lonesome eyes right before you pulled the trigger. Some men couldn't do it, and for those that couldn't it wasn't a badge of shame. A horse, an ox, a mule, they were all extensions of your own family. Without them the work wouldn't get done and the distance traveled would take twice as long, and you needed them like a man needed hands. Killing them was an act of mercy, but it was easily the hardest thing a man had to do. A young boy like Charlie, he'd have to have a lot of guts to do it.

Jacob had picked up what things he could find, Charlie's satchel and clothes, a few things that had been thrown from the wagon, and as he kicked around in the snow next to the fire he'd seen the burnt edge of the checkerboard. Charlie must have used it to start the fire and Jacob made a note to get him another one. It couldn't have gone to better use.

After they'd eaten, Jacob stopped at the dry goods store and bought Ethyl a new apron. He wasn't good at buying gifts but she was always complaining about how old and raggedy the one she had was, and for some reason it had just struck him. He picked up a checkerboard set while he was at it and then they walked back to the doctor's office.

"He won't be going anywhere for several weeks," Horace said. "His leg will have to be checked quite often for infection and I doubt he'll be able to make much headway with the other one either."

"I figured as much," Jacob said. "Is he awake?"

"He was. You can go in and see him, but don't stay too long, he needs the rest."

Jacob walked into the room where Beryl was laying. He was awake staring at the wall. The sweat from the ordeal he'd just been through was still sitting on his forehead.

"He says you're gonna live," Jacob said.

"I'm not sure I feel the same way," Beryl said with a weak smile.

"Is there something I can do for you before I leave?"

"I need to get a message to Josh Danner over in Berryville. He's taking care of my place for me."

"I can do that," Jacob said. "Anything else?"

"Charlie's at your place?"

"Yeah, he's there."

"Can he stay with you until I can come and get him?"

"Sure he can."

162

"Tell him I'll be there as soon as I can, and I'll be taking him home. He won't be going back to the orphanage."

"We'll pull your wagon out and fix it for you," Jacob said. "I'll bring it and Charlie up here in a few days. My neighbor's got some horses for sale if you're interested."

"Pick me out two good mares, Jacob, and tell him I'll settle up with him, and pick out a small horse for Charlie. A man needs his own horse."

Jacob smiled and turned to go.

"Jacob," Beryl said. "Thanks."

"I'll pick him out a good one," Jacob said.

It was dark by the time Jacob made it home. Ethyl was standing on the porch when he turned into the drive. She waved and he waved back, but he could tell she was troubled. He stopped by the house before going to the barn.

"He's sick, Jacob. He's been in bed ever since you left and he's not getting any better. I'm sure it's the grippe."

Jacob was tired. He'd been up since Charlie had first come to the door and the ride home had been long and cold.

"I've got to get the horses fed," he said. "I'll be in soon."

"What about Beryl Stinson?" Ethyl asked.

"His leg's broken but he'll live if the infection don't get him. When I left him he seemed better than I'd expected." He headed the team to the barn.

Ethyl went back inside and checked on Charlie. He was awake but not talking, and she checked his forehead for fever.

"You're still feverish," she said. "Jacob's back, Charlie."

"Is Uncle Beryl with him?"

"No, he's in Harrison with the doctor. His leg's broken, so he won't be going anywhere for a while."

"But he's okay?"

"As good as can be expected, I suppose. Quit worrying about him and get some rest. You're a sick boy."

"When will he come and get me? We're going home—he said so."

"I don't know," Ethyl said. "He'll have trouble getting around for quite some time. I wouldn't look for him anytime soon."

Charlie was weak and wanted to know more but he closed his eyes and turned his head away from Ethyl. She picked up the bowl of broth and tried to get him to swallow but Charlie didn't want any.

"You've got to eat something," Ethyl said. "Don't make me get stern. I've doctored my own boys when they were sick and they lived through it. I guess I can get you through this, too."

Charlie turned his head back and let Ethyl spoon the broth in his mouth. She gave him two more spoonfuls before he refused to take anymore. Off and on all through the day she'd been giving a few sips as he would take them—she knew he had to have something to give him strength. She had napped in the chair beside the bed, but now she was worn out and felt she could fall asleep any moment. She knew Jacob would be of little help; he had to be just as tired and she didn't want him getting sick too. At least that worry was over—Jacob being home. She couldn't remember the last time she'd spent a night without him and she was glad Charlie had been there. At least she had him to care for, and she was sure she wouldn't have gotten any sleep anyway.

"How is he?" Jacob asked. Ethyl hadn't even heard him come in.

"His fever won't break and he can't keep anything down. We may have to get the doctor."

"Charlie," Jacob said, touching is shoulder.

Charlie opened his eyes and looked at him.

"Your uncle's doing fine. He told me to tell you he'd be along as soon as he could and he'd take you home. He wants me to buy you a horse. You'd like that wouldn't you?"

Charlie's eyes widened a little and they saw a weak smile come to his lips. "A horse?"

"Yeah, he said a man like you needs a horse. What do you think?"

Charlie nodded with more energy than Ethyl had seen in the last twenty hours.

"When I can see him?" Charlie asked.

"I haven't gotten him yet, son," Jacob said. "But I will in the next day or two. You have to get better before you can ride him though, so do as Ethyl tells you and you'll be well soon enough."

"There's dumplings on the stove," Ethyl said. "I'll heat it up. You need to eat and get some sleep. I can see it in those tired eyes."

"I'm too worked up to sleep," Jacob said. "But I will eat something."

"I'll heat some water and you can wash up," Ethyl said. She got up and went into the kitchen and Jacob sat in the chair. The room was cool and silent, and he could hear Charlie's labored breathing and somehow it calmed him. He was glad he could help Stinson and he was glad the boy was at least well enough to talk. Maybe the news of his uncle coming to get him would lift his spirits and help him get well.

By the time Ethyl came back to the room Charlie and Jacob were both sleeping. She decided to let Jacob sleep for a while before she woke him, even though his chin was resting on his chest. She went back to the kitchen and made another pot of coffee—it would be another long night for her.

Beryl's teeth chattered with the cold. The pain from his leg was like nothing he'd felt before. He hated being down, not able to take care of his own needs, and he was worried about Charlie. He knew if it hadn't been for him he probably wouldn't be alive right then. He wondered if there was more to it than just chance, that Charlie would have had the gumption to run away from the orphanage in the middle of a snowstorm, and more than that, how he'd found him down below the road in the darkness and had been man enough to shoot the mare and build the fire. The fire had done more for him than anything. Lying on the cold ground for most of the night was enough to take the strongest life, and Beryl knew it. Without the warmth of the fire and the blankets Charlie had spread over him, he felt he would have frozen to death. He owed the boy his life, he was sure of it, and he wanted more than anything right then to be with him.

The feeling was new to Beryl, wanting to be around someone, and the strangeness of the feeling was confusing. He wasn't sure what it was. In some way he felt sad, and couldn't understand why, and in another way he felt lightheaded, not from the pain of his leg, but a feeling of a burden lifted, like there had been something weighing him down all the years and now it was gone and he was thinking clearer and seeing things differently. Telling Jacob to pick out a horse for Charlie had just come out of his mouth, he'd never thought about it before. For once in his life he'd thought about something for someone else, and it made him happy, and when he'd said it, as surprised as he was that he had, a pleasant feeling had come over him. Maybe it was the look on Jacob's face, a look that said you're doing the right thing, or maybe it was the wish that he could be there when Charlie first saw the horse, knowing how happy he'd be. Beryl knew there would be a big smile on his face, and because of him there had been few smiles.

As he lay on the small bed, unable to move, staring at the ceiling from the low light the lantern afforded, he thought about how so many people had helped him through that night and were still helping. For the first time in his adult life he'd had to depend on others. The feelings he had leaving the orphanage and leaving Charlie behind had something do with it, because he had never felt so guilty. He always figured the further a man distanced himself from the needs of others, the less guilt he would feel, but that night he had been racked by guilt, and it was what had made him turn around.

Beryl thought about all the times he'd declined help from others, not wanting to owe anybody anything, but now he couldn't remember anybody ever asking for anything in return. No one had ever asked for anything, not Josh Danner for taking care of his place, not Beatrice Hagen for leaving her shop all day and bringing supper to him and Charlie, not Jacob or his wife for saving his life and taking care of the boy, and least of all, not Charlie. He'd never asked for anything. All he seemed to want was a home and someone to lean on.

Beryl had no friends, at least that's what he'd thought, but now he knew different—they were there, regardless of how ill he'd treated them. Folks had helped him, folks he was sure didn't approve of what he was doing or the kind of man he was. Beryl was the most disliked man in four counties and he was aware of that, but it had made no difference to him. As a matter of fact it was just the way he'd wanted it. But now as the years and the people ran through his mind he understood they had not wanted to hate him; he'd made them do it. He'd brought it all on himself and no good had come from it. Folks wanted to help each other, and they wished for nothing in return but a hand when they needed it and a smile when they didn't.

Beryl's eyes were wet and he wiped them with his hands and a smile formed on his face. He felt good, he felt like getting up and running; he wanted to be at Jacob's place seeing to Charlie, making sure he knew they were going home. He wanted to telegram Beatrice Hagen and thank her for bringing supper and giving Charlie the clothes. He wanted daylight to come so he could see some people and talk to them and know how their day was going, and maybe he could help them with something. Betty was right—all he had was worth nothing. He had no one to leave it to but strangers. All that would change. Now he had Charlie, and he had friends, and he would become their friend.

Chapter Seventeen

Fifteen days had passed and Beryl was sitting in a chair across from Beatrice Hagen and Josh Danner. He was well enough to get around on crutches, although his good leg wasn't as good as he would have liked it, but Beryl wasn't one to lie around. He'd had the doctor, against his wishes, send a telegram to Josh and ask him to come and get him and Charlie and take them back home. He didn't know Beatrice was coming along but he was glad she did. The more time he'd spent in the bed on his back eating food either the doctor made for him or bought from the café, the more he'd thought about the fried chicken she'd made. He'd even asked her if she would teach him how to make biscuits, one of the foods he was loath to give up, seeing as how they'd seen him through so many years, but he had to admit they lacked a certain quality and he was sure it was something minor he was doing wrong.

Betty had come along with Josh for one reason and one reason only—she was going to make sure Charlie came home, but when they'd reached the doctor's office they met a man neither she nor Josh had known.

"It's got to be something I'm missing," Beryl said, deep in thought. "I've been making biscuits since I was old enough to pour water, but they never seem to have the taste others do."

"Always use fresh milk," Betty said. "That's—

"Milk?" Beryl said. "What's milk got to do with it?"

"What do you mix your flour and shortening with?"

"Shortening? Flour and water's the way I fix 'em. You see, I knew I was leaving something out. Milk you say, that might be it."

"And shortening, Beryl, you've got to have shortening."

"I believe I can remember that," Beryl said. "I wouldn't mind though if you'd write it down. It's two more ingredients than I'm used to."

Betty and Josh gave each other a glance while Beryl seemed to be forcing the art of biscuit making into his memory.

"Beryl," Betty said. "I want to talk about Charlie. I want to take him back with me."

"No, you can't take him back with you. He doesn't belong with you."

"I won't take no for an answer. I'll come and get him if I have to."

"I know you don't think I've done right by him," Beryl said. "But everything I've done I thought was best for him, and I think he knows it now."

"Beryl, I'll fight you till the day I die over this. I'll hire lawyers and take you to court if I have to."

"Go ahead and hire your lawyers. If they step one foot on my property I'll feed 'em to the hogs. Now tell me about that fried chicken you made. What is it that makes it so tender and tasty?"

Betty and Josh both felt that Beryl was talking crazy. He must have hit his head when the wagon turned over on him and done some damage that couldn't be seen. Even more reason, Betty thought, to take control of the situation and take Charlie with her.

"I'm not going to let him stay at the orphanage," Betty said, her temper rising.

"He's coming home with me, Beatrice," Beryl said. "He belongs with me and I'm gonna keep him as long as wants to stay. Don't try to take him away from me, I won't allow it. I want to go to the orphanage and see about that little girl too. Her and Charlie hit it off from the start, I could tell, and maybe she wouldn't mind coming home with us and being a sister to Charlie like the one he lost. Her name's Mindy. She was there when I left Charlie."

Betty had lost her voice and Josh couldn't get his jaws to work. They both sat staring at Beryl, who was scratching around the stitches on his shin.

"And another thing," Beryl said. "I like mashed tators but they don't turn out so good. Do you think I should try putting milk in 'em instead of water? In a way it makes sense, them being white like flour."

"Yes," Betty said. "By all means try milk. You're taking Charlie home with you?"

"Of course I am, and I'd like it if you'd come and see him. He likes you a lot, and Josh, I want you tell Harley that he can come over anytime he wants, and he can spend the night too. Charlie needs a friend to play with and I won't be getting around so good for a while. Now, if you two are through talking gibberish I'd like to be leaving. I haven't seen Charlie in a while and I'm wondering how he's getting along. He's fairly well attached to me and I don't like being away from him for to long a time."

Beryl pulled himself up with his crutches and swung himself between his two dumbfounded neighbors.

In the outer room Beryl stopped long enough to thank Dr. Greenbottom for his hard work.

"I believe I couldn't have been in better hands, Dr. Greenbottom," Beryl said, offering his hand.

The doctor took it, and said, "It's Greenbaum, with an 'a'."

"Oh," Beryl said. "Where'd I get that from?"

"I know where you got it, and when you see Jacob Demanche you can tell him I didn't kill his mule, it was old age that killed him, and I know he knows how to say my name."

"Pull into the orphanage," Beryl said from the back of the wagon, where he was laying. "I want to talk to Miss Winston about the girl."

Josh steered the team to the front of the building and set the brake. A few kids were outside playing and Beryl searched through them trying to locate Mindy but couldn't find her.

"I'll go inside," Betty said. "You don't need to get up, Beryl."

"Bring her out here," Beryl said. "She'll remember me."

"I'm sure she will," Betty said.

Betty walked to the door and several children ran up to meet her, tugging at her dress and asking questions. She answered what she could but it saddened her to see the kids, most of their faces needed washing and their clothes were ragged and dirty. She opened the door and went inside.

Even in the light of day the inside of the home was dark. Kids were standing around, some sitting in the floor, arguing and laughing, some just sitting cross-legged and staring. She stopped one of the girls and asked her where Miss Winston was.

"She's in her room," the girl pointed. "Downstairs where we eat. She don't come out much, only to shout at us and tell us what to do."

Betty walked to the end of the hallway and turned down the stairs. When she got to the bottom she saw a woman at the far end of the room carrying tin plates and cups through a door leading to the kitchen. She followed her through the door.

"Excuse me," Betty said. "I'm looking for Miss Winston."

The woman continued on with her business, dropping the plates into a large steaming washtub.

"She's on the other side of the fireplace," she said, not looking up. "Are you here to take a child?"

"I want to talk to her about a girl that's here," Betty said. "Her name's Mindy."

The woman stopped what she was doing and wiped her hands on her apron and stared at the wall.

"Don't recall a child by that name," she said. "But I don't know all of 'em. There's too many and the good ones don't get much attention. It keeps us busy chasing down the ornery ones." She went back to her washing.

Betty went back out the door and crossed the floor to the door on the opposite side of the fireplace. There was a small fire glowing, but it was very small, and the room was chilled, and Betty pulled her coat tighter. She knocked on the door and waited, but heard no voice from the other side. She knocked again, this time harder.

"What is it?" the voice yelled from inside. "You kids know better than to bother me. I'll get the stick after you."

Betty pushed the door open slightly and peered inside. The room was dark, lit only by a small window behind a large desk. In the corner was a bed and an old woman sitting on it, her hands resting on the mattress and her feet planted firmly on the floor. She had a scowl on her face and appeared as if she was ready to launch herself from the bed and meet head on whoever was interrupting her morning.

"Are you Miss Winston?"

"I am. I'm not expecting anyone."

"I didn't expect to be here either," Betty said.

"Are you wanting a child or leaving one?" Miss Winston asked. She shoved herself from the mattress and walked to her desk. "I hope you're wanting one, I don't have room for any more."

"I'm with a man that's interested in a girl he met here a week ago, a girl named Mindy. The man's name is Stinson."

Miss Watson cocked her head to the side and stared at Betty. "I remember him. He left his blood kin here. Why would he be interested in a small girl? The boy he left ran off the same night and we've not heard anything about him since. Leaving in the storm like he did I'd guess he's dead."

Betty was irritated by the way the old woman casually talked about the possible death of Charlie.

"Charlie's fine," Betty said flatly. "Mr. Stinson's taking him home."

"Had a change of heart, did he? Well, the boy was trouble anyway. I'm glad he's gone."

Betty's temper was rising. She'd heard stories about this orphanage, that the kids weren't cared for well and that many of the children were sick, and she had also heard that the graveyard in the field in back of the home always had fresh dirt showing.

"Mindy," Betty said. "They met a girl named Mindy the night they were here. I'd like to meet her."

"I have no child here named Mindy. He's mistaken. Why isn't he here himself if he's wanting to find her."

"He's outside, in the wagon. He's got a broken leg."

"He deserves it," Miss Winston said, sitting down in her chair.

"Mr. Stinson said Mindy was here with you when he left Charlie."

"There was no other child. He left the boy and ran out the door like he was on fire. I have no girl here named Mindy. Now, I do have other girls, and he's welcome to take any of them. I'd be glad to get rid of them."

"Maybe he's got the girl's name wrong," Betty said. "Can we see all of the girls?"

"I've only got twelve. Most folks keep the girls. They're not as much trouble. The boys now, they drop them off like hot rocks. You say he's in the wagon? I'll have them rounded up and meet you out front."

Miss Winston got up from her chair and walked past Betty through the door. She made her way to the kitchen and stuck her head inside the door.

"Greta, find all the girls and get them out front. They might want to take one of 'em."

"I'm busy," Greta said.

"You do as you're told," Miss Winston said. "It's one less mouth to feed that slop you cook. Now get on with it."

She let the door close and turned to Betty. "She ain't much help, but anybody can cook grits. You go on and she'll have the girls out there soon. How about the boys, maybe he'll want another boy since he's feeling Christian."

"Just the girls," Betty said. She turned and walked toward the stairs. She passed the dirty tables with dried grits pasted on their tops, and crumbs of food scattered on the tables and the floor. She stopped and turned around.

"Do you ever clean these tables?"

Miss Winston was already at her door ready to go inside.

"The kids clean up," she said. "They like the crumbs better than Greta's slop. They're just trash anyways." She walked into her room and closed the door.

Betty was mad and hurt. She had no idea the kids were being treated so poorly but she also didn't know anyone that had actually been here. She walked up the stairs and down the hall. When she came to the stairway she stopped and looked to see if any adults were around. When she didn't see any she started up.

The cots on the second floor were lined along the walls from the staircase to the fireplace at the far end. None of the beds were made and trash was strung from one end of the room to the other. The floor was thick with dust and dirt and there was no fire, the room colder than it was outside. There were only two small windows, both of them looking out the back over the graveyard. Nothing adorned the walls, no pictures, and no curtains on the windows, no lanterns to see by.

Betty almost cried, but didn't want to make a show in front of the kids. As she turned to go a small boy stood behind her and she almost tripped over him.

"Can I go home with you?" he asked.

"What's your name?" Betty asked.

"Willie."

The boy's eyes were sunk in hollows and had dark rings surrounding them. His nose was running and he had no socks on his feet, only worn out shoes with no laces to tie them up.

Betty reached in her pocket and took out a hanky and kneeled down and held it to his nose.

"Blow," she said. He did and Betty cleaned him up and brushed his stringy blond hair back from his face, away from his hopeful blue eyes.

"Which bed is yours?"

He pointed to the one closest to the stairway, the farthest from the fireplace. The blanket was thin and worn, with tears and holes in it, and the pillow was nothing but a wadded up rag.

"You can't go with me today," Betty said. "But I promise you I'll be back, and when I do you won't be cold anymore and you won't be hungry."

"I could go with you now," Willie said. "Miss Winston won't care."

Betty stopped herself from saying what she was thinking. She knew it would be bitter, and this little boy had heard enough bitterness.

"I can't take you home with me," she said. Betty reached in her pocket and pulled out a piece of rock candy she'd brought for Charlie and handed it to the boy. "I'm sorry, but I just can't."

He took the candy and ran to his bed and crawled underneath it.

Betty walked to the bed and bent down and looked at Willie.

"What are you doing under there?"

"They'll take it from me," Jason said.

"Who will?"

"All of 'em."

Betty took out another piece of candy and gave it to him. "You hide this real good, okay. The next time I see you I'll have enough for everyone."

Willie sucked on the candy and clinched the other piece in his fist, and stared at her.

"Bye," Betty said.

Willie scooted back into the corner until she could only see his worn out shoes.

She went downstairs and out the front door. Greta was there and had the girls lined up beside the wagon and Beryl was looking them over. When he saw Betty he waved for her to come over.

"She's not here," he said. "There's six girls here claiming their name's Mindy, but none of them's her."

"That old crow inside said she didn't have a girl named Mindy," Betty said, trying hard not to upset the children. Greta snickered.

"I don't get it," Beryl said. "I saw her with my own eyes. There was something special about her, something that seemed familiar to me."

"The light's poor in there, Beryl. Maybe it's one of these girls and you didn't get a good look at her."

"I'd know her if I saw her—she's not here. Have any girls been taken or run off?" He asked, looking at Greta.

She shook her head and shrugged her shoulders. "I don't count heads," she said. "That's the old crow's job."

"Nobody does anything around here that I can see," Betty said.

Greta shrugged again. "Take one or don't, it makes no mind to me. I make the same amount of grits no matter the count."

Betty leaned close to Beryl and said, "Let's go, Beryl. If I have to stay here one more minute I'm likely to kill somebody."

"Charlie'll be disappointed," he said.

"No more disappointed than these kids will be when we leave," Betty said. She climbed into the seat of the wagon and nodded at Josh. He slapped the reins and the wagon jolted away. Betty refused to let herself look back as they rode off.

Chapter Eighteen

When they pulled into Jacob's place Charlie was running down the hill to meet them. He'd been waiting at the front window for days. Ethyl wouldn't let him go outside. His fever had broken the third night and he'd been getting better ever since. By the end of the week he was able to get out of bed and she was having trouble keeping him down. He wanted his uncle to show up and had even tried to convince Jacob to take him to town, but Ethyl wouldn't hear of it. His new colt was in the barnyard but he'd yet to see it. Jacob was just as excited about him seeing the colt as Charlie was, but Ethyl wouldn't let him go outside, and Jacob had tried to sneak the colt around the house so Charlie could see it from the window, but Ethyl caught him in the act and made him take him back, saying it would just agitate Charlie and he might have a relapse. Jacob had told her he thought some of Stinson's meanness had rubbed off on her, and he'd had to make his own coffee for the last two mornings, and he liked his eggs runny and they'd been fried to a flat slat.

"Hi, Charlie," Josh said.

"Josh, and Betty," Charlie yelled. "Where's Uncle Beryl?"

"He's in the back of the wagon resting," Josh said. "Just 'cause his leg's busted he thinks he don't have to do no work."

Charlie ran to the rear of the wagon and jumped up and down to see over the edge. Beryl scooted his way down to the bottom and leaned over and gave Charlie a hug.

"How are you, Charlie? You look a little pale."

"He's had the grippe," Jacob said. "Ethyl's been staying up with him night and day since he got here, but he's feeling better now."

"Lord, son, it's good to see you," Beryl said. "Go give Betty a hug. She's been as antsy as a chicken in a fox hole ever since we left Harrison."

Betty was down from the wagon and Charlie ran to her and she picked him up and held him tight against her.

"You've had quite a trip, haven't you?"

"Uncle Beryl got hurt," Charlie said. "Jacob had to go help him."

"I heard you did your part, too."

"Rosie was hollering. If it hadn't been for her I wouldn't have found him." Charlie frowned and his eyes watered. "I had to help her die," he said.

Everyone grew quiet then and Charlie thought he'd said something wrong.

"Her back was broke," Beryl said. "Charlie had to put her down. I couldn't get to her to do it."

Josh looked at Charlie and smiled. He knew what it took to put down a horse and so did Betty.

"You did some growing up while you were gone," Betty said.

Charlie grinned. "I've been playing checkers too. Jacob bought me a new checkerboard."

"I saw a checkerboard in the fire," Beryl said. "I wondered where it came from. It was the only dry wood Charlie could find. Without it he might not have gotten a flame to catch."

"I'm glad it went to good use," Jacob said. "It's always been bad luck for me. The old woman beat me all the time on that board and I never could catch her cheating."

"Don't just stand there, old man," Ethyl said. "Show 'em where to put the horses. They'll have to stay the night and start off in the morning. I'll not let Charlie make the trip in the night air."

"Can I see the colt now?" Charlie asked.

Ethyl frowned, but knew it was time. "I suppose so, but make it quick. You've been out long enough."

Betty let Charlie down and he went with Jacob to the barnyard. Josh and Betty helped Beryl out of the wagon.

"You bought him a colt?" Betty asked.

"He needs his own horse," Beryl said.

"What's happened to you, Beryl Stinson?"

"Charlie's hope," he said. "As hard as I was on him, he never gave up wanting to be with me, and he never asked for nothing in return, none of you did, not Josh, or Jacob, and not you. It came to me lying in the snow when I first saw Charlie leaning over me. It's not doing something for yourself that counts, it's bringing others along that makes it worthwhile."

Beryl was embarrassed by the talking and fitted his crutches under his arms and headed to the house.

"Now, Ethyl," he said, as got closer to her. "I've learned a few tricks about biscuit making, and I was wondering if you had any."

"Put a pinch of salt in your dough," Ethyl said. "I think it makes them rise better and it mixes well with the sweet milk."

"I see," Beryl said. "And potatoes?"

"Same thing—always add salt, and put a dollop of butter on top after they're smoothed out."

Beryl looked back over his shoulder and winked at Betty.

After dinner everyone was in front of the fire and Beryl was playing checkers with Charlie. Josh had helped Jacob finish his chores and Betty and Ethyl had cleaned up the kitchen.

Jacob was waiting his turn at checkers and Josh was drinking coffee by the side of the fireplace.

"Well, you've won again," Beryl said. "My checker skills need some mending. I suppose you better play Jacob."

"Can we go back to the orphanage?" Charlie asked.

Everyone stopped and stared at him.

"Why would you want to do that?" Betty asked.

"To find Mindy."

Betty glanced at Beryl, and Beryl looked back at her as if to say he'd been right about Charlie being disappointed.

"We stopped at the orphanage and tried to find her," Beryl said. "But she wasn't there."

"She had to go back," Charlie said. "She had no place else to go."

"What do you mean, go back?" Betty asked. Then she saw the strange looks on Jacob and Ethyl's face.

"We tried to find her that night," Ethyl said. "Jacob went around the house and barn, but never did see her. Charlie thought he saw her down at the road, but I couldn't see her."

"What are you talking about?" Beryl said. "She was at the orphanage when I left."

"She walked with me," Charlie said. "When you told me to get Jacob, I got up to the road and the lantern went out, and I was scared to go on in the dark, and then Mindy walked up and warmed my hands and said she'd go with me."

The room was silent and still. Charlie looked from face to face and saw the same amazement on each one.

"Remember, Uncle Beryl, at the orphanage, she said you needed me, and you did?"

"She did say that," Beryl said quietly.

"And she knew right where to take me. I was tired and cold and sleepy and she brought me here." Charlie looked at Jacob and then Ethyl.

"There were two sets of footprints outside when Charlie got here," Jacob said. "Somebody was with him."

"And Betty, she knew Betty."

"What did she say?" Betty asked.

"She said you were right about the fire, how Rachael and Papa were in the light."

"Maybe she'll find you again," Betty said.

"We'll keep looking for her," Beryl said. "If she could find Jacob's place then she'll be able to find us."

"At first I thought it was Rachael," Charlie said.

"How about some apple cider, old woman?" Jacob said, ending the silence. "Charlie and I've got checkers to play."

The next day as they were getting ready to leave, Ethyl told Beryl to make sure Charlie took a few sips of coffee every morning at breakfast.

"One of my boys had the same problem, getting distracted all the time," she said. "His thoughts were so scattered he didn't know if he was getting out of bed or getting in. The coffee seemed to help. He grew out of it, one way or the other, but give it a try, it might help."

"Are you ready, Charlie?" Beryl asked.

"Yes sir," Charlie said.

"Let's go home, then."

Chapter Nineteen

"Are you ready?" Charlie asked.

"Give me another minute," Betty said.

Charlie held her hand as they looked at the grave. It was a clear November day and he was thinking back ten years ago in November when the day had not been clear and sunny. It had been dreary and cold, windy, and snowing. He held his hat in his hand and watched as the mourners walked away, on their way to the house where others were waiting, the rooms filled with food and memories.

"You need anything before I go?" Harley asked.

"No," Charlie said. "You go ahead, we'll be along soon."

"Stupid wagons," Betty said. "He was in decent health, there's no telling how long we could have had with him."

Three days earlier Charlie and Beryl had been cutting wood for the coming winter. The wagon was loaded full with spilt firewood when the brake broke free, spooking the horses and making them bolt. Charlie and Beryl had been standing with their backs to the horses when it happened, and Beryl had just enough time to push Charlie out of the way before the team and wagon ran over him. Beryl never regained consciousness.

"I should have checked the brake," Charlie said.

"It wasn't your fault. It was something he wouldn't have forgotten a few years back, but lately his memory was playing tricks on him."

It had taken Beryl a year after they'd come back from that November ten years ago to ask Betty to be his wife. She was taken by surprise, but she'd said yes immediately. Beryl's life had only gotten better after he'd brought Charlie home. He was a changed man. Not once in the nine years he and Betty were

179

married had he thought about himself. Everything he did was directed toward others. He was the first one there when a neighbor needed help and the last one to leave. He smiled and waved at everyone he saw, and when someone was sick he always made sure their chores were done before his own, and he particularly enjoyed taking them warm biscuits first thing in the mornings.

It had taken Betty quite a few weeks to teach him the method of fixing biscuits and it provided many times of laughter for them all, Beryl most often laughing the loudest, as he tossed the brown stones to the hogs on many of the first lessons, but he'd finally gotten the hang of it, and he was always the first one up making sure there were hot biscuits for breakfast.

After the first few months Charlie was getting quite tired of the same thing in the mornings, although the biscuits were good, but he'd taken to stuffing them in his pockets when Beryl turned his back so he could distribute them to his classmates at school. Beryl thought Charlie liked them so well he started making double batches, until Betty came to the cabin one day with a sack full of old biscuits she'd found lying by the road. Beryl was startled when he saw the sack and Betty thought his feelings might be hurt, but he admitted he was getting a little tired of them himself. The only reason he'd kept making them was because he thought Charlie liked them so well, so after that he mixed the morning menu up considerably, throwing in some eggs and salt pork every other day or so.

In the months it took for Beryl's leg to heal he got to be a pretty good cook. Betty came by every few days to fix dinner and he'd hop around on his crutch and help as he could, mostly just in the way, looking over her shoulder and bothering her with questions. She'd put him to work peeling potatoes or turning the fried chicken, something that would put him in a time consuming position while she finished getting the meal ready. She enjoyed those times though, being with him, knowing how much he'd changed and seeing the joy in his eyes just by being able to help.

Beryl bought Harley a colt too, and he and Josh taught the boys how to ride and care for their horses. After his leg got well enough he'd go for long rides with the boys showing them the things he'd learned about the woods, teaching them how to fish and hunt and track, something Harley never did get the hang of, but Charlie seemed to pick up quickly. Charlie never let on to Harley that he could do it better though, most of the time letting Harley think he'd been the one doing the best.

Beryl, Betty, and Charlie went back to the orphanage the next Christmas taking clothes, shoes, toys, and food with them, collected from the neighbors in Berryville. Betty had petitioned the Arkansas governor about the conditions of the orphanage and the women in charge. He met them on Christmas Eve. They were not received well by Miss Winston, and the two wagons were met at the door and told to leave, but the sheriff of Harrison also met them there, and the wagons were emptied and distributed among the children, and Miss Winston, along with the other women were dismissed and replaced by a newly appointed administrator and supervisors by order of the governor.

In the following months Beryl and Betty collected contributions from around the state for funds for a new home for the children and two years later it was built. It was the start of a revamping of the regulations for homeless children in Arkansas and much credit was given to the Stinson's.

They made many trips to and from Harrison over those next two years and always stayed with Ethyl and Jacob. Jacob had slipped on the ice in February of the second year and had broken his hip. It was a setback for him and his health never recovered from the injury. They were forced to sell their farm and move in with one of their sons. One year later Jacob was gone and Ethyl soon followed.

After Beryl's death, Betty signed the farm over to Charlie and moved back into town. Charlie married a girl named Evelyn and they had a daughter. They named her Rachael.

After they put Beryl to rest Charlie went back to Oklahoma to see the graves of Rachael and his dad. He visited the old sod house he knew so well, now just a storage shed for those that owned the land. A small wooden bridge had been built across the shallow creek where they had tried to cross that night, so long ago. Charlie stood on it and wondered why it had all taken place. Was it meant to be, that he was supposed to lose his father and sister in order to save his uncle? He thought about how his life would have been if things had turned out differently. Would he have stayed in Oklahoma like his father had, or would he have left the plains in search of something different? He missed his sister and always would, but somehow in that late evening as he looked down on the dry creek bed, he believed there must have been another hand in it. His uncle had been right—the droughts and floods took a man's youth and gave back very little. Back then leaving it behind was the only answer. Maybe the lost lives of Charlie's family were his salvation.

Charlie had more than his father had ever had, or his father before him, and it had been because of Beryl Stinson, the one man in the family that had enough sense, or guts, to leave the clay and wind and dust, and the tornadoes and the droughts behind. Beryl had fought for what he'd wanted, just the way Charlie had when he ran out the door of the orphanage after him. And it was probably because of Beryl Stinson that he'd had the nerve to run away. There was fight in Beryl, maybe some might call it stubbornness, but Charlie liked to call it perseverance. It was the quality in a man that pushed him forward even though he might be headed into the unknown. In the short time Charlie had been with Beryl before he'd made the trip to the orphanage he'd learned to take nothing for granted, that the world was hard, and there wasn't always someone there to take the knocks for you. Beryl had taught him that. Even though he'd been cruel and at first wanted nothing to do with Charlie, he had still shown him to stand on his own and fight for what he believed in. It's what had saved Charlie, and Beryl too, and in the end it had built a family, and maybe it's what Beryl had started out to do in the first place, he just didn't know it.

They never found Mindy. Some things in life go unexplained. Most people say it was just a small boy's imagination, but Beryl was no small boy and he had seen her too. And how could the extra set of footprints at Jacob's house be explained? Maybe there is no need to explain. Of course it was Rachael, even though the face was different, even though the voice was not the same. Beryl had never known Rachael and so the young girl was no surprise to him, and even Charlie mistook her for a kind stranger. But she was no stranger. Rachael had come to help him, and she was not afraid of Beryl Stinson. Perhaps she needed to meet her father's brother, the man who was abandoning her own brother. But she held no bitterness against him. She knew Charlie's future lay with his uncle, and she had shown him the way. Two lives had been saved that night—Charlie's and Beryl's, and Rachael had saved them, and there was only one person who needed to believe in her.

Charlie looked out over the land and the rows of crops and the glimmer from the water flowing through the canals. Irrigation was turning the once parched land into firm lush fields. Of all of the men and women that had been worn down to nothing, working and plowing land that defeated them at every turn, it had all come down to managing the water.

He felt the breeze on his face as it lifted across the open flats, and saw the tops of the corn bending with the whispering unseen weight of prosperity. He shook his head in wonder, that so many people had fought and died for the land, stretches of dirt that provided little more than a mud hut for shelter, knowing like his uncle had known that it would come to no good, but staying, out of determination, killing themselves and their families and leaving nothing behind but more of the same. And there they were now, abundant fields of progress and prosperity, sitting against an orange sunset, giving life where there was none and giving hope where it once was only a glimpse through the dust. Charlie's father had known it, and his father before him. It was a lesson only time could prove. There was always hope.

Printed in the United States
118358LV00002BA/49/P

81606 105078